THE SWORD AND THE CIRCUS

THE PHANTOM OF NEW YORK, VOLUME TWO

A. L. JANNEY

The Phantom of New York
Volume Two
The Sword and the Circus

Copyright © 2017 by Alan Janney

alanjanney.com

Cover by eBookLaunch.com
Crown Hotel by Anne Pierson
Illustrations by Georgia Stanley

eBook ISBN: 978-0-9996073-0-5
Paperback ISBN: 978-1-9814192-0-3

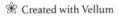 Created with Vellum

For Rima Grace
my daughter
Home from India
At last

PART I

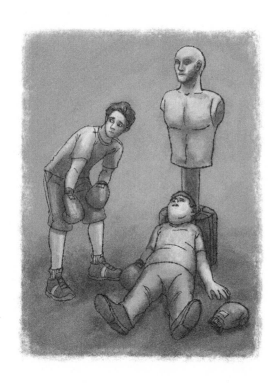

Some heroes are born. Some are made. And apparently some live in hotels, longing for adventure.

-Darci Drake
    New York Times

"YOU'RE NOT HIM."

Peter Constantine did not know a ghost was sitting on his wooden dresser, not even when he rolled out of his bed that morning and stretched. Peter smiled blearily at his eccentric pet mouse, who was glaring hatefully at the ghost, and he went into the bathroom.

The ghost wore a cockeyed hat, and under his tattered jacket there was a red scarf. Far-off battles had left his face crisscrossed with scars. He heaved an unhappy sigh, growled, "It's not him. I *knew* it weren't him," and vanished.

Peter, rather startled to hear a voice, stuck his head back into the room and asked, "Hello? Did someone...?"

The fat mouse twitched its nose, irritated.

Peter shrugged, finished his bathroom business, and went into the kitchen, which was free of ghosts. His mother Jovanna sat at the table in her blue robe, idly picking at pancakes. Though she was quite an attractive woman with olive skin and long brown hair, she was always bleary and slow until later in the morning. "Hello, sweetheart." She gave him a sleepy smile and ruffled his thick black hair.

"G'morning, Mom." Peter moved a box of his father's

tools in order to sit down, it being a very tight eating area. "Where's Dad?"

"Mr. Conrad rang for an emergency meeting. He'll be back later," she replied through a yawn, and she handed Peter the syrup. "I think you grew another inch last night."

"Mmmpf," said Peter and he rubbed his eyes. His mother *always* thought he'd grown the previous night.

"Do you know what today is?"

"Monday."

She nodded. "That's right. First day of school."

Peter hungrily filled his fork with four layers of pancake. His father had made them an hour ago and they'd grown cold, but Peter didn't care. Talking around a titanic mouthful, he said, "Not for me and Joey. We've been back at it for a week."

"But it's the first day for the other kids," she hinted.

He didn't reply because he was busy swallowing an enormous bite of buttery pancake.

His mother continued, "Which means, most likely Caroline Crawford returned home from England yesterday." She said Caroline's name with an extra dose of emphasis and she smiled behind her mug of coffee. "Doesn't that make you happy? Aren't you and Caroline friends?"

"MooOOOooommm," he said defensively. "I *don't* want to talk about this."

"Why ever not?"

Peter groaned. Truthfully, he'd been anticipating Princess Caroline Crawford's return for weeks. Her father was a British diplomat and the Crawford family vacationed in the United Kingdom for two months during the summer. Somehow the world was less magical without her in it, something he could never reveal. Today should be a good day because the beautiful little blonde princess would be walking the hallways of the Crown Hotel and possibly searching for him. She wasn't really a princess, more of a minor and wealthy celebrity, but Peter thought of her as royalty.

"She's my friend. That's *it*," he insisted.

"Peter, don't be so—ACK!"

"Wha—MOM!" yelped Peter, ducking, as his mother hurled the bottle of syrup. "Careful!"

The bottle thunked against the doorframe and syrup exploded, and the white rodent she aimed at scampered back into Peter's bedroom with a squeak.

"Where's the frying pan? It's that disgusting *mouse*!"

"I'll kill it," Peter said vehemently. "Wait here." He snatched the cast iron frying pan and bolted into his bedroom, banging the door closed behind him. He slammed the pan harmlessly onto the bed and into the side of his dresser. He stomped his feet and threw a book at the wall and yelled things like, "Come here! Almost... Ah hah, here you are! No biting!"

The mouse watched his performance safely from the corner and seemed to think, *You look absurd. Honestly, is this really necessary?*

It was necessary, in fact. Otherwise Jovanna would realize Peter didn't actually want the mouse caught, and that he'd been secretly setting off the mousetraps himself to be safe. He'd grown attached to his fat little friend ever since it saved his life during a fire last spring.

He clunked the pan into his dresser once more and hissed at the mouse, "Why do you always cause trouble?"

I'm not the one throwing syrup bottles!

"Stay *here*," he said quietly.

Hmphf.

Peter reemerged into the kitchen and said, "It got away."

"Ugh. It's such a clever little rodent," his mother groaned, crouched down and cleaning syrup from the floor. "At least you tried, and probably startled the neighbors with that racket. Where does it go, I wonder."

"Probably hiding from the crazy syrup lady," Peter said, returning to breakfast. "What was Dad's meeting about?"

She resumed her seat and drank more coffee. "He didn't tell me. I guess we'll find out. What are your plans today, sweetheart?"

He didn't respond immediately, as he was nearly choking on an even larger forkful of pancake. Peter was a boy who'd been given an unusually large amount of freedom by his parents. During the previous twelve months he'd proven to be responsible and reliable and hard working; as a result of his superior grades and test scores, he could essentially set his own schedule, a situation which baffled most children his age. Happily, his two best friends, Josephine and Hawkins, had similar freedom. Eventually he responded, "Reading and math with Joey, I suppose. We talked about helping her dad in the kitchen and then..." He paused, an idea occurring to him. "Mom, do you work today?"

"I do."

"What shift?"

She scrunched up her eyes thoughtfully and answered, "Mmmmm, I think I go in at ten."

"Ten," Peter repeated and he idly pulled at his lower lip. "Huh."

"Why do you ask? Want to come fold laundry with me?"

"No," Peter said, a little too quickly. He experienced a pang of guilt; his mother had been an up-and-coming realtor until Peter'd been born, and she'd envisioned returning to her career once he was old enough. But life could be cruel and now she toiled underground in a hot laundry room to help keep her family safe and hidden from the outside world. "Well, maybe. If I have time."

Despite the guilt, Peter had no intention to visit his mom today. In fact he planned to attempt a daring expedition, one he'd been putting off for months, and with his mom occupied for most of the day he would have his chance. All he needed now was the courage.

Hurriedly he finished breakfast, cleaned up both his dishes and his mother's, and he dressed. Jeans, Captain America T-shirt, and good walking sneakers. The shirt was a little snug around the shoulders and soon he'd need new shoes. He dug under his bed and through his messy drawers until finding what he needed—a shiny black trinket, the most bizarre key ever created. A gift from a ghost.

The mouse, which had been lazily reclining on his dresser, sat up with a squeak.

"Wish me luck, mouse," Peter said, shoving the key into his pocket. "Today is the day. I hope."

The mouse began hopping and bouncing off the wall, which Peter took for approval. This was no ordinary mouse; in fact, it had once belonged to the Crown's ghost, and Peter assumed it possessed all kinds of knowledge and secrets.

"*Hotel Chelsea*," Peter repeated from memory. "*Hidden door,* whatever that means. Right?"

The mouse stopped leaping and nodded solemnly.

Peter had been given a mysterious note from a mysterious girl, and he should have followed the note's instructions to the Hotel Chelsea a long time ago. The remainder of the mysterious note read, *You'll know how to get in. Otherwise don't bother.* Whatever that meant. But he assumed it had something to do with his key.

"I can do this," he said. "I'm going to get some answers."

The mouse nodded again.

Peter experienced the same pleasant jolt he always did emerging from his apartment into the golden hallway, which was lit with chandeliers and layered with squishy carpet. The hotel never stopped feeling new and magical to him.

Josephine Arora was sitting in the cozy second-floor Nook, a richly furnished common area he spent more time in than his own bedroom. She sat crisscross on one of the red overstuffed reading couches, dressed in her customary cooking garb and fussing over a collection of junk in her lap. Their friend Leo sat nearby, watching anxiously. Mrs. Love (the concierge director) and Ms. Briggs (the housekeeping director) chatted quietly over coffee near the large window with a view of 58th Street. Peter decided he needed more energy for his journey and he swooped past the kitchen area for a mug of steaming hot chocolate.

As a general rule, Joey held the Crown's powerful guests and residents in high regard, unwilling and often unable to be sociable. She was only a cook, she argued, and not even a cook of note. However, she relaxed her rules for Leo, whom she considered something of a hopeless mess. She held up the tangled disaster of electronic pieces and said, "This is the third time this month Leo has broken his video game controller. He needs a new hobby, you ask me."

Leo shrugged modestly. "I struggle with impulse control. When I get angry, I throw things."

Peter said, "If you stop fixing it, Joey, he might learn a lesson."

"I don't *want* to learn a lesson," said Leo with a frown. "If you play video games, you understand."

"Who has time for video games," wondered Peter. "I'm too busy."

Leo stared at Peter like he'd spoken a weird language.

"Oh, I don't mind fixing the controller, I suppose. It's kinda fun." In fact, she did look like she enjoyed the work. Her hands moved so quickly Peter could barely follow them. She was a green-eyed, light-skinned Indian girl, often dusted with flour. She stopped fiddling with the controller long enough to hold out her arms. "I tanned yesterday on the roof. Can you tell?"

"Oh yeah, sure," Peter lied, because he couldn't see a difference. "I didn't know Indians could tan."

"You think only white people can?" she snorted. "I have skin, don't I? But I don't get outside often enough. The kitchen is short-staffed at the moment, you know."

"I know," said Peter, picking up a newspaper. "You only mention it once an hour."

"Well...it is. There's no need to be rude."

Leo, a pudgy boy born in Japan, grew impatient waiting for the controller so he reached into the pocket of his sports jacket and withdrew a fancy virtual reality visor. He placed it over his eyes and soon he was weaving in his chair as though riding a rollercoaster, the device beeping and bopping.

People playing video games looked preposterous, thought Peter. He sipped his hot chocolate and scanned the paper for mentions of the Red Masque, a sophisticated treasure syndicate harassing the city. Syndicate, Peter had learned, was a fancy word for gang. He had a particular interest because in February the syndicate had set fire to the Crown, and they planned to return and hunt for hidden treasure in the hotel. Peter had heard that piece of dreadful news with his own ears, but no one believed him. As he read he also kept an eye out for photographs of a criminal known to Peter as The Evil Treasure Hunter, a man who wanted to murder his father because Manos had reported him to the police. He had been a high-profile treasure hunter, now a powerful fugitive, and the paper liked to show pictures of him. However, both the Red Masque and The Evil Treasure Hunter had vanished, staying hidden for months. Finding nothing, Peter folded and returned the paper.

The syndicate was coming back to steal secret treasure from the Crown. *Soon.* He just didn't know when or how.

"Have you heard the big news?" asked Joey, bent over her work.

"What big news?"

"It's so odd how boys live their entire lives with their heads stuck in the sand."

Peter retorted, "I don't even know what that means, so you hush up."

"It means—"

"I *know* what it means," said Peter, who didn't. "I just don't care about your big news."

"I do," said Leo, still wearing the visor and ducking his head. "I want to know, please. I get lonely."

"The circus is coming to town."

Peter said, "Hah! I knew that already. They're performing shows for two months straight at Barclays."

"But," she said, holding up an imperial finger, signaling he celebrated too early. "Did you know that most performers are staying at the Crown?"

"Here? You're kidding."

Leo responded loftily, "The circus is not an honorable profession. I am surprised the hotel owners allow that."

"Funny thing about Mr. and Mrs. Banks, they're huge circus fans. Gave them all discounts," she said. "I assumed the Banks would worry about the Crown's reputation with rich and famous guests, but apparently not."

Peter said, "Should be fun. There'll be jugglers and trapeze artists and stuff."

Joey rolled her eyes, as though already exhausted with the extra responsibilities. "Oh, it'll be a madhouse. The hotel is preparing to cater to their bizarre requests."

"Requests like what?"

"For starters, they're bringing animals."

"Animals!" Peter hooted. "HERE? Like elephants?"

"I don't know. Where would the elephants go? The garage, I suppose. I bet they'll bring smaller animals, like snakes and birds and goats."

"Bird and goats?" Peter frowned. "What kind of circus is *that*?"

"I'm just guessing! What do they have, seals and tigers? I've never been to a circus," she said defensively.

"Me neither."

"My parents would never allow it," said Leo. "They worry about disease."

Joey's face brightened and she lowered the broken controller. "Maybe we'll get tickets for free."

"If not, I bet Hawkins can sneak us in."

"Of course he can. And one day he'll sneak himself into *jail* and Social Services will whisk him off to foster parents and you'll never see him again."

"Joey! You say the worst stuff," Peter cried. "I would hate that."

"Which is why we need to discourage his lawless behavior. I wish he'd move into your room permanently."

Peter nodded. "Me too, but he's a loner. He likes his space. Now that it's warm he's only staying with me a couple days a week. Maybe he'll move in when he finds out about the circus performers. Wow, I wonder if they'll breathe fire and juggle swords in the Lobby."

There was a ding from the bank of golden elevators and crazy Mr. Hayes wandered in. He was the Crown's longest-tenured resident and most of his wits had fled long ago. When Joey noticed he held a gooey chocolate muffin she rose slowly and raised her text book as a shield. He'd been known to rampage and coat the Nook with pastry bombs.

"Mr. Hayes?" she said carefully. "Have you locked your nurse in the closet again?"

His eyes alighted on Peter and he cried, "Alexia, my boy! Just the scamp I came to see. You'll come up for checkers?"

"Yes sir," replied Peter, nervous. He enjoyed their weekly games but Mr. Hayes loaded with bakery ammunition was a scary thing. "Tomorrow afternoon, right?"

Sensing danger, Leo removed the visor and loudly called, "His name's PETER," as if Mr. Hayes was deaf. Which he wasn't.

"Tomorrow afternoon. Don't be late! I'm winning, a hundred and twelve games to eight," cackled Mr. Hayes. Mrs. Love and Ms. Briggs were hurrying over with stern looks so he said, "Oops! Better run." He returned to the elevators. Another ding and he was whisked away.

Leo marveled, "Is he truly beating you by a hundred and four games?"

"He's like a wizard," said Peter, nodding.

"Maybe you are of substandard intelligence," he suggested innocently.

"Or maybe he's just super great at checkers! Shouldn't you be saving Mario or something?" shouted Peter.

"Save Mario?" Leo grinned, almost completely hiding his eyes within his fat cheeks. "Mario is the hero. Don't you know *anything*?"

Joey sat down again and grumbled, "Crazy Mr. Hayes remembers the score but not your name. I thought for sure he was gonna stuff that muffin into my ear. Honestly. Should we begin our math work?"

Peter drained his hot chocolate and stood. "I can't, not until later. Gotta run out."

"Where to?"

"Oh, just somewhere. An errand," he replied evasively. "I'll be back after lunch."

"After lunch? But you never go anywhere alone. You're acting sneaky."

"Am not."

"Very sneaky," agreed Leo.

"Oh, just...hush up." It wasn't fair to make fun of Peter for not going anywhere alone—he hadn't grown up in New York like she had, or in Tokyo like Leo had. They were accustomed to the enormity of people. Before she could ask any more questions, Peter fled down the stairs.

The Crown Lobby sparkled brilliantly with light bursting from the chandeliers and windows and reflecting off the marbled floors. Vases of chrysanthemums and other fragrant flowers rested on the counters and tables. The tuxedo-wearing man at the piano spotted him and interjected a quick melody into his song, a whimsical tune he'd written specifically for Peter. He had short songs for most kids who lived at the Crown.

What with the sunlight, the exciting mission he was on, the circus news, and Caroline's return, it was going to be a great day. Peter waved at the pianist, and at the attendants behind the reception counters, and at the bell hop, and he plunged through the revolving doors.

"Hey Pete, whaddaya say," said Tony the doorman, a burly friend of Peter's. He was dressed in a heavy red uniform, and he stood attentively at the entrance. "Can't beat days like this, you know it? You off to the Park?"

Peter fingered the curious key in his pocket and didn't respond immediately. His spirits, which had been soaring, faltered slightly now that he was outside. This corner of the Crown was still blue with the shadow of skyscrapers.

Tony continued, "How long should I wait today, 'fore I come find you?"

Peter did some quick math. He needed several hours... He said, "How about lunch time?"

"Lunch? That's three hours, Pete. Manos will skin me, something bad happens to you."

"Yeah..." Peter replied in a shaky voice.

Why was he suddenly nervous? He shouldn't be. He went to Central Park most sunny afternoons and today wasn't much different. But for some reason his heart raced and his lungs couldn't find enough oxygen.

"I'll be fine," Peter said, mostly to himself. "I'll be okay. And I'll be back around lunch. Maybe a little after."

Tony gave him a friendly whack on the back and said, "Have fun, big guy! Don't kiss any girls, right?"

Peter turned the corner on wobbly legs and said again, "I'll be fine..." He maneuvered west through the crowds on 59th Street. To his right—the familiar vast expanse of Central Park, green as far as the eye could see. To his left—towers and people to infinity. He hurried past the Ritz-Carlton Hotel and across 6th Avenue, and two minutes later he stopped at the New York Athletic Club on the corner of 7th Avenue.

Looking south down 7th, the city had no end. The towers ran to a point in the distance, and Peter felt vaguely like Luke Skywalker about to travel the trench of the Death Star. The Hotel Chelsea was located two miles down the 7th Avenue corridor, which was walled with brownstone and glass. To get there, Peter would need to brave the riot of yellow taxies and hissing buses. The air was thick with gas fumes and the aroma of sizzling hotdogs.

"I can do this," he said and he dove into the jungle.

Or at least he tried. His feet refused to cooperate. He scowled at his unresponsive sneakers and attempted to pump his knees. Nothing happened.

A horde of businessmen wearing black suits stormed past, nearly knocking Peter over. He couldn't stand immobile on the corner very long, else he'd be trampled.

"C'mon," he told himself. "What's the big deal? It's only two miles...two huge, scary miles." But he couldn't stop marveling at the height of the towers and the fact that *millions* of people loomed above him. Securely tucked away inside the warm Crown, he never had to think about that.

Was this even a good idea? Who knew what waited at the far end of 7th Avenue. Maybe the Judge—the infamous and shadowy leader of the Red Masque. Or maybe even The Evil Treasure Hunter...

With an extreme exertion of willpower, Peter forced his feet to move. They promptly turned in the *opposite* direction, however, and scurried him across the street and into Central Park. He didn't stop marching until deep inside the trees, 7th Avenue safely out of sight.

He doubled over at the waist to rest and gasp for air. A coward. He was a coward! He'd been so sure he could do this, and now... Now he was a wimp.

He paced back and forth through the grass and fought off tears. Cypress Fitzgerald had given him the bizarre key for a *reason*. The mysterious girl dressed all in white had given him instructions for a *reason!* But neither the girl nor the ghost had reckoned Peter would be too afraid to walk down 7th Avenue. He paced back and forth through the grass and fought off tears. Last spring he'd assumed destiny was calling him and a great adventure awaited, but then summer arrived and so did the surge of tourists, and Peter never had enough time to go, and now...now he felt smaller than his pet mouse. Cypress Fitzgerald had hinted that Peter would be the next Phantom of New York, the successor in a long legacy of infamous heroes. A protector of the Crown. Of the city.

Peter scoffed bitterly at himself.

Some Phantom. The city terrified him. So he paced and rubbed his eyes, holding back tears.

Hawkins soon found him sulking near the Pond and called, "Jumping Jack Peter! You gotta run through the sprinklers with us!" Hawkins stood with the Raiders, a community of kids frequenting the Park. Hawkins was barefoot and without his usual pageboy cap. Rivulets of water streamed out of his hair.

That was *exactly* what Peter needed, some fun to remove his mind from the failed mission. He shrugged off his disappointment, dumped his shirt and shoes on the heap of the Raiders's stuff, and dashed through the sprinklers near Heckscher Playground. Immediately he felt better.

"Hawkins, guess what?" he said, waiting his turn and wiping hair from his eyes. "The circus is coming to town and they're staying at the Crown."

"Wicked! Is it the Circus of Doom?"

"The *what?*" Peter yelped. "Of Doom? I thought it'd be, like, the circus of jugglers and tigers."

"They got those. Circus of Doom is only a name, Peter. I saw them last year, July 15th. We can sneak in for a few shows."

"Or, you know, get tickets like everyone else," suggested Peter.

Hawkins chuckled and punched him in the shoulder.

"How we gon' afford that? I got two dollars to my name, right now."

"I'll ask Mom and Dad and they'll—"

"Oh no. The last thing I need is your mom throwing me out. Hawkins gets *himself* into places. Your family does too much already! I'm a man who can handle his own business and never overstays his welcome. You know?"

Peter fidgeted unhappily. He didn't want to sneak in but he also didn't want to offend his best friend.

Suddenly it was their turn to streak through the water again. They leaped and laughed and skidded for an hour until Park groundskeepers ran them off for wearing out the grass. Peter had been named an honorary Raider because he'd gotten Sneakers (the leader of the gang) a hat last autumn, and Peter felt accepted. All the boys laid out and dried on top of Umpire Rock, discussing food and girls and school and the Yankees. Peter couldn't contribute on any of those subjects, being the youngest and least experienced. Hawkins knew everything about the Yankees, and every other team too. Which pitcher was hot, who was cold, what the lead-off batters were averaging, all kinds of stuff.

As lunch drew near, the Raiders slid down the rock to fetch their clothing. Sneakers, a tall and brooding lout, shouted, "Holy crow! Where's my stuff?"

"Where's *our* stuff?" Peter asked, staring at the empty patch of grass. "Mine's gone too."

Peter and Hawkins and the others hunted through the trees and bushes, disturbing the birds and squirrels, wondering if they'd misremembered the location, but no, this was the small hill on which they'd disrobed—the clothes had simply vanished.

"I don't get it," Peter said, flabbergasted and turning in circles.

"I do." Hawkins's jaw was set and his fists clenched. "It's the Ritz kids. They did this."

"The who?"

"Ritz kids. Punks who want to start a war with the Raiders. They took my sack of books, too."

"Oy! Found them!" Sneakers roared, and the gang rallied near the Center Drive sidewalk. There, stuffed inside two foul garbage cans, was their stuff. The kids hauled handfuls from the trash and sorted through their gear. Peter found his shoes and his shirt, which was stained with mustard from a burger wrapper. Everything stank.

Hawkins trembled with anger. "Ritz kids! I know it's them. They pranked us last year, too, launching kitty litter at us and spray painting Umpire Rock. These are my only shoes and they're soaked with coffee. And the Librarian at your hotel will skin me if these books are ruined."

"But who are they?" Peter asked.

Someone else answered him, a Hispanic boy several years older. "Kids living at the Ritz Carlton. That hotel right there." The Raider pointed at a stately structure across the busy street, a building on the same city block as the Crown.

"This is just like the book *Hunger Games*. The Ritz Kids believe they're at the top of a caste system," growled Hawkins.

"The book what?"

"It's about kids fighting in the future, Peter. You should read more. And *those* are the Ritz Kids."

He pointed at a group of boys lounging at the intersection of Center Drive and 59th. While Peter, Hawkins, and the Raiders wore shorts and jeans and t-shirts, these boys sported khakis and monogramed oxford shirts and belts. Unlike Peter's shock of black hair and Hawkins's curly mess, their hair was perfectly parted and frozen in place. In short, they looked like Atticus Snyder...

...actually, that WAS Atticus Snyder, a vicious brat who lived at the Crown with Peter. He stood in the back, hands in his pockets and a smirk on his face. Peter said, "Hey, that's... what's *he* doing—"

"GET'EM!" roared Sneakers, and the Raiders raced toward the intersection.

"What's afoot, chums?" called the leader of the Ritz kids, a hand to his mouth like half a megaphone. He was a tall youth, broad-shouldered and handsome. "Only lending a hand! Now your clothes match your body odor!"

The Ritz Kids (and Atticus) howled with mirth and trotted across 59th into the safety of their luxury hotel. A few Raiders made attempts to pursue but the doorman cuffed them and ran them off.

Hawkins watched and growled. "Man, I *hate* Ritz kids. They were born with the entire world given to'em, and instead of being generous they're nasty." He was soaking the coffee out from his shoe with dirty napkins. "We'll get'em. We'll roast them, one of these days."

Sneakers and the rest trudged back and dressed sullenly. Sneakers grumbled, "Friends of *yours*, runt?"

"Me?" Peter asked. "No! I don't—"

"You hotel kids are all alike. The Crown, the Ritz, whatever, you're the same. Just like when we first met you, you was protecting that prissy little hotel girl."

Peter stiffened. "Her name's Caroline. She did nothing wrong, and neither have I. I'm not like them."

Sneakers said, "You may not be a Ritz kid, but if you live at the Crown then you're a *rich* kid. Maybe figure out whose side you're on. Let's go, Raiders. We'll wash at the lake near

Strawberry Fields." He glared at Peter and said, "Not all of us have a laundry service."

"But..."

The gang moved north, leaving Peter behind. He gaped at them helplessly. He'd done nothing wrong. His clothes had been trashed too!

Hawkins stopped and turned. "Don't feel bad, my man. He's just mad. Gotta take it out on someone, right?"

"I didn't—"

"I know, Peter, I know. Not your fault. Don't tell your mom about this? She'll get mad at me." Hawkins turned and followed Sneakers and the others.

Peter plodded home in a daze, wondering what'd happened. He'd gone from being one of the gang to an outsider in the blink of an eye. He wasn't a rich kid; his mom *worked* in the Laundry.

He was in such a funk that a yellow Chevy taxi nearly crushed him, swerving at the last second. The driver honked and stuck his head out the window. "Watch out, kid! Gonna get yourself killed, ya dope!"

Peter scampered out of the traffic, heart pounding, ears burning with embarrassment. "Jeez, Pete!" Tony the doorman called. "What's a'matter? I almost had to scrape you off the street."

"I don't know," Peter mumbled. "Wasn't watching..."

"What'cha got on your shirt?"

"Some bullies at the park threw it in the trash."

Tony gave him a solid pat on the back. Instead of making Peter feel better, he felt worse. Tony said, "Rough morning, Pete. Guess you ain't used to New York yet, huh."

"Guess not." He walked numbly across the Lobby and up the stairs. He needed a change of clothes. Joey looked up from her schoolwork as he walked past the Nook and her nose wrinkled.

"What happened to you?" she asked.

"Found out I'm not a New Yorker yet," he sighed.

Nor a Raider, apparently.

Nor was he the Phantom, despite Cypress Fitzgerald's prediction. Phantoms weren't scared of the city and they *didn't* get their shirts stuffed into the trash.

Using his room key, Peter let himself into apartment 201. His mom had gone to work and his father hadn't returned, so their apartment was quiet. He threw his stained shirt into the laundry bin and fetched another, one of his clean superhero shirts. Iron Man was on the front. He held it in his fists, examining the golden face, and he wondered if he'd outgrown it. The shirt fit but...was he childish to still enjoy Iron Man? To watch Batman movies? Older kids didn't wear stuff like this. He stuffed the shirt back into the drawer, unwilling to pull it over his head.

Men in masks were only fantasies.

He'd been foolish to believe he might become one.

No sooner had he changed into a plain shirt than an awful banging erupted from the door.

Peter rushed to the kitchen and yanked the door open, and he gasped. Mean old Victor Webb, the Crown's nastiest resident, stormed in and howled, "WHERE'S MANOS? Where is that confounded Greek man?" Victor's wrinkly skin was pinched tight across his face and hands. As usual he wore a dark shirt and slacks, and he smelled like onions.

"Oh! Mr. Webb," Peter stammered. "I'm not sure. Umm, Mr. Conrad called for a meeting and—"

"I don't give a single cent about any meeting, boy! I've left THREE messages for Manos! My sink is clogged and my chicken livers need washing."

"Chicken livers? Sir, I could unclog your sink if you—"

"I don't allow punk kids into my apartment, noooo thank you! Where's Manos?" he asked again, peering distastefully at the apartment as though Peter's father was hiding.

"Like I said, sir, he's at a meeting. But I'm happy to help."

"I called for Manos! And you, you little twerp, WON'T DO. You're not him. Just a boy. I need an ADULT. Find him and get him upstairs or I'll have his job!" With that, Victor Webb stalked out and slammed the door.

Peter collapsed onto a kitchen chair. *Good grief*, he thought, his ears ringing and his eyes pooling with tears. What an awful day.

2

A ROYAL REUNION

Peter was staring blankly into the refrigerator the following morning, wondering what he should make for breakfast, when his father emerged from the bathroom, dressed for working on greasy pipes in the basement.

Manos was a handsome man with dark eyes and prominent cheekbones, and he said, "There's bacon, behind the milk. Make your mother a few pieces too."

"Yes sir," said Peter, snaking his arm to the rear of the shelf.

Manos poured a mug of coffee. "Did you hear the news? The Circus of Doom is coming to town."

"I heard. Some of them are staying here, right?"

"It'll be hard work, son. The performers are very picky about their animals. Think you can help me out?"

"Of course! What kinds of animals?"

"Tandra—their prized lioness—will be delivering a litter of cubs any day. And the Crown never turns away animals, so we've got to prepare a nursery in the guest rooms."

Peter grinned. "Hah! Baby lions staying in a Crown suite?"

"The lion handlers insist on sleeping near the cubs, who will be too young to be in the circus. Also, the bears and elephants might stay at the Crown when they need a day off."

"Bears and elephants? This'll be great!" Peter cried, but as he spoke he felt a shadow fall over his heart. A sense of dread that had no source. For reasons he couldn't explain, he was suddenly and intensely worried. But why? Something in his subconscious about the circus, perhaps? What could be wrong with a circus staying at the Crown?

"Peter?" his father said. "Are you okay?"

"Hm? What?" said Peter, returning to his senses. His hand was flat on his chest.

"Did you hear me?"

"Oh. Um, sorry. I'm listening now."

Manos said, "You should know, I informed Mr. Conrad that I intend to hunt for jobs outside the city."

"You *did?*" blurted Peter. "But...but why?"

"Don't panic yet." Manos took a sip of coffee and continued, "Mr. Conrad practically turned blue in the face, like yours is now. He started blubbering about the importance of the circus. Offered me a raise to stay."

"A raise? That's great news, right?"

"Your mother thinks so. She said it's just in time for you to get new shoes. And hers are a disgrace too, apparently, though they seem fine to me. I still don't make near as much as at my old job in accounting."

"But *why* did you tell him you wanted to leave the Crown?" One of Peter's hands was shoved into his pocket, fingering the weird black key. The other hand rubbed at his chest—his heart hurt. Not only did the circus inexplicably fill him with dread, but this fresh bit of news could be even worse.

"Well..." Manos said and paused, casting a glance back at the bedroom. Yesterday Manos and Jovanna had received word that Manos's old accounting firm burned to the ground and police suspected arson. Scary news, especially because his former client, Gordie Abaddon the infamous treasure hunter, was still in hiding and searching for the Constantine family. Manos and Jovanna didn't want to worry Peter and so they hadn't told him. "Being the superintendent at a hotel isn't why I went to college. I'm an accountant. But we'll live at the Crown at least until the circus leaves town and then we'll reevaluate. Sound good?"

Peter nodded but he wasn't fully pacified. He didn't want to leave his new home.

Manos left for work and Peter started cooking bacon, but the feeling of dread and shadow stayed with him until lunch.

PETER DIDN'T SEE Caroline Crawford that day nor the next despite his best attempts at a casual encounter. An awful thought occurred to him and he nonchalantly asked the front desk if the Crawfords had moved, but he was assured that the Crawford family had returned safe and sound. The attendant, a lady who'd watched Peter escort Caroline to the Valentine's Ball last February, tried not to smile as she delivered the good news. Peter also tried not to smile as he heard it.

On Thursday he and Joey busied themselves with schoolwork inside the Nook, sitting around a coffee table and drinking raspberry lemonade. They both wore pajamas. After finishing his math, Peter snatched the newspaper and scanned the pages.

Over the summer, a new kid had moved into the Crown. Grover Ivory had been born with the rare condition of being allergic to sunlight, so his family kept him inside all day. He'd fallen in love with Joey at first sight, trailing her around and often waiting in the Nook for hours, much to Joey's chagrin. Her friendship with Peter irked Grover to no end so he verbally abused Peter whenever possible, despite being two years younger and thin as a twig.

Today Grover was sitting in a reading chair near the corner, wearing black socks but no shoes. He snickered. "Look'it Peter Constantine pretending to read a newspaper! It's adorable, like a dog watching television."

"Grover, be nice," said Joey.

Peter didn't hear him. An article had caught his eye; displayed prominently on page three was a photograph of The Evil Treasure Hunter. Peter stood and nervously paced the Nook, weaving through the luxurious furniture and absorbing the article.

THE INFAMOUS FUGITIVE and treasure-hunting Gordie Warren suffered another setback yesterday, as police raided his midtown bank vault...

GORDIE ABADDON WAS A WEIRD NAME, Peter thought. Not very scary. But his picture sure was.

...DISCOVERING a trove of bizarre historical and religious arti-facts. Authorities are still pouring over the collection, but an unnamed source revealed that the confiscated pieces are not collector's items, or valuable in and of themselves. Items such as voodoo dolls, rosary beads, a prayer mat, and an oil lamp, the kind which summons a genie in fairy tales.

In fact, the only connection between the artifacts is the supposed ability to grant the user immense power...

"PETER? HELLOOOO?"

He lowered the paper, realizing he'd heard his name called several times in a row. He said, "Yes?"

"What're you reading about?" asked Joey.

A terrifying man trying to capture my family, he thought. Out loud he said, "Um...uh, fish?"

"Fish?"

He winced. Why on earth did he say fish? "Err, fish...sticks."

"The kind you dip into tartar sauce?" One of her eyebrows arched.

"No, the other kind," he said, folding the paper and clamping it under his arm. Not even Joey knew about his family's terrible secret, that they were hiding from a dangerous man. What did the article mean, grant the user immense power? Was that what The Evil Treasure Hunter was searching for in the Crown, some sort of magical weapon? Peter would have to finish the article later.

"Boys are so weird, always thinking about food," said Joey. "Are you going to the Park today?"

"Maybe, dunno."

"You're still upset with Hawkins."

Peter stopped at the Nook's window and peered at the intersection of 58th and Grand Army, jammed with traffic. "I'm not *upset*. It was mean that he took sides with Sneakers, is all."

"Can't you see, Peter? Hawkins didn't take sides. He

simply left with his family."

"They're a gang, not a family."

"Poor Petah! Shame on 'dose mean kiddies!" called Grover. "Did they hurt your feewings?"

"Ignore him, Peter. And don't stress about Hawkins picking sides. We've known him for a year, but who knows how long he's been a Raider. Family is family. And they're family."

Peter huffed.

She continued, "And if you're not upset, go find him."

"Why should *I* have to find him? I did nothing wrong."

"You're funny looking. Doesn't that count?"

Peter growled, "Grover! Go home, you little twerp."

The skinny boy smirked.

Joey did her best not to enjoy the insults but her eyes were shinning with mirth. "Focus, Peter. You have parents who teach you right from wrong and how to be generous. Hawkins doesn't."

He scowled and walked back to their homework table. "I'm not apologizing to him. Or to Sneakers."

"You don't have to."

"What do you think happened to Hawkins's parents? How could they simply be gone?" asked Peter.

"Maybe he ran away. Maybe they died. Maybe he never knew them," she said, and she blew eraser crumbles off her paper and started another math problem. "You could ask him. Point is, he needs you."

"If I go back, they might think I'm groveling for forgiveness."

She sighed. "Don't be such a baby, Peter. It's been several days. They're mad at the Ritz kids, not at you."

"Yeah Peter," muttered Grover. "Don't be such a baby."

Peter crossed his arms and fell backwards into the overstuffed reading chair, crossing his ankles on the table. "Those Ritz kids are jerks. And do you know? Atticus Snyder was with them. Figures."

Joey groaned and threw her pencil at him. "You *must* stop this pouting. It's unmanly. You know what I like about you?" she asked, screwing up her eyes in concentration. "I'm only now realizing it—you're a positive person. You're optimistic and you see the best in people. You've got a good heart. Now quit being so sour."

Peter tossed the pencil back and opened up a novel, one Hawkins had suggested, titled *Hatchet*. After a minute of silence, he grinned. "Thanks, Joey."

"You're welcome."

"I guess my heart's pretty good, huh."

"Nope," said Grover. "You're basically a toilet."

Joey smiled down at her paper. "Yes, Peter. Sometimes. Now hush. I'm working on dividing variables."

DARCI DRAKE WAS the only person who took Peter's story seriously. She believed he'd seen the Red Masque the night of the fire. She also believed the claims of Caroline Crawford and the fire fighter, who had seen the Phantom of New York inside the smoke. Three eyewitnesses in a matter of two months was too much of a coincidence for her to ignore. She was, after all, a famous writer who focused on New York City.

Last May she'd written an opinion piece for the Times newspaper and caused a minor sensation. She openly suggested that the eyewitnesses HAD seen the Phantom but that he wasn't flesh and bone; instead he was the long-rumored ghost who lived on the Crown's tenth floor.

. . .

"Perhaps more is going on at the Crown Hotel than meets the eye," she'd written. "Perhaps there is more to our beloved city than the physical world. This writer, for one, is rooting for the Phantom's return even if he does it as a ghost. With the Red Masque's mounting terrorist activity, we need all the help we can find."

Just like that, the Phantom was in the news again. Peter hoped during the course of her investigation she would uncover information about the Judge, the shadowy leader of the Red Masque. No one knew anything about him.

Peter stumbled across Darci that afternoon as he went to fetch the mail. She perched in her usual spot, feet tucked under in the cushy chair near the coffee shop, pouring over her black notebook. Although her presumptions in the article were wrong, she was too close to the truth for Peter's comfort. Moreover, she'd developed the frightening habit of glaring suspiciously at Peter.

She spotted Peter before he could hide in the ficus plants. She appeared ready to grill him for another hour about that fateful night, but he was saved by Ms. Ernestine Parker, who entered the Lobby from the outside doors, balancing two bags of groceries. Despite the warm weather, she was dressed in a brown scarf and long sleeves. "Peter, be a dear," she said, setting the heavy paper bags into his hands. "I'm just about all used up."

"My pleasure, Ms. Parker," Peter said, peeking over his shoulder at Darci, who sat back down unhappily. He walked with Ernestine toward the golden elevators. "Is that a new necklace? It's lovely."

Ernestine Parker's face broke into a pleased smile. She was responsible for Peter's cordial education, teaching him about correct, incorrect, and inappropriate behavior. "Aren't you a scoundrel, Peter Constantine. But, as a matter of fact, yes, it's new."

"You might want to wear something less flashy, ma'am, unless you're chasing bachelors."

She laughed and swatted him on the shoulder. "You rat. You shouldn't tease old women so. A gentleman only compliments when appropriate. You'll come up for tea, yes? At four o'clock? I need to hear about your school work, I think."

Peter didn't respond.

The golden elevator opened and Caroline Crawford stepped out. Her blue eyes widened and locked onto Peter's.

"Peter? You'll join me for tea?" Ernestine Parker asked again, but she followed Peter's gaze to the elevator. "Ah. The Crawfords have returned, bringing home your Valentine's date. Close your mouth, dear boy, you're a gentleman."

It'd only been two months since he last saw Caroline, but she looked like she'd grown two years. Her hair was brighter, her eyes bluer, her smile wider. She'd tanned in Europe and a ribbon of freckles lay across the tops of her cheeks.

"Hello Peter," she said. "Fancy meeting you here."

Peter had to search for his voice, but finally he said, "H-hi Caroline. Welcome home."

Ernestine Parker gave her a hug, the kind of small hug only rich people do, Peter thought. She said, "Yes, dear, so good to see you again. Here, Mr. Constantine, give me the groceries. Don't you think you should take Miss Caroline for a walk in the Park?"

"That would be lovely," Caroline said and she bounced

on her toes.

Peter said, "I can walk your groceries to your apartment, Ms. Parker, and then—"

She interrupted, "Nonsense, young man. Give them here. You two have a good time, and we'll have tea another day. Yes?"

Peter handed her the bag. "Sure. Ahh, I mean, yes, thank you."

"You're welcome, dear." She gave them her blessing by way of a smile, and the elevator whisked her away.

Alone for the moment in the Lobby, Caroline said, "Peter, you've gotten bigger."

"So have you. But, um! I mean, not in a bad way. What I mean to say was, errr, you look...older. But, you know, it's nice. S-should we go for a walk?" he asked, suddenly and shockingly nervous.

Tony the doorman gave Peter a wink on their way out, and soon they were strolling through sunlight at the Park. The awkwardness of infatuation gave way to warm affection and they chatted the way friends should.

"I bet Europe was fun," said Peter.

"Magical! We spent a month in London and then toured Switzerland and Spain and France by train. Have you ever vacationed on a train, Peter?"

"No, never. We've never gone on a real vacation."

"I hope you get to," she said. "You see the world's most beautiful sights from a comfy chair while servers bring you treats."

"Wow! That does sound magical."

Caroline said, "We even slept on the train. We saw the Alps, and the Rhine, and we went through tunnels in the mountains, and...oh, did you know that people in Europe talk about the fire at our hotel?"

"You're kidding! How'd they know?" he asked as they passed the Hallett Nature Sanctuary. As it often happened with Caroline, he didn't know what to do with his hands, and his feet felt too big. He clasped his fingers behind his back, changed his mind, shoved them into his pockets, and then tripped and stumbled.

"Careful, Peter. Anyway, it was international news, apparently. And passengers riding in our train car discussed the Red Masque," said Caroline. "They believe New York City is in danger and the syndicate is worse than we realize."

"That's what I believe! Except no one listens to me. Did they...did anyone, you know, mention the Phantom?"

Caroline looked down at her shoes and Peter thought she might be blushing. "No one thinks he's real. Yet. But I think, I *hope*, one day they will. Because he's incredible."

"He is?"

"I know you might not believe me. Not everyone does. But Peter, I promise I saw him. He *carried* me. He's big and strong and he wears a mask."

Peter grinned helplessly. "Strong, huh? He had big muscles, you think?"

"It sounds silly, even to my own ears. It's almost a cliche, I know, but it *happened*. My brother saw him too, even if he doesn't talk about it," she said.

"I believe you. The Phantom was real. And he promised to return." Peter gazed south, towards scary 7th Avenue and the distant Hotel Chelsea. If only the new Phantom wasn't a coward...

Who am I kidding. I'm no Phantom.

A magical world, just beyond my reach...

A breeze blew strands of blonde hair into her face and she pushed them back. "I'm talking about myself too much, aren't I. Sorry, Peter. My father would throw a fit."

"I don't mind. I think the Phantom's fascinating."

She asked, "What about you? How was your summer?"

"Nothing happened, really. But, oh, the circus is coming, that's news."

"The circus!" Caroline beamed. "I enjoy a circus. Cirque du Soleil?"

"It's called the Circus of Doom. And the performers will be your neighbors for two months."

"They're staying at the Crown?"

"Mr. and Mrs. Banks like circuses, apparently," said Peter.

"How charming. Something to look forward to."

Peter started to reply but at that moment he felt a shadow fall over him, the same sensation he experienced in the kitchen with his father. It wasn't physical, nothing he could touch—more of an anxiety. The feeling wasn't painful but it wasn't pleasant either. He winced and tried to shrug it off.

Oblivious to his discomfort, Caroline continued, "I saw Hawkins at school today. He's something of a legend."

"I didn't know you went to Trinity," remarked Peter, and he turned in a quick circle to make sure no one was following them, just in case, but they were alone. *Why* was he suddenly so worried?

"Of course. Where else would I go?" she said.

"Why is Hawkins a legend?"

"He hardly ever attends and when he does he's never in dress code. He's three grades ahead of other kids his age. He scores a perfect on all his tests, and there is a rumor that his tuition is entirely covered by the school."

Peter nodded in appreciation. "Hawkins is a genius, I think. He only started reading novels last year, and he's already gone through half the Library. Ack—" he grunted, because the shadowy sensation grew worse.

"Ack? Are you okay?" Caroline asked.

"I think so, it's only..."

It was only *what*? He didn't know. He turned and glared down the path they'd been traveling and understood *somehow* the shadow came from that direction.

He was staring directly at the Crown, noble and glittering in the sun like a pink castle.

"The Crown..." he whispered. "Something's there..."

"What's wrong? Can you tell me?" Out of concern, Caroline placed her hand on Peter's arm.

All thoughts of discomfort disappeared, blasted into oblivion. Her fingers—touching his bare skin. Their eyes connected and each reacted as though jolted by electricity, jumping and pulling away.

"I'm so sorry, Peter! I—"

"No, no, I didn't mean—"

"Did I startle—"

"No! That is, I'm not, uhhh, it wasn't—"

"Only, I thought you were upset and—"

"I liked it—"

"Crawford!" called a new voice. "Caroline Crawford, here you are."

Atticus Snyder was sauntering their way. His red hair was precisely parted and his khaki pants were cuffed, and he wore leather boat shoes. Peter thought he looked ludicrous, exactly like a Ritz kid.

"Hello, Atticus," replied Caroline coolly, recovering from the shock of touching Peter's arm. His *strong* arm, she thought.

"Welcome home, love. I hope your summer vacation was as fierce as my own. Look, it's Peter. Good to see you, chum," said Atticus, inclining his head backwards so he could look down his sharp nose at them.

Love? Chum? Good to see me? What was wrong with Atticus? Peter wracked his brain, recalling Ernestine Parker's lessons, but he didn't know how to respond.

"Where did you travel, Atticus?" Caroline asked.

"Australia, and of course the Polynesia islands, as one must, that time of year. Listen, Crawford, I've been introduced to the most elite gang of chums. You've got to meet them. They'll adore you."

"Who are they?"

Peter, feeling shabby next to Atticus, answered, "The Ritz kids, I bet. I saw Atticus following them around."

Atticus shot him an annoyed glance. "Great fellows. Yes, they live at the Ritz Carlton, so what?"

"So they shoved our clothes in the trash, that's what."

Atticus grinned and his face reddened with glee. "You were with that pack of rats? Whatever for? Got what they deserved, running half-naked around the Park and destroying our grass."

"I've seen those boys, Atticus," said Caroline. "They're cocky jerks."

"No no, Crawford, wait till you get to know them. They've got the Crown hopelessly outclassed," he said, gesturing towards the hotels. His other hand was still in his pants pocket.

"What do you mean?"

"The Ritz is newer and nicer, and the residents are top tier."

Caroline tsk'ed at him. "How can it be nicer than our hotel? The Crown is one of the nicest hotels on the planet."

"They've got us beat, love, no way round it. But they're willing to mingle with us. Me and you, maybe Leo, though he's a bit fat, couple kids I don't know well on ninth floor, and some older teenagers—"

"Atticus, you've changed. You're mimicking their words, and stop calling me 'love.' You can be friends with whomever you like. What's that got to do with me?" she asked.

"It matters, Crawford," he said, and he strained with urgency. "It *matters*. It says a lot about who we are. What if they see you with Peter? I mean, don't get me wrong, he's a great sport, but he pals around with the Raiders. The *Raiders*, Caroline. They'll think less of us."

He's a great sport? Was Atticus taking snarky manners lessons at the Ritz?

"What's wrong with the Raiders?" asked Peter.

He scoffed. "Look, I'm trying to be civil, Peter. But I don't know where to start with that question. Just...shush."

"The Raiders stole my hat and punched you in the stomach, Peter," said Caroline. "Remember? Why would you befriend them?"

"Because...because..." Peter couldn't think of a reason, all the sudden.

"They're homeless rats, chum. I know your family only gets to live with us because they work there, but *technically* you've got a place to live. Right? Listen, Crawford, I'll put in a good word for you. You'll do great with this crowd."

She offered a slight shrug. "Whatever you say, Atticus, but I really don't care much for them. Maybe if they learn to be kind."

"You'll see, Crawford." He turned to go. "Just as soon as you grow up. Cheers."

He walked away, hands in his pockets and looking smugly upon the world. Peter muttered, "Cheers? Who says that?"

For some reason neither could explain, Atticus had sucked the fun out of their walk. They made an effort but it was no use—neither felt much like talking anymore. Soon they turned for home, a quiet march, each worried what the other was thinking.

At least the shadow had evaporated from Peter's mind. Completely gone. What *was* that?

They reached the Lobby and the doors hissed open. The hot September heat surrendered to the cool and perfumed air of the Crown. Immediately Peter spotted his father Manos talking with Mr. Conrad (the hotel's senior manager), and they waved him over.

"I should go," he said glumly.

"Peter, I'm sorry our walk turned out so...bleak. I don't know why I let Atticus bother me," she said.

"It's my fault, I—"

"No, no, I looked so forward to seeing you—"

"Me too," Peter said.

"You did? Because I... well, and then—"

"Atticus showed up—"

"Exactly! And he—"

"Ruined it, somehow..."

"Yes."

The two kept interrupting and talking over one another, trying as best thirteen-year-olds can to express friendship and loyalty and guarded affection, but in the end Caroline covered a giggle with her hand and she dashed off to the elevator with a, "Bye Peter!" over her shoulder.

Unbeknownst to either, behind them and hidden near the ficus plants, a girl dressed in white was watching. She'd spotted Peter in the park and followed. As Peter trailed his father up the stairs, she sniffed in disapproval, slipped on a pair of white sunglasses, and snuck out.

3

MARLOWE BLODGETT

Like he did every morning, Peter rose, yawned, stretched, said hello to the mouse, and went into the bathroom. On this particular morning however, when he returned, an unhappy ghost was sitting on the dresser.

"Yer not him," the ghost half-moaned, half-snarled.

Peter, startled almost to the point of a heart attack, jumped into the air. He was quite a good leaper and he struck his head against the ceiling, a sharp blow that surely woke anyone sleeping on the level above.

The fat white mouse rolled its eyes as Peter staggered around the room and held his ringing head.

He collapsed onto his bed and said, "Oooooowww!"

The ghost watched all this with grim confirmation. "Definitely *not* him."

"Who are you?" Peter asked, blinking away stars in his vision. "Do you work here? What're you doing in my room?"

The ghost scoffed and began to fade from view. "Nothing but an under-fed cabin scamp, don't know why I bother..."

Peter gasped, only now realizing the unhappy man

sitting on his dresser was *see-through*—more of a mist. A mist wearing a cockeyed hat and red scarf. "Hey, wait!"

The ghoul froze in mid-evaporation. "You'll address me as Captain, boy."

"You're a ghost!"

"Course I am," it growled. "Y'think I look like this because'a scurvy?"

"What'd you want?" Peter asked, rubbing his head but thinking a little more clearly. "Why're you here?"

"Wasting m'time, so it seems."

"Are you...errr, were you...friends with Cypress Fitzgerald?"

"Bah," the ghost hissed. "Friends with that landlubber? I think not. With his fancy pants and shoes..."

At these words, the mouse jumped and made angry noises.

"Ghost, listen, I need your help," Peter began. "About the Chelsea Hotel—"

"Pipe down and I'll give ye some advice," the ghost sneered, and it faded from view. "Give that key to the *real* Phantom..."

The words echoed hollowly around the room. "Hello?" Peter asked and got no response. He and the mouse stared at one another. The fat rodent shook its head, and Peter got the impression it was saying, *Don't listen to that stupid stupid man!*

"The real Phantom," Peter repeated. "I knew it. There's a real person. An adult, I bet, not just a teenager, like me." In his heart, Peter had been holding out hope that Cypress was right, that he was the next Phantom. But really, he told himself, that was absurd. He felt embarrassed he ever assumed otherwise. The real Phantom was probably a giant man with huge shoulders, fists the size of a Toyota. "I have to find him," Peter said.

The mouse emitted an actual hissing noise.

"What's your problem, mouse? We can help him! He's probably looking for this key," Peter said.

The mouse, with a shocking burst of energy, leaped onto him and bit his finger.

"Hey, ouch!" Peter cried and flung the rodent into the far corner. "That hurt."

The mouse picked itself off the floor, gave a full body shake, and glared malevolently.

Peter glared back and said, "Hmphf."

Hmphf, it said in return and wobbled unsteadily under the bed.

FOR THE FIRST time in two months, Peter knocked on Arthur Graves's door. He'd arrived five minutes early, which meant he was on time. Barely.

The door was flung open and he was greeted by his boxing coach, an older but powerful man. Arthur Graves was probably in his sixties and he kept his white hair and beard trimmed close. His nose looked puffy, as though it'd been broken several times when he was young. "Get in, Pete. Let's get started."

"Welcome back, sir," Peter said. He knew the routine— he hustled to the hallway closet to fetch an old pair of boxing gloves and pull out a thick mannequin on wheels. Arthur's apartment was furnished with only a television and cushioned reclining chair, leaving ample space for exercise. The air smelled of bacon and ointment, and he kept the temperature at sixty-four degrees.

Atticus Snyder had already arrived. He'd been boxing longer than Peter and he was good at it. He wore boxing

shorts and a t-shirt (they matched), and he brought his own
shiny pair of new gloves. Next to him, Peter's old clothes and
gloves looked dingy. Atticus said, "Coach Graves, I hope
your trip was as fierce as my summer vacation."

"Fierce? That's a nonsense description of a holiday, and
it wasn't, Snyder. Boxing's a dying sport. Kids today are soft
and so am I. I'm getting tired of Las Vegas. Missed my bed.
Missed my—" Arthur's rant was interrupted by a knock at
the door. He yanked it open and Peter was astonished to see
Leo in the doorway. "You're late, Tanaka."

"Wha...?" Leo glanced at his fancy watch. He was unac-
customed to being yelled at. "I'm on time."

"Which means you're late. Get in here and get some
gloves on," Graves grumbled.

Peter showed Leo to the closet. "What're you doing here,
Leo? You want to box?" he asked doubtfully.

"No," snorted Leo. "My parents forced me. In my
country—"

"Less talking, you two. Tanaka! Get those gloves on!"

"I'm trying!" complained Leo, waving his chubby hands,
stuck halfway in the gloves.

Graves bopped him on the back of the head and said,
"Where's those famous Japanese manners? I need a lot more
respect outta you, boy." He shoved the gloves over Leo's fat
fingers and dragged out another boxing mannequin. "Set
your feet. Watch Synder and Constantine, Tanaka. We gotta
strengthen those weak hands and arms. I said set your feet!
Atta boy, Peter. Ready?"

For three minutes, the boys smacked the heavy
punching dummies. Arthur Graves called, "Left, left, right-
left. No, no, snap that wrist, Pete! Jab, jab, hook! Like this,
Tanaka, like *this*," and they did their best to keep up. It was
only three minutes but Peter's shoulders were screaming at

the end. His knuckles stung and he dripped sweat. The long summer break had deteriorated his muscles and it showed.

Leo turned a bright purple and he stared with horror at Graves, like the boxing coach had grown another head. He tried to ask a question, but between wheezes it came out as, "Heee-eeeee-eeeooooo-ooooohhhhh..."

During the second grueling three-minute round, Atticus lowered his gloves and collapsed. He was pale and looked as though he might throw up.

Leo was feebly swinging his shoulders, unable to get his fists above his belt.

Arthur brought them water and said, "See what I mean? Soft! What'd you do this summer, Atticus, sit on a beach and eat cookies? I was your age, I had *two* jobs. Look at Pete, here. Worked all summer. Got them strong arms and hands. Atta boy, Pete."

Peter didn't *feel* strong. His hands refused to function at the moment...but at least he was standing. Last year, Atticus had been stronger and quicker—not anymore.

Graves called, "Three minute break."

Atticus sneered at Peter when the boxing coach's back was turned and he muttered, "Not all of us carry garbage every day."

"Need help getting up, *chum?* Don't the Ritz kids exercise?" Peter asked.

"I don't need exercise," said Atticus. "My family manufactures robots that will one day do everything for us."

Peter rolled his eyes.

"Buu...buu...hooow...hooo...I...I," huffed Leo. The poor boy could neither breathe nor concentrate.

After the break, Arthur Graves returned from the closet and said, "Here. Gonna try something new. These are punching mitts. Put these on, Pete."

Unlike boxing gloves, which curled the fingers, the punching mitts kept his hands flat and the cushioning was in the palm. "You hold these up, and Atticus hits them. Make sense? It'll make you quicker and stronger. You dig?"

"No," they both said.

"Here, I'll show you." Arthur held up his bare hands, which were thick and tough, palms facing out. "My hands are the targets, Atticus. Hit'em. Left, left, right."

Atticus eyed him suspiciously. "You sure?"

"Hit'em, boy! Left, left, right."

Atticus obeyed, punching Graves's palms.

"Just like that, 'sept you hit like a newborn baby. Pete, hold your mitts like targets. Steady, that's it. Now, Atticus, jabs only. Go."

Gradually they got the hang of it. Instead of hitting a big thick dummy they had to concentrate on smaller targets. Holding up the mitts was almost as hard as punching, and the bones in Peter's hands ached from jarring collisions. Atticus snarled and smacked Peter's mitts as hard as he could, like he wanted to break them. Soon they swapped and traded rolls. Peter jabbed and hooked savagely, enjoying the popping sounds. Atticus was exhausted but didn't dare drop the mitts, else he might take a fist to the nose.

Leo kept swatting the dummy, resorting to kicks and head butts when his arms lost muscle power entirely.

By the end, none of the boys could lift his hands. Their knuckles bled and fingers throbbed. Peter wanted more water but couldn't squeeze the bottle or bring it to his mouth.

Arthur Graves watched them with a cheerful and devilish glee. "Hard work, growing into a man, ain't it?"

"Yes sir," Peter panted.

Atticus was unable to respond. Leo was lying on the floor and trying not to die.

Arthur said, "Want to be tough? Strong? There's no easy way. Gotta work. Gotta want it. And who knows, one day it might pay off. Might save your life."

PETER GOT out from the shower, dressed, and discovered a surprise sitting at the kitchen table.

"Hawkins!" he cried.

Hawkins looked up from his book and grinned. His tattered backpack was hooked over the chair. "Is it...is it okay if I'm here?"

"You don't need to ask. That's why you have a key."

"Your mom won't mind?" he asked.

"Of course not, she thinks you're great."

Hawkins's smile widened and he looked down at the book in his hands, something by Jules Verne. "It's nice, having someone's mother think I'm great."

Peter sat next to him. "Can I ask a personal question? What happened to your mom?"

Hawkins gave a half shrug. "Not sure. Prison, probably. She was dating the wrong guy, last I saw her. Getting in trouble."

"Should we try to find her?"

"Nah, she wasn't that great of a mom. The worst, actually. I hope she's okay. But...I like my new families better, you and the Raiders. Yikes, Peter, what happened to your hands?"

"Boxing," Peter answered, examining his swollen knuckles. "They hurt."

"You're a weird guy, you know that, Peter? Not many kids these days box."

"Atticus does."

Hawkins set the book on the table and chuckled. "I bet he quits soon. Probably just something his dad makes him do to keep him busy, cause his kid's a creep."

"Are you hungry?"

"Starving!"

The boys investigated the Nook where they discovered spiced apple cider and an entire birthday cake leftover from the Windsor. Joey joined them and soon they were sitting around their usual table, laughing at the frosting on each other's face.

"I'm supposed to be eating steak," Peter said, eyeballing his fourth piece of buttercream-frosted lemon cake. "Or hamburgers or chicken."

"I can get you those, Peter," Joey said, eating her cake with a fork. "But why?"

"For the protein, a'course," answered Hawkins. "Rebuilding the muscles. Else he'll never build up wicked awesome strength. Can you really get him steak and hamburgers?"

She nodded and handed Hawkins a napkin, because he was wearing so much icing he looked like Santa. "We dispose of meat near the expiration date. The trash, or we give it away. I'll ask my dad but he'll say yes. He's crazy about Peter."

Peter's father strode into the Nook, accompanied by Mr. Conrad and a newcomer. Manos called, "Peter, over here. You too, Joey and Hawkins. Come meet someone. This is Marlowe Blodgett, the senior circus director. He's visiting early to make preparations."

Marlowe Blodgett was tall and darkly handsome with a friendly face. His lively green eyes twinkled over gaunt cheeks and a thin mustache. He shook Peter's hand with long fingers and said, "Ahhhh, yes. Zee boy, Peter Constantine!" He pronounced it, Pete-AIR. "You will be helping zee circus, yes?"

"I will help, yes sir," Peter said, decoding the thick accent. "Extremely honored, Mr. Blodgett."

"Look, zee boy has manners! Well done, Manos!" Marlowe Blodgett said and he threw up his hands in theatrical praise. "I knew we came to zee right hotel. Together we will make beautiful magic!"

Another man trudged into the room, carrying Marlowe Blodgett's luggage. He wasn't as tall as Marlowe. In fact he wasn't as tall as Joey, who was short. He was a little person, rising to the height of Peter's elbow. Peter tried not to stare, because that would be rude, but he'd only seen them in pictures.

Mr. Conrad, a kind man who'd gone bald early and who always wore a tweed jacket, was also trying not to stare, and doing a poor job of it. He said, "Ahhh, Mr. Blodgett, should we, ummm, show you to your room? That way your, ahh, midget can unload?"

Hawkins released a burst of laughter. "Mr. Conrad! C'mon, man, you can't call him *that*. Everyone knows they're either dwarfs or little people, right?"

Mr. Conrad went purple with embarrassment. "Oh! Was that...was I...s-surely you understand—I meant nothing...oh dear..."

Marlowe Blodgett laughed good-naturedly and wrapped his arm around the humiliated hotel manager. "Or even better, my friend, call him by his name! Zis is Keith. His family performs in zee circus."

Keith, a sturdy man with a stoic face, appeared not to hear a word.

"But yes, please lead zee way to zee room. Children, you come too!" he cried and swept them all toward the golden guest elevators, a luxury the kids weren't often allowed. Instead of clunking and banging like the service elevator, the guest elevator zoomed and chimed.

Peter found Marlowe Blodgett fascinating. His hands and neck had been tattooed with words, like "LIVE FREE" and "DOOM" and "MOMMA," and silver hoop earrings pierced the tops of his ears. His belt was a thick strand of leather cords and his jeans had patches all over. Both his mustache and hair were the color of midnight. He kinda looked like a pirate, Peter thought. He asked Marlowe, "Where's the circus now, sir?"

"Zee Circus of Doom is...is..." he said theatrically, "...is somewhere. Keith, where is zee circus?"

"Atlanta," Keith answered.

"Atlanta!" Marlowe cried. "A charming city but nothing compared to zee mighty New York. We will be here in...in... Keith, when will we be here?"

"End of November," Keith answered with a bored expression.

"Yes, zee end of November. And we are SO looking forward to it. Many of us are from here, you know."

"End of November?" asked Hawkins. "But that's over two months away."

"Yes, but zee lioness Tandra will deliver cubs soon, and zey represent a considerable investment. I'm visiting zee hotels now to make arrangements. You see, I do not perform in zee circus. Zis is my job."

Peter had never been on the nineteenth floor because it was reserved specifically for the wealthiest guests. The carpets were so thick his shoes sank into them, and expensive rugs were laid out in the central floor lobby. The chandeliers looked like diamond starbursts and they cast rainbow prisms on the wall. A butler waited at the elevator bank with crystal goblets of bubbly drink for the adults. Marlowe Blodgett took glasses and pressed them into the hands of Manos and Mr. Conrad, who otherwise wouldn't partake.

Mr. Conrad led them to 1919 and opened the set of double-doors with a key. The children oooh'ed and aaah'ed. The room looked nearly as big as the Lobby and it sparkled and gleamed. The marbled entryway alone was bigger than the Constantine's entire apartment. An enormous window overlooked Central Park. Peter breathed, "Oh wow."

"Yes, oh WOW!" Marlowe cried.

"Look at that," Hawkins said, rushing to the window. "I've never been this high, I suppose."

"You children must visit and enjoy zee view! For zis is where we will keep Tandra and her cubs."

Joey, finding this too illogical to comprehend, spoke for the first time since meeting Marlowe. "Here? In *this* luxury suite? But...but..."

"Zee lioness and her cubs will stay out of zee public eye for three months, other zan select publicity shoots. A necessary precaution, and her handlers insist! So naturally we must create a den in zee hotel suite."

Manos handed Joey a set of sketches and schematics. "What do you think, Joey? With you as my helper, can we build a den in this suite?"

Her ears reddened with pleasure and she gave him a nod, glancing through the papers. "I would love to, Mr. Constantine, although I'm already quite busy. Do Mr. and Mrs. Banks approve?"

"They do indeed," replied Mr. Conrad. "Not all the owners agree, but the majority have been convinced. The circus will stay with us and the Crown will fully accommodate them."

"Some animals have better lives than people," Hawkins noted.

Peter glanced out the window. This was the same view he'd seen from the Crawford apartment last February, when he'd been trapped in a fire. That meant the Crawford's unit was directly five stories below. Idly he wondered if the abandoned dumbwaiter shaft ran all the way up here. Probably. That shaft had saved his life.

"A toast to zee circus and to zee Crown," Marlowe cried and he raised his drink. Manos and Mr. Conrad and Keith clinked their bubbling glasses. "May our partnership make beautiful magic!"

"Hear, hear!" Mr. Conrad drained the golden liquid in one gulp.

"Gentleman, and Miss Joey of course, I am very tired after zee long day of travel. I'm sure Keith is too, yes, Keith? But first, if you don't mind, I would like to see zee basement. Zee circus is hoping to build additional pens for animals in need of a rest."

Mr. Conrad said, "Of course, Mr. Blodgett, I'd be happy to show—"

"Perhaps, Mr. Conrad," interrupted Marlowe, "it would be better if zee children show me? It's late and I've kept you too long."

"Not at all, Mr. Blodgett, it's my pleasure."

"I insist! Zee children will show me zee basement, and zey'll be home in fifteen minutes. Yes? I insist!"

Manos shared a curious glance with Mr. Conrad, but he

nodded. Carefully he said, "Fifteen minutes is fine. After that, I'll come fetch them."

"Fifteen minutes, children! Let's hurry! Keith, follow us!" Marlowe cried and he rushed to the elevator. Keith and Peter and Joey and Hawkins hurried after, and the golden elevator plunged them toward the depths of the Crown.

Inside the elevator, Peter asked, "Mr. Blodgett, why didn't you want the adults?"

"Please, Peter! Call me Marlowe. Adults, ugh, you know...we can be so..."

"Stuffy," said Keith, leaning in the corner with hands in his pockets.

"Yes, Keith, stuffy. And..."

"Boring," Keith added.

Marlowe agreed. "Yes! Boring."

"And nosey."

"Zey get zee idea, Keith, don't be so talkative! Besides, children always know zee best ghost stories!" Marlowe said, with a gleam in his eye.

"Ghost stories?" the children yelped.

"Yes! Certainly zee famous Crown has ghost stories. I love to hear zem."

"Peter *met* the Crown's ghost once," said Joey knowingly. "On the 10th floor."

"You did?" Marlowe asked, turning his attention onto Peter. "You must tell me!"

"Ummm..." Peter stammered, furious with Joey. He didn't like to talk about it. "Well, sir...ahh, I mean Marlowe... there's an old legend. About Cypress Fitzgerald."

"Yes! I know zis one. You *met* him?"

"Well..."

"You met Cypress Fitzgerald?" Keith asked, as though he didn't believe him. "Really met him?"

Peter gave a noncommittal shrug. "Sometimes I think maybe I imagined him. You know, sir? It doesn't make much sense, when I think about it."

"What did he say? I love a good ghost story, and Cypress Fitzgerald was famous!" cried Marlowe.

Peter very much wanted to disappear. He felt silly talking about Cypress because he doubted anyone truly believed him. Furthermore, he wouldn't dare reveal the parts about the Phantom, especially not to a stranger, even a kind man like Marlowe Blodgett. He said cautiously, "Cypress told me...um, that he died along time ago. That he died protecting the Crown."

"Zats true! I heard zis!" Marlowe was leaning forward, his hands clenched in excitement.

"And that he stayed at the Crown afterwards, as a ghost, you know, but now it was his time to go," Peter said, carefully choosing his words.

Marlowe gasped. "His time to go? He left?"

"I think so, sir."

Hawkins blurted, "Wicked! How come you never told me about this?"

"Because I'm not sure I believe it actually happened," Peter lied. He *did* believe it happened, but he also thought maybe Cypress had been confused. Or insane. But he didn't want to explain it all.

"Anyzing else, Peter?" Marlowe asked.

"Umm...I think maybe he had a pet mouse." Peter gave a half laugh, expecting Marlowe to disbelieve him but Marlowe seemed thrilled with the oddity.

"Fascinating! A pet mouse. Ahhh, zee Crown Hotel, so full of surprises! It must be wonderful to live here. I am a kid in a candy store."

Peter nodded. "I love the Crown. It's my home." The

elevator chimed and opened into a concrete cavern, a section of the basement Peter'd never seen. He asked, "What's this place?"

"The garage, of course," Joey said, and her voice echoed off the steel rafters. "Can't you see the cars?"

Peter stepped from the elevator, but suddenly he was struck once again—by the anxious shadow sensation. Same as last time, an absolute certainty that something was wrong. Marlowe Blodgett walked circles around the garage, proclaiming that this space was "Perfect!" but Peter grabbed Hawkins arm.

He asked, "Hawkins, do you feel anything...I don't know, funny? Or hear something?"

Hawkins paused and tilted his head. "Like what?"

"I don't know, I just...feel weird. It's happened before."

"Peter, did you drink bubbly stuff?"

"What, *no!* I felt the same way the night of the fire. Remember? I knew the Crown was burning."

"You think there's a fire now?" Hawkins asked.

"No," replied Peter, staring at his shoes. "I think...I think it's below me this time." He walked in circles, inspecting the walls and the floor and shrugging his shoulders.

"What's below you?"

"I don't know. *Something.* Are you positive you feel completely normal?" asked Peter.

"Everything's normal except you, my man."

Marlowe and Joey and Keith returned from their quick circuit of the garage, "Children! Our time is half up. We must return or Manos will hunt me down. Zank you for zee tour! Zis spot will work nicely for zee bears and elephants, when zey need a vacation. Out of zee sun, away from zee people. We'll use truckloads of zee straw."

"Bears and elephants!" hooted Hawkins. "November can't get here soon enough."

"But there's so much to do first," Joey said.

Peter agreed, though he kept his eyes firmly fixed on the concrete floor, and the mysterious unknown *something* far below.

4

THE KEY

Summer gave way to a golden autumn and the leaves turned, and Peter's life settled into a comfortable rhythm. In the mornings, he and Joey worked through school books and went on field trips to museums, often taking breaks to help their mothers in the Laundry, or Mr. Arora in the kitchen, or Manos with whatever project he had that day—no matter the season, the Crown remained a buzzing hive of activity with constant work to be done. Peter eventually returned to Central Park and to the Raiders and their wild games. Even though their quarrel was never mentioned, Sneakers was cooler to him than he used to be. Peter had gone from being a member of the Raiders to merely a questionable ally.

Any afternoon Peter didn't go to the Park he spent with his mentors, for that was how he thought of them. He played checkers with crazy Mr. Hayes and he practiced magic with Max Freeman, who was teaching Peter the subtle art of distraction. Ernestine Parker insisted on meeting at least once a week for tea, a visit during which she probed and tested his manners.

Peter couldn't decide if Ms. Ernestine Parker was tougher on him or if Arthur Graves was. Under his boxing coach's grueling tutelage, Peter rebuilt the lost muscles and soon he was smacking the heavy mannequin more forcefully than ever. At first he wondered if he was imagining things, but over time it became apparent—he was now bigger, faster, and stronger than Atticus. His lungs turned robust and his hands hardened, despite weekly applications of Ernestine Parker's expensive lotion.

Halloween came and went. In early November, Joey and Manos began the process of transforming room 1919 into a partial lion's den. Peter tried to help but only slowed them down. Joey was truly gifted with her hands, and even Manos marveled at how she built the things she did. To safeguard the spare bedroom, they replaced the carpet with absorbent pads, hung heavy floor-to-ceiling claw-proof drapes, hid the electrical outlets, and installed a fancy steel door. Marlowe Blodgett returned in mid-November to inspect the updates and he declared it, "Magnificent!"

The work in the garage was more industrial, welding together a heavy bear cage and bolting it to the floor.

Excitement in the Crown swelled. The front desk attendants wore animal name tags, and purple posters of famous Circus performers were hung from the ceiling, most notably of Lino Kang, the celebrated ringmaster.

Unfortunately for Peter, he was prevented from being wholly enthusiastic about the circus's arrival. Two things nagged at him. The first was intermittent bursts of shadow, the sensation that something awful was about to happen, during which he became so stressed he could barely think. He decided it was like Spider-Man's supernatural awareness of danger, but Peter himself was never in danger that he saw. Could the Crown itself be trying to tell him something?

Maybe something about the shadowy Judge, the leader of the Red Masque? He searched the Laundry and mechanical rooms and the garage but discovered nothing amiss.

The second thing was the bizarre black key he'd taken to wearing round his neck. *If* the story was true, *if* the Phantom was returning, *if* the Red Masque was gaining power in the city, then the key might be of massive importance. But what did it go to? And who was the rightful owner?

The burden weighed on him until finally the calendar turned to November 30th, the day the Circus arrived, and Peter could no longer bear it. He was no Phantom. He was a wimp who couldn't even walk to the Hotel Chelsea.

With the arrival of the circus imminent, he decided to do something drastic—he would mail the bizarre key to the Chelsea, with instructions for it to be delivered to the hidden door. Surely someone there would know what that meant, even if he didn't.

Bright and early that morning, with a heavy heart, he addressed, stamped, and sealed an envelope containing the black key. The mouse lolled lazily on his dresser, unaware of Peter's intentions. Else it would have been jumping and biting him.

He made his way to the Lobby with ponderous footsteps, growing anxious as he neared the mail slot. *This is the right thing to do,* he told himself. *I'm not meant to have it. Someone brave is.* He felt like crying. Adventure had been thrust at him, but he simply wasn't up to the task. He stopped at the Crown's outgoing mailbox and took a deep, shaky breath.

"Peter Constantine!"

Peter was so startled that he dropped his letter onto the floor, and Max Freeman scooped it up before he could retrieve it. Max was the flashiest man Peter'd ever met. His hair glistened, his teeth sparkled and he dressed as though he might spring onto a stage any minute. "Just saying hello, my excellent friend!" Max cried, and he gripped Peter by the shoulders. It was a friendly greeting but it made Peter nervous because Max was prone to cause mischief up close. After all, he was a world famous magician. Behind Max waited a beautiful woman who looked as flashy as he was.

"Good morning, sir," Peter said, trying to reclaim his letter but Max kept spinning it through his fingers.

"Today's the day, isn't it? The day that half-rate, two-bit circus hauls itself into view," Max said with a flat chuckle. Somehow, someway, even though Peter was watching, the envelope vanished.

"You aren't excited to see the circus?" asked Peter curiously.

Max sneered. "Of course not, the con artists. They're all cheap tricks and no talent. Plus, they steal half my audience while they're in town!"

"I'm sorry to hear that, sir. Who's your friend?"

"That's my fiancé! I've just fetched her off an airplane." Max beamed. "Or at least, my driver did. Isn't she a doll? My fiancé, not the driver."

"Mr. Freeman, I didn't know you're engaged. Congratulations!"

"Well, let's hope she sticks around." Max winked playfully, as though sharing a dirty secret. "Most of my fiancés don't."

"But...how many times have you—"

"Too many!"

"Oh. Does she know—"

Max interrupted him. "Peter, my boy, what do I do to escape a sticky situation? I've taught you this."

"You create a diversion, sir."

"Exactly. Ka-zam!" He grabbed Peter's ear and tugged,

and without warning colorful M&Ms poured out. "Careful Peter!"

"What!" cried Peter, frantically trying to catch the candies as they cascaded onto the marble floor. "But I didn't—"

"Clean up your mess, my friend, and we'll talk soon!"

Peter dropped to all-fours and hurriedly scraped the M&Ms into a small pile. How'd Max do *that*? When he glanced up, the magician and his beautiful fiancé were gone. But Clint Banks, the majority owner of the Crown, was hurrying over.

"Peter?"

"Yes sir, sorry. I didn't mean to." He scooped up the candy and dumped the pieces into a golden trashcan.

As usual, Mr. Banks wore loafers and a sports jacket. He'd always been cordial with Peter but he was very serious when it came to his hotel. He clasped his hands behind his back and bent slightly, as though Peter had a hearing problem. "Good morning, young man, do you have a moment to speak with me?"

"Certainly, sir. What can I do for you?"

"It's about the circus, Peter," he said, but he was forced to stop and step aside as two men walked past carrying hay bales. "A busy day, eh? A busy day, indeed."

"Yes sir."

It *was* busy. The Lobby teemed with frantic activity as guests checked out and workers carried supplies in all directions. Mr. Banks suggested, "Perhaps it would be easier if we spoke outside."

Peter held the door and Tony the doorman greeted them both, but Mr. Banks didn't notice. It was a chilly November day and brown leaves from the Park scuttled past on 5th Avenue.

"As I was saying, it's about the circus, Peter. A very important event, you see, and the eyes of the city will be watching."

Peter nodded. He'd heard as much. "What can I do to help?"

"An excellent question. I knew you were just the lad to speak to, always lending a hand. Peter, you certainly know of the Ritz-Carlton Hotel," said Mr. Banks loftily.

"Yes sir, I do. Just down the block."

"I received word yesterday that...what's this?" asked Mr. Banks, puzzled. He reached behind Peter's neck and yanked a letter out from his collar. "Do you always keep stationary tucked into your shirt?"

"No sir. That was...well, Max Freeman must've put it there...somehow," Peter said and he shoved the letter with the key into his front pocket.

"Ah yes, Mr. Freeman. He once snuck a frog into my jacket. An illustrious yet confusing man. Anyway, as I was saying. The Ritz-Carlton was the victim of a vicious *prank*, played by Central Park ruffians."

"Uh oh," Peter said. "What'd they do?"

Mr. Banks shook his head and made an unhappy tsk'ing noise. "Spray painted vulgar pictures on the main entrance, for goodness sake. Can you imagine. Just awful."

"I think I know why, sir. The kids in the park are in a fight with—"

Mr. Banks interrupted him. "Yes, well, here's what worries me, Peter. The youths in the park like to cause trouble and they could badly embarrass us, if they so choose. I don't know *how* they'd do it, but you've heard the expression about idle hands, I assume?"

"Umm...yes?" said Peter, who hadn't.

"I know you like to play in the park with your little

chums. Seems to me like you could find a more advantageous use of your time, but that's for a different day. I hope I can count on you to convince your ruffian pals to keep away from our beloved Crown, especially while we have such prominent guests."

"Sir, the Raiders would never—"

"The *Raiders*?" he asked, pronouncing the word as though it was covered in manure.

"That's what they call themselves, the kids in the Park. They have a feud with the Ritz kids, and—"

"Yes, Peter, exactly. The *Raiders*, what a degrading name. They must be kept far away. You agree?"

"I can try," Peter said. "Err, that is to say, Mr. Banks, I'll do my very best."

"It would be awful, Peter, if I find out that the neighborhood youths interfered with our operations. You understand, I assume? How bad it would be? For everyone?"

Peter understood. Mr. Banks was threatening him. Keep those kids away. Don't let the Raiders embarrass the Crown *or else*.

As Peter searched for a reply, he spotted someone familiar from the corner of his eye. A girl, wearing white sunglasses, dressed in a bright leather jacket.

It was the girl in white! Peter had been on the lookout for her since April. She was passing the hotel on 59th, searching the Park and peering into the Crown's Lobby. Could she be looking for him?

"Peter?" Mr. Banks asked again. "Are you listening, young man? You understand what I'm asking you?"

"Oh, yes sir! Sorry, I...yes sir, I understand."

"Excellent. Now, let's get back to work. The Circus should be here before dinner, and there's not a moment to lose!" Mr. Banks clapped his hands and strode inside.

Peter waited until Mr. Banks was out of sight and then shot off around the corner, racing full speed after the girl in white. She wasn't really a girl, probably closer to eighteen... The KEY. He could ask her about the key, finally get some answers! She was a half block ahead of him, weaving gracefully through the walkers and joggers, but Peter gained steadily.

As he neared, she turned onto the dreaded 7th Avenue. Peter skidded to a stop, his heart hammering. Of course she had to walk *this* way. Could she be on her way to the Hotel Chelsea? She was the one who'd given him the paper, the paper which read, "*Hotel Chelsea, hidden door.*"

Should he follow? Definitely he should, but...but the gigantic towers and the floods of people.

What would the Phantom do? The Phantom would race after her. Too bad he was wimpy ol' Peter.

His hands balled into fists. *No.* This once he would be brave. Right now he needed to be the Phantom and not a coward. Cypress Fitzgerald would go, and so would he.

His mind made up, he surged forward into the 7th Avenue corridor. But his plans had changed—he wasn't going to question her, he was going to *follow* her.

She stayed on the left-hand side of 7th Avenue, walking against traffic. Following her was easy, even when the streets opened and Peter found himself in the middle of Time's Square, perhaps the most famous city block in the world. Neon signs blazed and adults in funny costumes danced and towering televisions blared and tourists snapped pictures. Advertisements for Pepsi scrawled across the buildings and police rode horses and a man with a python around his neck strolled past. Peter wanted to stay and gawk at the sights but he'd lose the girl in white in the sea of elbows and shoulders, because she looked neither right nor left. If anything, she sped up.

To avoid being spotted, he hung back twenty feet and kept pedestrians between them. Twice he had to scamper across streets before the lights changed, else he'd be trapped on the wrong side. Peter was so engaged in the chase he didn't notice how far they were traveling. The Crown was on 59th Street and they were moving south out of the 50s and into the 40s, then the 30s.

His stomach growled. After forty-five minutes of the chase, Peter began questioning whether this was a good idea. He hadn't eaten breakfast and he was thirsty, and because he forgot his jacket he'd grown quite cold. Yet the girl kept walking. And walking. And walking.

Finally, as Peter was on the verge of turning around, the girl in white crossed to the far side of 7th Avenue and turned right, onto 23rd Street.

Peter was stunned. How'd he get all the way down here? This was over *thirty* blocks from the Crown.

He was deeply lost, but that problem could be tackled later—first he'd follow the girl in white for one or two more blocks before giving up, and then...well, perhaps he'd ask a police officer for help getting home.

23rd was narrower than 7th, and the lanes were painted unusually bright colors, and the buses roared and taxies honked, but suddenly...there it was.

The Hotel Chelsea.

If the Crown Hotel looked like a castle fit for a king then the Chelsea was a palace built for a queen. It had *personality*. It wasn't made of glass or boring brownstone as most surrounding buildings were, but instead it was painted a rich red color. It had gothic black balconies on each level and peaked gables on the twelfth floor—this was the type of hotel Peter Pan would pluck Wendy from, while famous authors smoked pipes on the balcony next door. Other than the Crown, and maybe the Met Museum, this instantly became Peter's favorite building in the city. This hotel *mattered*, it was important.

To Peter's surprise, the girl in white strode past the main entrance, reached the far end of the Chelsea, pivoted directly into the hotel's wall, and...disappeared.

Peter muttered, "What the heck... Where'd she go?" He dashed past the Chelsea's curiously small entrance and a delicious-smelling Spanish restaurant built into the bottom floor. He stopped where the red hotel ended and adjacent building began. He looked left, he looked right, he looked way way up. There was nothing. She'd vanished.

"Crud, I can't have lost her *again*." His teeth chattered and he stamped his feet, turning in circles to look for clues. There was no sewer, no ladder, no window, just plain brick. Could she have gone into the restaurant? No, it hadn't opened yet. The temple next door? No, it was locked. He searched the sidewalk for trapdoors until passing New Yorkers gave him angry looks. "This makes no sense," he grumbled. He ran his fingers across the brick surface and pushed but the wall remained.

On his second try, his finger passed over a small divot in the brick. He took a closer look—it was hole, not a divot, barely visible. Not big enough to insert his pinky, but maybe a pencil or...

Peter heard faint chimes between his ears and he grew goosebumps. Could it be?

He stuffed a hand into his pocket and tugged out the sealed envelope. His fingers shook as he tore it open and dumped the funny-looking black trinket into his palm. Probably it was only his imagination, but the key felt warm.

"*Hotel Chelsea, hidden door. You'll know how to get in. Otherwise don't bother,*" Peter repeated from memory.

The key slid into the lock and emitted a soft pulse of light—a perfect fit, like they'd been made for each other. There was a click and a small section of the wall swung inwards, revealing a steep staircase plunging under the Chelsea.

He'd discovered the hidden door.

PART II

Had I known how important the mouse was, I would have arranged to have been introduced before its untimely demise, the poor little thing.

-Darci Drake
    New York Times

5

PHANTOMS

Peter descended the steps cautiously. There were no lights and the rough concrete staircase pitched at a dangerous angle. He was halfway down and in sight of the bottom landing when a gust of wind swung the exterior door closed, leaving Peter in total darkness. The air smelled cool and damp.

"Well, this wasn't smart," he mumbled, unable to see anything. Probably he should have been more nervous, but instead of fear he felt inexplicable determination and he told himself that if the girl in white discovered him trespassing then he'd simply remind her about the note.

The bottom caught him by surprise and he stumbled, creating scuffing noises that echoed madly in the stairwell. He steadied himself, strained his ears for angry guards (none appeared), and tiptoed forward, his arms roving to detect protrusions.

What did he expect to find? His imagination ran wild. Was this the former home of the mysterious Phantom? Had Cypress Fitzgerald been here? Could it be something like the Bat Cave? A secret lair full of powerful weapons? Or maybe a prison? Or a military base hidden far underground? Or a cave stuffed with an army of angry trolls?

...Well, probably not trolls.

His hands struck a wall, smooth and flat, and then a knob—it was a door. A doorway to destiny, he thought.

"No turning back now," he whispered. "...Right?"

He waited, hand on the doorknob.

And waited.

And waited some more, working up the courage, as would any boy about to enter a new world.

"C'mon, Peter," he said, feeling a little light-headed. "Don't be a wimp."

He should have left a note at home, because his parents would never know what happened if he died here. *Dear Mom and Dad, if I don't come back it's because I was murdered by evil trolls under the Hotel Chelsea, in a secret passage that you can't find. PS. Hawkins can have all my stuff, and please let him sleep in my bed whenever he wants.*

He was stalling.

What would the Phantom do?

Peter took a deep breath, turned the knob, and pushed. Blazing light spilled onto the floor of the hallway, and Peter peaked into the room beyond...

...and nearly fainted—a man stood there, waiting. At first Peter thought it was the Phantom himself, because he wore a cape and a mask. But, on another second glance, the man didn't have a face. It wasn't a human after all, only a mannequin.

After Peter's heart restarted, he glanced curiously around the room. It was lit with naked lightbulbs dangling from the dark ceiling, and the bare walls were cinderblock. The room was laid out like a maze, tables set this way and that way, covered with piles of gear and knickknacks. The room was empty of people, though music played somewhere in the back.

The more he inspected the space, the more convinced he became it was an old workshop. Someone had once used the scattered tools to build here. What, he didn't know. He slipped inside and closed the door. It was nothing like the Bat Cave and Peter suppressed his disappointment.

He tiptoed carefully to the mannequin. This was the outfit he'd seen in old Phantom drawings. A dark jacket, a cape, and a mask to hide the eyes. There was even a fancy sword clipped to the belt.

"Wow," he breathed, fingering the jacket. This was it. This was really it. But he didn't remember the Phantom of New York being so...round. This jacket could fit four of him, especially round the middle.

The maze of tables held a fascinating collection of gadgets and tools. There were old maps, piles of sports helmets, bits of electronic doohickies, hammers, screwdrivers, rusty swords, faded newspapers, dusty boots, gloves, radios, clubs, rope, and so much more it would take days to inventory.

A cork board was set into the back wall. Pinned to the board were old magazine articles and newspaper clippings titled...Peter squinted and drew closer..."The Dangerous Red Masque" and "That Dynamic Rogue, the Phantom! But Is He Even Real?"

Peter laid flat the curling edges of the yellowed articles. They were dated from the 1930s. At his touch, one of the scraps broke into pieces and fluttered to the ground.

This *was* the Phantom's former home. This was hallowed ground, the most well-kept secret in the city. A sacred space.

An elderly man walked out from a nearby doorway, spotted Peter, and cried, "WHOA!"

"AUGH!" Peter cried in return. He recoiled, stepped on a pile of oily rags, slipped, and fell onto a table of walkie-talkies. The table broke and sent Peter and the radios cascading across the hard floor.

"Blast it, boy! I spent a lot of time on those radios!" the man growled. He wore black jeans, a white t-shirt, and a jean jacket—a surprisingly hip outfit. He was entirely bald and his hard face was etched with wrinkles.

"I'm so sorry!" Peter cried from the floor, and the music from the next room scratched and stopped. "I didn't mean... that is, I'll clean it up."

The man scrutinized Peter, as if taken aback. "I'm impressed, ya little intruder. A boy your age with a pure heart? Don't see many of those anymore."

The girl in white appeared, still in her leather jacket. In her fist she carried a hard-looking baton, the kind police used, raised and ready to bash Peter's head in. Her eyes widened and she shouted, "*You!* How'd you...what're you...? You're *here.*"

The old man said, "The pipsqueak was looking at the articles on the wall."

Peter said again, "I'm really sorry. I tripped and knocked...well, obviously, you can see, I suppose."

"You're here," she repeated, lowering the baton. "I can't believe it."

"This is the place, right?" asked Peter. "From the note?"

"Easy!" the man called as Peter scrambled to his feet and righted the table. "Fixing those radios is a son of a gun."

"Do they still work?" Peter asked.

The girl shook her head. "They're useless junk, need to be thrown away."

"You don't throw something out just because it's old," the old man argued. "We keep the relics to help us remember where we've been."

She continued, "But that's not the point. What're you doing here?"

"This is the Phantom's lair," Peter said, forgetting the mess for a moment. "Isn't it."

The girl didn't respond but her eyes narrowed. This was the first Peter'd seen her without her glasses on, and her eyes were a piercing blue. She wasn't really a girl, he kept reminding himself, probably old enough to vote and do the things grownups can.

"Those articles are about him," Peter said, pointing at the cork board with a shaking finger. "That's why you were at the Crown. Because of the Phantom. Right?"

The old man whistled softly in surprise, a noise he made between his teeth.

The girl asked, "What do *you* know about the Phantom of New York?"

"I know he promised to return if the city needs him."

She crossed her arms, the leather jacket making a creaking noise. "What's that got to do with you?"

"I...I-I don't know yet."

"Do you remember that day in the hallway? Outside of 1010?" she asked.

"You were there to investigate the haunted room," Peter said immediately. He started to sweat; two angry adults were glaring at him. "You were worried the Red Masque would find secrets."

"Of course I was. You asked me if I knew Cypress Fitzgerald. Kind of a weird question, don't you think, kid? He's been dead for over eighty years."

"But..." Suddenly Peter felt a little confused. Did these

two not know about Cypress's ghost? Did Cypress hide from them? Was he a secret? Cautiously he asked, "What do *you* know about Cypress?"

"I asked first," she said. "Tell me what you know."

"I can't," Peter complained. "Maybe if you—"

"NO. You tell *me*."

The old man threw up his hands and said, "Blast it, Dot! The boy knows. It's as plain as daylight. He knows, we know, and we can all stop pretending we don't."

"I know," Peter agreed in a shaky voice.

"You know what?" she asked coolly.

"I know Cypress Fitzgerald was the Phantom. At least one of them."

The girl and the old man fell silent. She uncrossed her arms, fidgeted, and crossed them again. Half-heartedly, Peter picked up a few walkie-talkies.

Eventually the old man growled, "First excitement we've had around here in decades."

"Cypress Fitzgerald's true identity was a well-guarded secret. How'd you find out?" asked the girl.

"Is your name really Dot?"

"Yeah, so?" She glared murder, surprised and insulted he would dare use her name.

"Nothing. Just..." he stammered. "...you know, Dot's an unusual name, that's all."

"Your name's Peter Constantine," she said. "We checked you out too."

"Call me Rory. Rory Franklin," the old man said."Dot's last name is Franklin too."

"Nice to meet you," Peter told them. "Did you know Cypress?"

"No," said the girl irritably. "I already told you that. You can't do math?"

Rory said, "The boy's not talking to you, ya rascal. And I knew Cypress. True, he was a flashy know-it-all, my opinion, but also an extraordinary man."

Dot rubbed at her eyes with the heels of her hands and walked a circle around Rory. She said, "No one's been here in years."

"We needed a change. Desperately," Rory noted. "Especially you, cooped up in this dungeon."

"What's Grandpa gonna think?"

Rory shrugged. "You know Ollie. He'll be flummoxed, the great buffoon."

"Who?" Peter asked.

As if they called for him, the door burst open and an old man bustled through, carrying groceries in both hands. He waddled straight to one of the tables and set the bags down, humming all the while. "Great news! Really terrific news— the bologna was on sale. Fried bologna sandwiches for lunch! Life doesn't get much better, I can tell you that!"

"Ollie, open your eyes for once," Rory grumbled. "You have a visitor."

The family resemblance between the two was obvious. Peter would bet his entire piggy bank that the newcomer was Rory's son.

Ollie turned and jumped at the sight of Peter and the mess. "Wha...who...HUH? Goodness gracious me! What's going on here?"

"This is Peter," Dot explained. "The boy from the Crown."

"Oh yes. Yes yes yes, I remember," Ollie said, rubbing his round stomach. "I remember him perfectly."

"No you don't," Rory said grouchily.

"No, I don't remember," admitted Ollie. "Tell me again?"

"He's the boy from the Crown that I met in front of 1010.

He saw the Red Masque the night of the fire. Is this ringing any bells?" Dot asked, frustrated.

Ollie was rotund, a polite word for fat. Peter glanced from the mannequin (with the huge jacket) back to Ollie, who said, "Yes! Yes, yes, I remember the youngster. How are you, Patrick?"

"Peter."

"That's what I meant. Peter. How are...better yet, WHAT are you doing here?"

"Uhh..." Peter replied. "Well, so..."

"I told him to come here," Dot said, her arms still crossed. "I said we needed to talk. He knows about Cypress."

"Who?"

Dot rolled her eyes. "Cypress Fitzgerald. Peter knows."

"Ah. Good. Excellent." Ollie nodded knowingly. "He knows, splendid. But, my dear, refresh my memory...who again is Piecrust Fitzpaddy?"

"Cypress Fitzgerald," Peter corrected him. "He was the Phantom of New York."

Ollie's eyes bulged and he sucked in air, making a high pitched whine. After a good ten seconds, Peter began to worry for the man's health.

Rory groaned. "Oh for Pete's sake, come off it, Ollie. *Exhale.*"

Ollie spoke through a hoarse whisper. "Ah yes, then, very good. Well, well. How about that. Hmmm. Hmm indeed. The Phantom. Okay. Well, Peter, answer me this...do you like bologna sandwiches?"

Peter's head was spinning. This was his only link to the Phantom of New York, and he'd come all the way here, and what he'd found was not what he'd anticipated, not in the least. He asked, "Is this all of you? Like, is there more?"

Rory chuckled. "Not what you were expecting, huh."

"I was expecting...I don't know. A secret society fighting against the Red Masque, I guess," admitted Peter.

Dot snapped a nod. "That's exactly what we are."

"Well..." Ollie blubbered. He looked around the room and winced. "It doesn't look like much now, but back in our heyday...you know...it was less dusty."

"How long ago was that?" wondered Peter, skeptical Ollie ever had a heyday.

Rory coughed and said, "Far too long. Lifetimes! Makes me furious."

"Doesn't matter, does it. This is our lot now," Ollie said, reaching for his grocery bags. Peter backed out of his way and bumped into a table. There came a hiss from the pile of gadgets and sudden bursts of light.

Ollie cried and ducked while Rory cackled. Fireworks erupted from the heap—explosions of red and silver, and ear-splitting pops. It was the Fourth of July crammed into a few seconds and shoved inside the workshop. The streamers bounced off the walls before finally silencing, leaving them in a cloud of smoke.

"Wow!" Peter cried, barely able to hear himself. "S-sorry about that."

Dot's hands were on her hips. "I didn't know that still worked."

"Course it works. *I* built it," said Rory. "Ideal for blinding your enemies at midnight."

Ollie's pants had caught fire and he hopped around the room on one foot, swatting at it. "Help! Help!" No one moved to help him, but soon he smacked the flames out himself.

Peter rubbed at his ringing ears, cleared his throat, and said, "No one believes me that the Red Masque came to the Crown."

"I believe you," she said.

"The treasure syndicate? At the Crown? Nonsense," Ollie cried, returning to his bags of groceries. "Such foolish talk, can't imagine it. Parker, watch out for that table."

"My name's Peter."

"That's what I meant. Don't need anymore surprises, do we. We lead quiet lives here. Poor Dot's already too obsessed with the syndicate as it is."

"I live at the Crown," Peter said. "And I saw them."

"What's that? You live there?"

"My father's the superintendent."

"He is? Your father." Ollie paused and an eager glint came into his eyes. "You're pulling my leg."

"I'm not. I live there. And I came here for help. I *saw* the Red Masque. My home's in danger because they're coming back, and the police can't stop them." He debated telling them about The Evil Treasure Hunter, the awful man after his father, but that might only confuse the Franklin family.

Dot asked, "How do you *know* the Red Masque is returning to the Crown?"

"I was in the same room and I listened, during the fire," said Peter earnestly. "They set the fire too early and had to evacuate. But they plan to return soon to keep searching."

Dot shot her grandfather a worried glance. "I knew it! I *knew* that's what happened. They're returning to power."

"Tell me, Percy, does your father have a key to all the doors?" Ollie asked.

"*Peter*. And yes."

"Oh ho ho! The old Crown's full of surprises. More than you realize, my boy. Yes indeed. What a fascinating turn of events."

"Grandpa, why don't you put the groceries away?" Dot said.

Ollie bent at the waist and lowered to look Peter in the eye. "You want to help defeat the syndicate, Peter?"

"Yes sir, I do."

"Then help old Ollie find the hidden secrets before they do. That'll show 'em!"

Rory groaned and coughed. "Ollie. You're being a fool."

Dot called a little louder, "Grandpa, your bologna will spoil."

"Indeed, indeed! I'm going, my dear, aren't I?" He hefted his grocery bags and waddled towards the door at the rear of the room. "The Crown calls again, who'd have thought."

As soon as he was out of sight, Peter pointed at the mannequin in the corner. "That's your grandfather's costume. Ollie used to be the Phantom, didn't he."

"A long time ago."

"Did Cypress Fitzgerald train him?" Peter asked.

"No. Cypress trained Rory," she said. "My *great* grandfather."

Rory pointed at himself with his thumb. "Me. And then Ollie took over. Unfortunately. He turned out to be a blasted screwup. Not totally his fault, though."

Peter nodded, looking between them. "And Ollie was the last Phantom?"

Dot nodded, her hands still on her hips.

Rory said grimly, "He didn't last long. Got scared and quit."

"What about the prophecy, that the Phantom will return if the city needs him?"

"Or her," Dot said.

"Huh?"

"Each Phantom has named his successor," Dot said, walking to the mannequin and touching the cape affectionately. "There can't be another Phantom until Ollie picks one."

Peter's heart sank. "So...there isn't one right now?"

"Not yet."

"He'll pick you?"

"The Red Masque is returning. Grandfather doesn't believe it, but I do. The city will need the Phantom. And he will return. Or...*she* will."

Rory gave his head a little shake and he sighed, which turned into a cough. "We've been over this, kiddo. It ain't you. Get that confounded idea out of your head. Let some other idiot try, not my Dot."

"Grandfather can pick who he likes, and I've been training my whole life," she said fiercely. "I'm ready."

"Ain't so easy," grumbled Rory. "The *city* has to pick you. Not that you ever listen."

"What did Ollie mean? About the Crown's hidden secrets?" asked Peter.

"Legend has it that the Crown is a place of power, dating back hundreds of years. The very land it was built on is magical, and somewhere within are ancient artifacts. The syndicate believes the legend and so does Grandfather. Supposedly the artifacts are the key to great strength," Dot explained. "He's always talked about getting his hands on one."

"Do you believe the story?"

"I don't know. Room 1010 didn't look that special."

Peter asked, "What about the Judge, do you believe he's real?"

"The who?"

"The leader of the Red Masque. Our Librarian told me he's called the Judge."

Dot said, "Never heard of him. By the way, how'd you get in here?"

Peter's hand was in his pocket, tightly clasping the black key. It was warm and heavier than usual, and Peter was gripped by a sudden realization—if the syndicate was truly returning to power, he would need more help than he'd found in this old lair. Ollie was *not* the Phantom, he was goofy and too old. Rory seemed smart and solid, but he was even more ancient.

If Dot was gonna be named the next Phantom, perhaps she should have the mysterious key? He felt a tremendous reluctance to hand it over, though. True, he'd found the remnants of the Phantom line...but this quirky family didn't strike him as the solution to the Red Masque. Perhaps Cypress had been right to hide himself from Ollie? Even if Peter wasn't meant to have the key permanently, he felt he ought to find someone worthier to give it to. Or at least hold onto it until Dot was ready. To do otherwise would be a betrayal of Cypress.

"Kid? How'd you get in here?" she asked again, waving at him. "Are you hiding something?"

Without planning to, he lied. "I followed you and the door was open."

"Good grief," Rory said. "Open?"

Dot's mouth dropped. "That's *not* like me."

"I do that sometimes at my apartment." Peter shrugged evasively. "It happens. By the way, how old are you?"

"Sixteen."

"Sixteen?" yelped Peter. "Wow, I thought...you look... you're *not* a grown-up."

"I'm older than you are, shorty."

"We're the same height. It's only—you look...older."

Dot said, "I do that on purpose. Keep my hair short. Glare at people. That kind of thing."

"So now what? What am I supposed to do about the Red Masque?" asked Peter, gripping the key more tightly. He definitely wasn't surrendering it to a sixteen-year-old. "Am I supposed to simply wait around until they show up?"

"You won't have to wait long," said Rory. "They're coming."

"You're not doing this by yourself, kid. I'll help. We know they're after the artifacts, so they'll get into the hotel somehow," she said.

"The blasted Red Masque could simply rent rooms and search the place," Rory scoffed.

Dot asked, "Has anything unusual happened there recently? Weird guests? Things like that?"

"Nothing out of the ordinary," Peter said. "The circus is coming, I guess that's new. They're staying with us a few months."

She snapped her fingers and said, "That's *it!* The circus."

"What about it?"

"The Red Masque will have hidden themselves inside. They'll be posing as clowns or support staff or performers. Staying a few *months*? They'll be able to search every inch!"

Peter gulped. Could that be true? A year ago he wouldn't have believed her. But since then he'd met Cypress Fitzgerald's ghost and everything changed. In fact, it made complete sense. "What kind of powerful artifacts are they looking for?"

Dot shrugged and Rory shook his head.

"No one knows," she said.

"We should tell...someone," Peter said. He felt frustrated. The police wouldn't believe him, and neither would his parents. The person he wanted to tell was the Phantom, except he hadn't returned yet. Or *she* hadn't.

"Like who?"

"Like a grownup," he replied grouchily. "But I don't know which one."

"That's the thing about the Phantom," Rory said and his eyes were trained steadily on Peter. "He doesn't get to call for help. And he never feels ready."

"I have to get back," Peter said, turning for the door. "The circus arrives today."

"Peter," said Dot. "You can't tell anyone. Ever. About this place."

"I know, I know." He stopped with his hand on the door.

"And stay out of danger," Dot warned. "You might get hurt. We'll take care of this."

Rory's face fell into a sad expression and he coughed. "Dot, the city hasn't picked you, sweetheart. I fear this could end in disaster."

"I'll tell Ollie about the circus," she said. "He'll know what to do."

"No," Rory sighed. "He won't."

Peter opened the door into the stairwell and looked up at the dark. "Umm. I forgot—I don't know where I am. I'm lost."

Dot rolled her eyes. "Just retrace your steps, kid. It's not hard."

"C'mon, Peter," Rory said, limping into the hall. "I'll point you in the right direction. That's the least an old fool like me can do, before I'm gone."

Peter took one last look at the Phantom's dusty old lair, closed the door, followed Rory into the dark.

6

THE CIRCUS

Thanks to Rory's advice, Peter made it over halfway home before getting lost. He reached Times Square and stopped to watch famous celebrities waving from a passing black limousine, and by the time he stopped gawking he'd gotten turned around. Possessing a dreadful sense of direction inside New York City's canyons, he traveled several blocks east before remembering the street numbers should be going UP. He was saved by catching sight of distant Central Park.

Soon the landmarks grew familiar. Directly ahead was the Ritz-Carlton, meaning he was close. Peter would really prefer to avoid the Ritz and its bullies. Should he cut down the side street near Angela's sandwich shop? This alley led home, didn't it? Anything was better than trying to sneak past the Ritz kids. He turned off the busy street and tore down the corridor.

Technically, he'd been correct—this alley ran in the direction of the Crown. But first it dumped into a shady courtyard shared by the Park Lane hotel and the Ritz Carlton. It was empty except for...

"Hey," a boy called. "I recognize that kid. He's a Raider."

Six boys lounged on cast iron chairs near a gurgling fountain. In his efforts to avoid the Ritz kids, he'd ran smack into them. They stood, led by the tall handsome kid Peter'd seen hanging out with Atticus.

"That true, chum?" he asked, peeling off his jacket. He had a wild grin on his face. "You a Raider?"

"No," said Peter. "Well, kinda. But—"

"Horace, fill that watering pitcher. We have ourselves a hobo in need of a shower," the handsome kid ordered. The boys had quickly surrounded Peter, still standing near the entrance to the shady courtyard. His escape was cut off. Where were grownups when you needed them?

"I'm not a hobo," said Peter. "I live at the—"

"But you're a Raider. Right?"

"That's complicated," Peter answered, truthfully.

"Complicated?" the kid laughed. His friend Horace was in the corner, filling a watering can from a spigot. "If you're not a Raider, who are you? You reek like one."

"I don't reek!"

The big kid got his nose near Peter and sniffed. "Bus fumes and hot dogs. You're a stinking mole person. Aren't you?" He shoved Peter backwards. A kid behind Peter shoved him forward again. "If you're not a Raider, then who are you?"

Peter ground his teeth, trying to rein in both his fear and his anger. "I'm Peter. And I hate bullies."

"Oh you do? Peter who? Peter nobody. Peter nothing." He shoved Peter again. "Listen up, Peter. We don't like the Raiders. We don't like mole people. And we especially don't like them in our courtyard."

They were pushing Peter back and forth, like a pingpong ball. Someone kicked him forward and he stumbled into the handsome kid. On instinct and quick as a flash, his hand darted into the boy's pocket. He came away with a wallet, just as Max the magician had taught him.

"Hey, what..." the kid blurted, patting his pocket.

The boy named Horace jumped onto a chair nearby, raising the heavy watering can. "I got the water!"

"Gimme my wallet, you thief," the handsome kid demanded.

Peter examined it curiously. "Lotta cash. Be a shame if it blew away. Is this your credit card? Your first name's Capulet? That *can't* be correct."

"Here's the water, Cap!" called Horace, wildly swinging the can.

Peter grinned with more courage than he felt. "No, be serious. What's your real name? Nobody is named Capulet."

Horace shouted again, "Want me to soak him? I got the water!"

The handsome boy growled, "My real name is Capulet." He balled a fist. Peter stayed calm, thanks to hours of training with a boxing coach. Things were about to get out of hand, but he was ready. Capulet continued, "And no stinking homeless rat gets to make fun of me."

Capulet threw a punch at the exact same time that Horace shoved the bucket upwards, tossing a jet of water into the air. Peter caught the punch with his free hand, exactly as he did with Arthur Graves during boxing practice. He wasn't wearing a mitt, however, and it hurt. Using his grip on Capulet, he pulled the boy into Horace's soaking spray. Peter got drenched but so did Capulet. It was like ice.

"W-wha—wha... H-HORACE!" gasped Capulet.

Peter sputtered, "W-who wants a m-magic trick? It's called d-distraction." He threw the wallet straight upwards and the dollar bills exploded like confetti, the chilly air snatching the paper.

"My m-money!" Capulet cried.

Peter slipped away in the confusion, the Ritz kids scampering after the cash. As he exited the alley, the boys got on their knees and shouted at each other.

The Crown lay only one block away but it was a long and miserable shamble in the cold air. He crossed his arms and shivered, grumbling about bullies. When at last the Crown came into view, he was frozen, exhausted, and covered with city grime.

A television news van had parked at the Crown's eastern entrance, ready to document the appearance of the famous circus. The Lobby felt warm and it sparkled even more brilliantly than usual. An actual red carpet was rolled out across the marble floor.

Peter shuffled to his room, changed, and crawled under the covers to help stop quivering. He was hungry, having missed lunch, but first he needed to warm up. The mouse climbed onto the bed too.

Peter pulled out the odd black key and ran his thumb across the worn surface. Could this be one of the powerful artifacts the Red Masque was after? All it did was open the Chelsea's hidden door. Not so special in his opinion. "I don't know what to do," he sighed.

The mouse tilted its head to the side and twitched its nose. *What do you mean?* it seemed to say.

"The circus arrives today, mouse. And I think maybe the Red Masque is hidden within. Posing as performers, maybe."

The fat white rodent squeaked in surprise and if Peter didn't know better he would've thought it was more of a gasp.

"They're looking for hidden treasures buried in the Crown. Artifacts that will give them...I don't know, some kind of power."

The mouse nodded knowingly and paced across the covers, climbing up and down his stomach.

"The police can't catch them. And The Evil Treasure Hunter is still out there. No one believes me except Dot and she's only sixteen. And...I feel like I'm supposed to do something but I'm even younger than her. It's a lonely feeling."

The mouse stopped pacing. *I'm here*, it seemed to say.

"Yeah but you're just a mouse. A really great mouse, don't get me wrong. I just wish Cypress was around."

Gradually Peter's eyes grew heavier as he lay under the comfy covers...

...UNTIL THE DOOR to his bedroom banged open.

"Peter, wake up," his mother said, grinning. "The Circus is here!"

He sat up sleepily. "Huh? Wha...?"

"You fell asleep. Hurry, sweetheart!"

Peter shoved his feet into sneakers and stumbled after her, rubbing his eyes and yawning. The entire second floor was pouring into the stairwell, eager to see the world-famous performers. In the excitement, Peter almost didn't recognize the shadow sensation descending on him. But there it was, the inner alarm—something was wrong.

Jovanna and Peter reached the Lobby in the nick of time. There was an enormous flash and purple smoke mushroomed from the long bank of exterior doorways. The overhead lights dimmed and lasers jetted from the smoke and music like thunder blared from speakers.

"**Ladieeeeeeees and gentlemeeeeeen, and boooooooys**

and girrrrrrls," came a deep voice. "**You are all witnesses.
Witnesses to GREATNESS! To the brilliant, to the magnificent, to theeeeeeeeee Circus ooooooooof Dooooooom!**"

Acrobats leaped from the smoke, landing on their hands
and turning somersaults in the air. They wore dazzling skin-
tight outfits. The crowd ooooh'ed and aaaah'ed.

Next came little people, also dazzling, and they wore
masks and flung knives. The crowd screamed and ducked,
but the somersaulting acrobats neatly plucked the
dangerous blades from the air. Joey squeaked and hid
behind her mother.

Jugglers emerged from the smoke, tossing swords and
torches dangerously close to the chandeliers, exactly as
Peter had once predicted. A tall magician in purple robes
materialized, laughing theatrically and shooting fireballs.
Peter and the audience screamed and clapped.

The acrobats walked on their hands around the Lobby
and pretended to run away from the little people. It was a
comedy act, but Peter found it a little frightening because of
the masks.

An enormous giant stepped into view and—Peter
blinked and looked again—his muscular arms were raised,
carrying Mr. Conrad in one hand and Manos Constantine in
the other. Neither man looked particularly happy or secure
bouncing so high in the air. The giant was over seven feet
tall and he laughed theatrically. The Crown employees
howled with amusement.

"Hah!" Peter cried. "Mom, do you *see*?"

She laughed. "I see! Your poor father."

Suddenly the purple smoke parted and an elephant—an
elephant!—reared back and released a trumpeting blast that
rattled the windows.

Impossible, how'd that get in HERE, Peter wondered.

Performers poured into the Lobby, emerging from under the elephant. And then...there she was—Tandra, the prized lioness. All the Crown guests and employees gasped and stepped backwards. She was tall and beefy, her eyes glinted with gold, and she wore no restraint of any kind.

"Thank you, denizens of the Crown Hotel, for this warm welcome!" cried a man sitting on top of the elephant, tossing his long black hair, much of it braided. Peter recognized him from the photographs—this was Lino Kang, celebrated ringmaster. In each of his fists he carried a lion cub. If Marlowe Blodgett looked like a pirate, then Lino Kang looked like the pirate captain. He wore golden jewelry and black eye-liner. Unable to help himself, Peter examined him closely for clues that might link him to the Red Masque. Lino slid off the elephant and landed gracefully next to Tandra. "The Circus of Doom is *honored* by your adoration, and we hope our stay at the Crown will be as magical for *you* as it will be for us!"

The audience cheered and applauded.

The giant set Mr. Conrad and Manos down, neither of which looked steady on their feet. Mr. Conrad and Mr. Banks both stepped forward to greet Lino Kang and each made a little speech but Peter had stopped paying attention.

In all the confusion, three new guests had entered without being noticed. Tony the doorman hauled luggage until the newcomers were surrounded by a small mountain of dusty duffle bags, and they quietly waited for service.

"Oh my gosh," Peter said.

It was Dot, Ollie, and Rory Franklin. Peter could see Dot was glaring through her sunglasses. Ollie wore a happily befuddled expression, and Rory rubbed his knee like it hurt.

"Ollie's here to get the artifacts," Peter mused, pinching at his lower lip. "Before the Red Masque does."

"What's that, sweetheart?" asked his mother.

The performance was over. The smoke lingered but the circus performers began gathering their bags from outside. Handlers soothed the elephant and the awestruck Crown employees assisted any way they could, under the watchful eye of Mr. Banks. The Lobby, which was nearly as large as his old school in New Jersey, had transformed into a cluster of chaos.

"I'll help with luggage," Peter said and pushed his way through the crowd. Peter's dad was already hefting Lino Kang's bags, careful to keep a safe distance from Tandra and her cubs.

Peter was edging round the elephant on his way to meet Ollie and Rory and Dot, when from out of nowhere Marlowe Blodgett appeared and clapped both hands on Peter's shoulders. "Zee boy, Peter! We have arrived at last! Zis will be legendary, I zink."

"Errr, yes sir, Mr. Blodgett. Happy to see you again. Welcome back."

Keith was with Marlowe, and he acknowledged Peter with a slight jerk of his chin.

"Your father Manos is helping with zee bags. You can lend a hand, too?" asked Marlowe, pointing with a thumb over his shoulder.

"Yes sir, I'll...that is, there's a lot of baggage and I'll help with all of it."

"Such manners! The adventure begins! Room 1919, please."

"I remember, sir."

Ollie caught sight of Peter and called, "Yoo-hoo! Paco! Over here!"

"Did zat strange man call you Paco?" asked Marlowe.

"Yes, ahhh...it's a long story. I'll see what he wants. Be

right back." Peter fought his way to the reception desk and said, "You're here! That didn't take long."

"Of course not. There's mischief afoot, Pablo," cried Ollie happily. He was bundled tight in a heavy coat, scarf, and red knit cap. He looked ridiculous next to Rory, who still wore the jean jacket.

"My name's Peter."

"That's what I said, don't interrupt. Can't let those valuable relics fall into the wrong hands, can we? Did I say valuable? I meant priceless! I mean, that is to say, powerful."

Dot said, "Grandpa, keep your voice down. We're moving in, Peter. I convinced Grandpa. The Red Masque is here and I'm gonna stop them. We, I mean. We're gonna stop them."

"Give us a hand, then," said Ollie, resting his hands peacefully on top of his belly. "We're checking into room 1011 and there's too much baggage for an old man."

"1011? That's beside—"

"I know," said Dot. "We're next to 1010, the haunted room. That's where we'll begin our search."

"It's not haunted anymore," Peter replied.

Rory stood a little straighter and looked as though he wanted to question Peter, but remained quiet.

Ollie said, "We'll cross that bridge later. Percival, these bags won't carry themselves, now will they?"

"Yes sir, I mean no sir, but..." Peter stammered. He'd already promised to help Marlowe, but the man had disappeared into the mayhem. Golden elevators were opening and whisking the circus upwards in small groups. The circus folk were tired and hungry after a long day of travel and they'd left mountain ranges of luggage for the hotel staff to carry. With a twinge of guilt, he saw his father Manos pushing two carts of suitcases towards the service elevators. Everyone was helping except Peter. "Ummm..."

"Peter?" Dot asked. "What's the matter with you?"

He turned back to the ragtag group of three. For the first time since the fire, he was uncertain if he should disobey a direct order. He knew his father, Mr. Conrad, Mr. Banks, and Marlowe Blodgett all expected him to accommodate the circus. The Crown had been preparing for this moment for months, and now here he was, faced with a decision—whose luggage should he carry? It seemed a silly decision because it was just toting suitcases, yet Peter stood at a fork in the road. What if his dad saw him ignoring the circus? Where did his loyalties lie? Certainly with his family and with his home, but perhaps Ollie and Dot and Rory represented his best chance to keep the Crown safe? But he didn't want to disappoint his father...but his father didn't fully appreciate the danger...

"Peter?"

Making up his mind, he snatched the dusty bags at Ollie's feet and said, "Yes, absolutely, I'll help carry your bags. I'm glad you're here. The Crown is in danger and we need to keep these people safe. Right?"

"Right," Dot said. "Let's go."

Rory nodded his approval and Ollie cried, "That's my boy! Come on, then. Ol' Ollie could do with a bit of food."

7

CHAOS AT THE CROWN

The next morning, Manos shook Peter awake and whispered, "Peter. Peter? Joey and I are heading up to the nineteenth floor. Do you want to come?"

Peter sat up and rubbed his eyes. "What time is it?"

"Six in the morning."

"*Six?*" Peter repeated. "Is something wrong?"

Manos smiled in the dark. "Nothing major. The circus has already broken everything but, other than that, no."

"Sure, I'll come," Peter replied through a yawn. He rolled out of bed and tripped over Hawkins.

His best friend cried out, "Who's that? Don't touch my stuff!"

"Hawkins, relax! It's only me."

Hawkins blindly swung his arms and said, "Huh? What...Peter? Why're you taking my stuff?"

"What stuff? You're in my room."

"Huh?" Hawkins said again. He still hadn't opened his eyes.

Peter, who had fallen asleep in jeans and a t-shirt, quickly pulled on his shoes. "Nothing. Go back to sleep."

Mumbling something about crazy white people, Hawkins laid back down and snored.

Peter was especially exhausted because he'd helped clean the Windsor Restaurant last night after the circus performers started a food fight. Butter had to be scrubbed from the curtains and Joey's dinner rolls carefully removed from the crystal chandeliers. Mr. Banks, responsible for bringing the circus to the Crown, had looked like a man having second thoughts.

The first thing Peter saw when he and Manos got off the elevator on the 19th floor was a woman on the ceiling. She smiled at them but didn't speak, which made her even creepier.

Mr. Schwartz was one of the only butlers Peter knew by name, and he was currently on duty. He nodded politely to Manos and Peter from the golden guest elevators. "Can I help you, sirs?" he asked.

"No thanks, Mr. Schwartz, we're answering a call."

Peter asked, "How is that woman...how does she...is she flying?" This was Peter's worst nightmare—not only was he worried about the Red Masque, but now he worried they could fly and stick to walls.

Mr. Schwartz smiled and said, "I haven't the foggiest idea. And I'm not going near her to find out. I'm a little spooked, to be honest."

"I think," Manos whispered, "that she's holding onto a sprinkler. It's very impressive. And we'll certainly have to fix it before long."

"Looks cold, doesn't she, sirs? I offered to fetch a blanket. That outfit can't be warm."

Manos and Peter edged carefully around her in the hallway, in case she decided to drop on them like some sort of exotic jungle cat.

The next surprise waiting for Peter was a man balancing five feet in the air on a vertical staff in the middle of the hallway. That would be impressive enough, but he was holding himself in place with only one hand braced on the stick, like a sleeping flamingo. The man's eyes were closed and he didn't acknowledge Manos and Peter as they passed.

"Don't these people sleep?" Peter whispered.

"I'm not sure. I've never been around circus folk before."

"Why are they practicing in the hallway?"

Manos shrugged. "They love an audience, I suppose." He knocked on room 1925 and the door was flung open with a bang.

"Ah hah! Help has arrived!" cried the heavily bearded man inside. Peter stifled a laugh; the man was dressed only in red underwear. He hit himself in the chest and said, "I am Bruno! Bruno thanks you for coming on short notice, my friends!"

"Our pleasure. You say your power is out?" Manos asked.

"The overhead light, it won't work!"

"I think I see the problem..." Peter observed. There were knives, DOZENS of knives, stuck in the walls. Some of them had punched straight through, buried to the hilt.

Even Manos was stunned. "You're...you...throw knives for the circus, I'm guessing?"

"With eyes closed. Bruno is impalement artist! Never miss."

"And you're using the walls as target practice?"

"Of course," the man said, stroking his bushy beard. "How else will Bruno stay sharp? You want me to practice on your son? I think not! Besides, Bruno was trying to kill a fly."

Joey arrived and they carefully removed knives until discovering the severed power cord. In order to patch the wire, Manos had to remove a section of the wall. Bruno thought this was fascinating and he stuck his head into the hole to look around, saying, "Bruno heard there are secret passages in the Crown. Could this be possible?"

Manos chuckled. "Not that I've found." He restored power and made a note on his to-do list: build a reinforced wall for Bruno's target practice.

Peter ran his finger over a blade. It was black and heavy. He said, "These aren't like regular knives. They don't have a handle."

"Throwing knives don't need hilt! They upset balance. You will learn to throw! Bruno will teach you."

"Really?" asked Peter. "You think I could learn?"

"Bruno is excellent teacher! You come back soon and we begin."

"Thanks! I will!" said Peter.

They stopped next at Adolfo's, the strongman. He shared a suite with his wife, a sultry woman who watched them from the couch while playing with a heavy green python. Adolfo had accidentally broken the sink and a doorknob by squeezing too hard.

As they worked, his wife purred, "It is said that the Crown is a magical hotel. Full of wonders beyond a mere mortal's imagination. Is this true?"

Joey pointed at Peter and said, "Peter met the Crown's gho—"

Peter interrupted her. "Errrr, the Crown's...gourmet chef. He says, umm...that the Crown is *totally* normal. Nothing magical. Right Joey?"

Joey and Manos glanced at Peter, curious at his bizarre outburst. For the rest of their visit, the woman didn't take her eyes off him.

After Adolfo, they changed broken lightbulbs and swept up glass in a room shared by jugglers. In the adjacent hotel room they reset a door onto its hinges. On and on they worked until lunch, and the entire time Peter suffered from the nagging shadow, the sensation that something was wrong. Like always, he didn't know what and he couldn't shake the dread.

Finally Peter, Manos, and Joey trudged into the service elevator. "Goodness," she said. "We're only halfway through the first day. These people are a mess!"

"Mr. Banks might have bitten off more than the Crown can chew, you reckon?" Manos said.

Struck by last second inspiration, Peter pressed the button for floor ten. He explained, "I helped a nice family move in yesterday. I figure I should check on them."

"That's very kind of you, son. Do you often visit guests?"

"No, never. They seemed....uh, extra needy."

Peter exited at ten, turned the corner and was surprised to find none other than Lino Kang in the hallway. The circus's ringmaster held a lion cub in his hand and a boy about Peter's age stood next to him. Both Lino and the boy had black hair and swarthy skin.

There was someone else too—a big man, dark eyes, bald, with a mustache. He spotted Peter, whispered something to Lino Kang, and walked off around the corner like he didn't want to be seen, which struck Peter as highly suspicious.

Lino called, "Come closer, boy! You work here. Manos's son, I think."

"Yessir, that's me," Peter replied, trying to ignore the butterflies launching in his stomach. "How can I help?"

"Open this door. I hear it's haunted. I would like to meet the spirit inside." He and the boy were standing in front of 1010.

Peter said, "I...I-I don't have the key. And I think that's just a legend, sir. Mr. Banks himself inspected it and—"

"Open it immediately. I am Lino Kang, Ringmaster of Doom, and I wish to enter!"

"I apologize, Mr. Kang, but I don't have—"

"Ghost!" Kang called in a shockingly loud voice. "GHOST! I summon thee!"

Nothing happened.

Kang said quietly, "Marcellus, what was the ghost's name?"

"Cypress Fitzgerald, I think, Father," replied the boy in a quiet voice.

"Cypress! CYPRESS! Thou art summoned by Lino Kang!" he bellowed. Held like a football, the lion cub looked curiously as Peter.

The door to room 1009 burst open and mean old Victor Webb stormed out. "Blast and darn you! What's the meaning of this *racket*? What're you circus freaks doing on MY floor?"

Lino Kang asked reverently, "Art thou Cypress?"

"Am I WHO? I'm calling security!"

"Then be gone, old fool."

Peter wished he could sink into the floor. Marcellus shot Peter an unhappy and shy glance. Clearly he was not enjoying the shouting either.

"SECURITY!" screamed Victor Webb.

"Cypress!" roared Lino Kang. "Come OUT!"

Peter cried, "Sir! I can arrange to get a key and show you the room later today." He was thinking fast because he suspected Lino Kang would get into the room one way or another, and Peter wanted to be there when it happened. If Lino Kang was involved with the Red Masque...

"Father, his idea is a good one," Marcellus said in a

soothing voice. "We can return later and upset no further guests."

"Except we have rehearsals tonight, Marcellus. I cannot! And I wish to enter."

"Then tomorrow?" asked Peter.

"Very well! Be here tomorrow, same time. I am Lino Kang! Come, Marcellus." Lino stalked off without a glance at Peter. His son, Marcellus, offered Peter a slight bow and hurried after.

Could Lino Kang be an ally of the Red Masque? He was the first guest who'd ever demanded entrance into 1010.

Victor Webb sneered but didn't say anything else. Perhaps while the circus was here, it would replace Peter as Webb's number one enemy.

Peter bolted to the stairwell and leaped down, descending each level in two jumps. He reached the second floor, ran into his room, snatched the set of master keys hidden in his drawer, and returned to ten. Slightly winded, he knocked urgently on room 1011.

Dot answered it, wearing white jeans and a white t-shirt. "Peter? What's wrong?"

Peter panted, "The circus ringmaster Lino Kang demanded to inspect the haunted room, 1010. I'm showing him tomorrow morning. Didn't you hear the shouting?"

"It's hard to hear anything over Ollie's snores," she replied.

"He's still *asleep?* It's lunch time!"

"Old fool thinks he needs naps twice a day," Rory grumbled, walking up behind Dot.

"Let him sleep. We'll inspect the room now," she said. "I looked once before, but not thoroughly. Maybe it's best Grandpa isn't there."

Rory snapped a nod. "Now you're talking sense."

Peter used the master key and pushed open the door to Cypress Fitzgerald's old room. It hadn't been rented for years and housekeeping never bothered cleaning it. The floors and all other surfaces were covered with a thick layer of dust. In February when Peter had talked with Cypress, the room had been full of furniture and sunlight and newspapers and everything else he'd expect to find in a room from the early 1900s. Now it looked as though it'd been vacant for a century.

Peter flipped on the overhead lights, one of which popped and burnt out immediately. Dot walked into the living room, hands on her hips. "There's nothing."

Rory circled the kitchen with a pronounced limp. "Cypress Fitzgerald was here. Not long ago."

Peter was still unsure if Cypress would want this family to know about his ghost. He cautiously asked, "How do you know?"

Dot turned. "It's just a hunch. Right? We all get those."

Rory shuffled behind Peter and whispered, "We'll talk about my hunch later. Now's not the time."

Peter and Dot walked through all the rooms. They pulled at the carpet, knocked on walls, removed the mirrors, looked in the cabinets, anything they could think of to discover secrets. Eventually she rubbed the dust from her hands and said, "As I told you before, there's nothing special about this room."

Rory winked at Peter. He knew. Somehow he knew this room WAS special, and the hairs on Peter's arms raised. Perhaps Peter'd found someone who would believe him. But why couldn't they discuss it in front of Dot?

"Do you know what this room would be good for?" she asked. "Wait here." She hurried out of the room and came back with two swords. She tossed one to Peter, who gasped and nearly dropped it. "Relax, you big baby. It's still sheathed."

"This is a real sword?" he marveled, visions of swash-bucklers swirling in his head. "And I can use it?"

"Of course, but it's old. Like *really* old."

"What do you want me to do with it?"

Dot scoffed. "Help me practice, obviously. I'm training to be the Phantom."

"I read the real Phantom used a sword. Is that his?" he asked, pointing to hers.

"I wish. His is long gone, I think."

"Mine's light." Peter slid off the curved sheath. The sword was long, thin, and scarred with notches and rust. Dot's sword looked equally ancient. "But it's dull."

"It's a fencing saber. For practice. A real saber has a sharp point and edge," she said. "But a particular *grump* I know won't buy me a real sword yet."

Rory scoffed. "Bah. Too young to play with swords, you ask me. He who lives by the sword, dies by the sword. Or she. I'm going to rest. Don't poke your eye out." He shuffled from the room, leaving the two alone.

Peter thought this might be the coolest moment of his life; he'd never held a sword before. He jumped and swished it. Accidentally he whacked the wall and the blade vibrated, painfully shaking his arm. "Ouch! Good thing it's not sharp, huh?"

"Don't be such a little boy. This is serious."

"How can this be serious? We're barely teenagers."

She glowered. "I'm sixteen, Peter. Almost an adult, and don't you see? This battle isn't just about us versus the Red Masque. This is an epic rivalry, going back decades, or even centuries! Ages don't matter."

"I think they kinda do," Peter muttered under his breath.

"I'm gonna cut you in half," she said.

"What!" hooted Peter.

"Don't let me. Okay? Block it." She swung at Peter's stomach and he knocked her sword down, the same motion he used to smack his bed with a frying pan. "Good! Again." She swung once more and he easily smacked it to the side. She attacked with a forehand slash, then a backhand, then a thrust, and an overhand chop. By the end she'd kicked up a small cloud of dust, and she frowned. "You're good at parrying."

"What's that mean, parrying?"

"Blocking, basically. Knocking my attack aside. It's frustrating."

"You're not trying very hard," Peter replied.

"What do you mean?"

"You're swinging slowly. You know, taking it easy on me. These blades can't cut us," Peter said, and he rubbed the sword across his arm. The edge was dull and didn't hurt. "Try harder."

Dot inhaled deeply and tried the same thing again. Forehand slash, backhand, thrust, and a chop. This time Peter didn't block, he merely moved out of the way. "Stop taking it easy on me," he said. "It's insulting."

Dot was panting. "I'm not! Attacking is hard. You try it, then, if it's so easy."

"I don't know how," admitted Peter sheepishly.

"Just try to hit me. It's not complicated."

"I think it is, though. People train really hard at this kind of thing."

"Peter! Just...ugh. Swing at me."

So Peter did. He swung his sword the same way he'd swing a tennis racket. She smacked it down. He did it again, but this time he pulled back and she missed. She stumbled off balance and Peter whacked her on the arm.

He grinned triumphantly. "Gotcha!"

"Beginners luck," she huffed furiously. "Try again."

Peter tried her combination of forehand, backhand, thrust, and chop. She blocked two and he landed the others.

"Again," she growled.

Peter found the sword easy to maneuver. He could make the blade's tip go wherever he wanted, something Dot seemed incapable of. He swatted at her knees, her elbows, her midsection, her shoulders, and soon she was hopelessly lost. He whacked and nicked and poked her a dozen times.

Finally she threw the sword down and demanded, "How are you DOING this?"

"What do you mean?"

"Let me see your hands."

She took his sword away and examined his palm and fingers. She squeezed his forearms and biceps, and Peter tried not to blush. They were about the same height and standing a little too close. She asked, "Why are you so strong?"

"I don't think I am," he replied honestly. "I'm normal."

"Don't lie. Why're your hands so hard? You have more muscles than most boys. Look at this," she said, squeezing his forearm. "And look at this," she said, scrapping her nails against the rough callouses of his fingers. "Your hands are like rock."

"That's from boxing."

"You box? Like with gloves?"

He nodded, still blushing. "I'm not very good yet. Still learning."

"Is that why you're not tired? I'm sweating and you're not even breathing heavy."

"I play in the park a lot too."

"Okay," she grumbled. She stalked back and forth across the living room area. "Okay then. This will be good. For both of us."

"What do you mean?"

"It means I can teach you how to fight with a sword," she said, like she was better than Peter, which he found odd. "And you can make me stronger. This is a mutually beneficial arrangement. You can be my sidekick, and together we'll thwart the syndicate's efforts to find the hidden treasure and...ACK!" Without warning, Dot picked up her discarded sword and hurled it at the fireplace mantle.

It was only then that Peter noticed they were being watched by his fat pet mouse. The mouse dodged the incoming saber with an indignant squeak, and vanished into a tiny crevice behind the mantle.

"Ugh!" Dot glared and shivered and said, "I DESPISE mice."

"I happen to like that particular one."

A voice from the hallway called, "Peter! Here you are!" The door, which had been partially closed, opened and Joey entered. "Sorry to spoil...whatever *important* thing you were doing, Peter, but I need your help. A circus clown got himself stuck in the laundry chute. Who knows WHAT he was doing in there. If we hurry I'll have enough time to finish pastries for tonight's dinner. I just KNEW this circus would be impossible."

8

DINNER AT THE WINDSOR

The next three weeks were the longest of Peter's life. It was as if the Crown was infested with spoiled toddlers who broke everything they touched and made demands all hours of the night. Peter helped his father fix or replace splintered doors, smashed overhead lights, collapsed furniture, punctured floors, torn beds, shattered mirrors, ransacked refrigerators, wrecked walls, and even the caved roofs of two elevators. Mr. Banks and Mr. Conrad were in a constant state of nervous panic about the amount of money being spent on repairs. Yet the circus was never reprimanded or asked to leave. It was beyond suspicious.

It soon became apparent to Peter that the Crown was being thoroughly searched. Anytime Manos removed a floor or wall or cabinet or roof, someone in the circus would demand to see the exposed area. In addition, Lino Kang arranged for performers to visit the hotel's residents for private shows. This was great fun for the guests, but Peter knew the truth—disguised Red Masque henchmen were inspecting every inch of every room.

Peter himself was daily called upon to give Lino Kang a

tour. He wanted to see the gardens and pool on the roof, the kitchens on the thirteenth floor, the lounges and Library and Laundry, and the offices and mechanical rooms and custodial closets, and he wanted Peter to take him. His son Marcellus usually joined them on the tour, a quiet and observant boy—a welcome change from the rest of the loud circus.

"Are you sure you've shown me the *entire* hotel?" Lino Kang demanded, growing irritated as the days flew by. He paced a loud mechanical room in frustration.

Marlowe Blodgett, who had accompanied Lino, emerged from a steam tunnel, laughed and said, "Lino! You push zee boy too hard. We've seen zee entire hotel and it has been wondrous. Let's leave him alone, eh?"

Marlow was right—Peter bordered on exhaustion. In addition to school work and field trips and boxing lessons and visiting crazy Mr. Hayes and tea with Ernestine Parker and helping his father and sword fighting with Dot, accommodating the circus was nearly enough to break him. Often he and Hawkins stayed up until midnight, Peter working on balancing chemistry equations while Hawkins read novels and assisted Peter when he got stuck.

The only positive aspect of the circus was that Bruno made good on his promise to teach Peter the art of knife throwing. Whenever he caught sight of Peter, Bruno clamped on and hauled Peter upstairs and they hurled sharp knives at the reinforced wall Manos had built.

"Count out ten steps," Bruno told him during their first lesson. Once again, he was dressed in red underwear only, but Peter had learned this was his official circus outfit. "Is all about distance."

"What do you mean?"

"Knife turns at certain speed. At seven feet, knife bounces off target. At ten, blade sticks. Like this."

He threw—WHOOSH THUNK—and the heavy black knife stuck, quivering in the bullseye.

Peter counted ten steps, held the knife the way Bruno taught him, and chucked it.

Instead of making a satisfying thunking noise, Peter's knife clanged off the board and onto the floor. He winced at the racket.

"Is okay! Don't snap wrist," Bruno told him, and repeated it over and over as they worked. "Use natural throwing motion. Let knife do work. Watch—easy throw."

WHOOSH THUNK. WOOSH THUNK.

After several lessons, Peter's knife was consistently burying itself deeply in the wood, even if he couldn't hit the middle of the target. For a few lessons, Marcellus joined the fun. He'd been practicing his entire life and possessed exceptional aim; Marcellus wasn't in need of practice as much as he needed a friend, and Peter liked him.

"Of course someone's teaching you to throw knives," fumed Joey when she discovered the lessons. "Of COURSE they are."

Nevertheless, no matter how much he enjoyed knife throwing, it didn't remove the threat of the hidden menace. In his heart, Peter felt the danger every day.

Winter came to New York City, bringing heavy snow in December. His father Manos took the morning off to participate in the snowball fight at Central Park. He and Peter sided with the Raiders, a huge mistake; that meant fighting opposite the circus. Bruno and Marcellus in particular were deadly accurate, shattering them with ice. Even during the fun, Peter couldn't shake the lurking worry.

Afterwards, bundled in dry clothes at the kitchen table,

Peter complained for the tenth time that month. "Dad, please listen. Isn't it kinda suspicious? I really think—"

Manos smiled patiently but he was frustrated. Peter spoiling lunch with conspiracy theories had become commonplace. "I know what you think, son. I heard you. But I don't believe in magical treasures, certainly not in the hotel."

"But these guys are creepy! Have you seen the bald guy? With the bushy mustache?"

"No, I haven't met that one yet."

"I only see him in the evenings," Peter said, drumming his fingers thoughtfully. "He's not a performer. I think he's with the Red Masque."

"Son, our hotel has a thousand surveillance cameras. Let our security team keep an eye on them, eh?"

"But what if our security team is part of the Red Masque too?"

"This would be easier to believe if you revealed the source of your suspicion. *Where* did you learn about hidden treasure?"

Peter balked. What could he say that his father would believe? He certainly couldn't mention Dot and her family. "It's just..."

"Just what?"

"A hunch, I guess," sighed Peter.

"You look tired, Peter. Are you sleeping enough?"

Peter rubbed at his eyes. No, he hadn't been. He really wanted a nap but it was almost time for boxing lessons with Arthur Graves.

"Besides," his father continued. "If there was anything special hidden in the Crown, it'd be in the Caves."

"The *what?*"

"The Caves. That's the nickname for all those underground storage rooms we don't use anymore. Have you never been there?"

"No! Where are they?"

His dad took a sip of coffee from a standard hotel mug. "Below the garage. The old rooms go far into the earth, as low as the subway lines and old sewers. It's like a labyrinth down there. Full of junk, and in my opinion the circus would be doing us a favor if they took some of it with them."

Peter slapped his hand to his forehead. "Dad! That's where the artifacts will be!"

"Then we're safe. Those rooms are too big for the circus or the Red Masque or whoever to hunt through, especially with shows at Barclays every night."

"You don't believe me," Peter said miserably.

"Son, I believe *in* you. But if this was as big a problem as you say, more people would be concerned other than a thirteen year-old boy."

"Just because people aren't concerned doesn't mean it's not a problem," he grumbled, slumping into his room. His pet mouse watched him worriedly. Too bad mice were worthless as allies.

THAT EVENING after boxing and a shower, Peter was thinking about opening a pack of hotdogs for dinner when Dot knocked on his door.

"Come eat dinner with us," she demanded, dressed all in white. "Grandpa wants to hear how the search is going."

"Eat where?"

"On the thirteenth floor. At the Windsor," replied Dot.

"I never eat at that restaurant."

"You're not allowed?"

Peter shrugged. "I am. But it's expensive."

"We're paying. C'mon."

Peter didn't own any formal dining clothes so he pulled on an old pair of khakis and his black cashmere turtleneck —a gift from Caroline Crawford—and hoped no one would give him a hard time.

Even though everyone else at the Windsor was wearing dinner jackets, the hostess waved them through without a second glance. The Windsor smelled like pine trees and spiced apple cider. Green garland festooned the central chandelier, and underneath sat a sparkling Christmas tree and red packages. Menorahs burned happily along several walls, all in the spirit of the holiday season. Peter'd been so busy he forgot Christmas was only a few days away.

"Patrick, my boy!" cried Ollie Franklin. He stood from his place at the table, spilling breadcrumbs everywhere. A white cloth napkin was tucked into his belt and another into his shirt. "Good of you to join us. I've got a head start on you, I'm afraid. Can't resist the clam chowder!"

Rory Franklin was there too, looking sour as usual. His arms were crossed over his chest and he wasn't eating. Peter hadn't seen him for two weeks.

The waiter, dressed in black pants and a crisp white shirt, brought Peter water and tea and bread, and suggested Peter might enjoy tonight's special, the rigatoncini bolognese, whatever that was. Dot asked for "my usual, please."

Ollie set his silver spoon into an empty crystal soup bowl and dabbed at his forehead with a third napkin. "Oh dear. Haven't eaten this well in ages."

"You ate this well for lunch," Rory grouched.

"Peter, did you know there's a painting of you near the restrooms?" Dot was slathering butter onto a roll. "I should say, of a boy who looks like you."

"It's my great great grandfather. He was partial owner of the hotel."

"So you've got blood in the walls," Rory mused, watching Peter carefully. "You're *related* to the Crown. For a pipsqueak, your story keeps getting more interesting."

Peter shrugged. "Eventually my great grandfather sold his share and moved back to Greece, or so the story goes."

"A shame, dear boy, an absolute shame." Ollie shook his head, looking genuinely heartbroken. "Had he kept his shares you'd be wealthy beyond imagination, owning part of the Crown. Why, it's costing us a small fortune to stay here!"

"I wondered about that," said Peter. "I hope you're not going broke."

"Nonsense, we won't stay forever. And besides, one can't very well be the Phantom without quite a bit of wealth, as you can imagine."

No, Peter had never imagined that bit of depressing news.

A small troop of circus hands barged into the Windsor, laughing and catcalling loudly. Most circus performers were at Barclays preparing for the evening show; these men must have a night off. The Windsor was a hushed and severe restaurant and most patrons studiously avoided looking at the obnoxious newcomers, but not Ollie—he stood and clapped wildly. "I just love the circus. Bravo!"

The large bald man with a bushy mustache was with them, hidden behind sunglasses and a hat. Peter couldn't be sure, but he thought the man was staring at him behind the dark lenses. His henchman friends paid Peter no attention.

Peter wondered if any of them new The Evil Treasure Hunter.

"Grandpa, sit down," insisted Dot.

"What? We can't express appreciation?"

"You're making a scene. And this isn't the place. We don't want people thinking we're weird," she whispered angrily.

Peter noticed Atticus Snyder sitting with his family on the far side of the restaurant. He had a swollen eye from when Leo accidentally popped him during practice. He openly sneered at Ollie. And at the circus hands. And at everyone in general.

"Those aren't performers," said Peter, nodding toward the circus hands. "They're support staff. I think the circus leaves men here each night to continue the search."

"The search!" said Ollie. "Yes indeed! Tell us how it's going, won't you? Give us your full report please."

Peter leaned forward conspiratorially. "Lino Kang demands I show him someplace new every day, but so far nothing's turned up. I don't let him go anywhere without me, but the trouble is he's got circus staff going throughout the hotel. I can't keep track of them all. It's possible they've found artifacts and I don't know."

Rory asked, "You think Lino Kang is working with the Red Masque."

"I can't decide about Lino. He might simply be a curious guy," said Peter, fiddling absently with a yeast roll. "There's no way the entire circus is one big group of evil henchman. But I *know* something's wrong. I feel it."

Rory leaned forward, interested. He covered a cough with the inside of his elbow. "I thought you might."

Dot said, "What do you mean, you feel it?"

"It's like this shadow hanging over me. I know I sound stupid, but it's as if the hotel is warning me. The Red Masque is here. Somewhere."

Rory made a sound like "Hmmm."

"That's just weird, Peter," said Dot.

"So...no artifacts then?" Ollie asked. He was visibly disappointed. "None at all?"

Peter shook his head. "Not yet. What about you guys?"

"Oh...well..." Ollie and Dot shared an uncomfortable glance. He blubbered, "These things take time, you know. It's best we don't rush."

"Where have you been looking? This place is huge," Peter asked.

"Um, so, you see..."

Peter got the distinct impression that Ollie and Dot were behaving like kids guilty of stealing cookies. "Well? What have you been doing?" he demanded.

"Acting like pigs," Rory said with a snort. "That's what."

"Enjoying the food, as I'm sure you understand," Ollie stammered. "And visiting the spa, and...resting. Rest is important, naturally. Got to stay healthy."

"That's it?" Peter cried in dismay. "Dot?"

"I've been practicing fencing," she replied, focusing hard on her buttered roll.

"And?"

"And...swimming in the pool. To stay in shape."

"And?"

"And, I did a bit of school work," she said defensively.

Peter couldn't believe it. He got so mad his ears turned red. "So I'm the only one! The only one who cares, who's been on the lookout? Going to all these places to make sure the Red Masque doesn't discover the powerful...whatever they are!"

Ollie cleared his throat and Dot looked at the ceiling, going a little pink at her cheeks.

"I have school TOO," he said. "AND I practice fencing. And boxing. And I help my dad. And my mom. *And* I'm keeping an eye on the circus. But I *don't* go to the spa and I don't stuff my face with fancy food. I'm too busy."

"You're right, pipsqueak," Rory said. "But don't be too hard on Dot. Ollie's kept her locked away in that dungeon for much of her life. He's terrified. Of everything. For Dot, this is her first chance to live."

Ollie mumbled something about seeing no reason to be nasty. Dot asked, "Okay smartypants, what do you suggest I do?"

"Follow those men from the circus," replied Peter. "See the big one? He's bald under that hat, and he's trouble. I want to know where he goes."

"He's *huge*," said Dot, peering over her shoulder at the circus hands. "And he keeps stroking his mustache, like an evil villain. But I can do that, sure. Anything else?"

A new voice interrupted them. "Hello Peter Constantine. I didn't know you ate here." Caroline Crawford and her family had just entered for dinner. Peter's heart lurched into his throat. He'd been so busy, he hadn't seen her for weeks.

He stood and said hello to Caroline's mother (she didn't look at him but she did say, "Hello strange child,") and he shook the outstretched hand of Lord Crawford, who cried, "Brilliant to see you, sport! What have you been up to?"

"Thinking about joining the circus," Peter joked, as Ernestine Parker would have insisted. A gentleman always has a quip ready. "And fixing everything they break."

Lord Constantine laughed and said, "Indeed? As you should. Carry on, old boy!" He pounded Peter on the shoulder and walked to his table.

Caroline finally took her eyes off Peter and noticed his dinner companions. Her complexion paled a shade and she said weakly, "I...I didn't mean to intrude, Peter. Are you here with...are you on a...I mean..."

"These are my friends, the Franklin family," Peter said, indicating the table. "Franklin family, this is Caroline Crawford." The introduction felt awkward and uncomfortable— clearly he'd done something wrong, but he didn't know what.

Caroline politely greeted them and hurried to join her family. Peter sat, puzzled. A server brought their food but Peter didn't touch it.

"That little girl is gorgeous," said Dot. Her "usual" was a plate of chicken nuggets and french fries, further proof Dot wasn't as old as she appeared.

"I think so too," admitted Peter.

"She's a little insecure, but nobody's perfect," she said, and she shoved french fries into her mouth.

"What's that mean?"

"Cheesh jea'ash," Dot replied with a mouth full of food.

"Dot said, 'She's jealous,'" Rory translated. "Caroline's feelings are hurt, boy. She thinks you're on a date, with our Dot."

Peter glanced at Caroline's table; Caroline quickly averted her eyes. Peter experienced a curious cocktail of emotions—intense pleasure, confusion, and guilt.

"She's jealous," repeated Peter, wondering why this revelation seemed to build a warm fire in his chest. He never would've guessed a girl as pretty as Caroline could get jealous, especially not over him.

After a few minutes Caroline excused herself. The Windsor restrooms were located in a hallway at the back, the same hallway where the painting of Peter's likeness was hung. Peter caught her there.

"Wait!" he called before she entered the ladies room.

"Peter?"

"Um...hi! I just...I mean...it's not...uhh..." he said lamely, because his brain and his mouth suddenly quit communicating. What he wanted to say was, *How on earth could you be jealous of Dot? You're Caroline Crawford! You're the sweetest, kindest, prettiest...*

"The blonde girl is lovely, Peter. Are you two...?"

Peter thought his chest would pop. "She's my friend. I mean...she's my only friend. No! No, I mean, that is, she's *only* my friend. Does...d-does that make sense?"

Caroline tried and failed to repress a relieved smile. The truth was she thought about Peter most days, completely charmed by the beautiful boy and his long lashes.

She said, "It makes perfect sense, somehow."

"Good."

"But you shouldn't mind me. That was silly. I'm in no position to be jealous."

Peter's head swam. A gentleman should say...something...he had no idea.

She continued, "After all, you and I never see each other. We're *only* friends, too."

She stated it as fact, but Peter heard her question underneath. Caroline wanted to know how Peter would react. Poor Peter, he was a little overwhelmed with Caroline's ability to express herself and willingness to do so. He said, "Y-yes? Err...what?"

"We're friends, Peter. Like you and Josephine are friends," said Caroline in a shy sort of voice, and again Peter heard a question underneath.

"Uh..." Peter said, close to fainting. He could hear Ernestine Parker instructing him on what he should say, but the words were garbled. He tried to say, *I want to be more than friends, Caroline*, but what came out sounded more like, "...eerrrmm..."

"Never mind," Caroline laughed. "This is a silly conversation. Especially outside the ladies room."

"Okay...I guess. I'll...go back to my table."

"Bye Peter. And I like your shirt."

He returned, floating like a Macy's Thanksgiving Day Parade balloon, to find Ollie and Dot already gone. Peter asked, "Where'd they go?"

"Ollie went to sleep off his meal, the old fool," answered Rory. "And Dot followed the circus hands."

Peter stared at the exit and said, "I hope she stays safe."

"Me too, kid. Sit down, we need to talk. Eat your food."

"Yessir." For a moment all was quiet except for the murmur of nearby patrons and clinking silverware. The rigatoncini bolognese was tasty pasta that Peter gulped in large mouthfuls.

He heard snickering from an adjacent table. It was Grover Ivory, the annoying boy allergic to sunlight, and his parents, as thin and pale as their son. Grover cried, "Lookit Peter eating at the Windsor. So strange. It's like a dog using utensils. Hey Putrid Peter, ever heard of a napkin?"

Grover's parents didn't hear the insult because they were busy on their phones, despite Grover calling loudly.

Rory said, "Blast it, boy, ignore him. And you're about to choke. Smaller bites. Now listen. Just me and you here. We both know Ollie and Dot aren't up to the challenge."

Peter's mouth was full so he made a "Huh?" noise.

"You've got the gift. They don't. You can hear the city. You can *feel* the hotel."

Peter swallowed. "Can you feel the shadow too?"

"Long time ago, yes. Lemme ask you, pipsqueak. Be honest with me. Did you meet Cypress?"

Peter wiped his mouth, thinking furiously. If there was anyone he could trust with the truth, it was probably Rory.

Besides, he had no one else and he was desperate. He nodded cautiously. "I met him."

"Thought so. Cypress saw what I see."

"What's that?" asked Peter.

"Courage and a pure heart. Strong enough to resist the enemy."

"You mean the Red Masque?"

"We're not ready for them, are we, kid? You saw Ollie's lair. That's what happens when we lose focus. When we get comfortable, we grow fat and lazy. Better to be lean and mean, that's what Cypress taught me."

"He trained you. Right, sir? Cypress picked you to be his successor. You became the Phantom."

Rory scratched at his stubbly beard. "I was the Phantom after him, yes. Didn't work like Cypress hoped. That's a story for another day. If you're smart, kid, you won't tell Ollie and Dot about Cypress."

Atticus Snyder and his family had finished and they were leaving. Grover Ivory waved and said, "Atticus! Hey Atticus! Lookit Peter eating. What, he couldn't find a hair brush? Could you smell him from your table?"

Atticus chuckled and smirked at Peter on his way out. Grover held up his hand for a high-five but Atticus, his elder by a few years, ignored the gesture.

"Hah," Peter said to himself. "Serves Grover right."

"What's that?" asked Rory.

"Nothing, sir. Sorry. So, Cypress Fitzgerald didn't trust Ollie? I mean, Cypress's *ghost* didn't trust him? Or Dot?"

"Bah." Rory waved the question away. "They aren't believers. They never listen. All is not as it seems, boy. You've still got some surprises ahead of you. You'll understand soon enough, I'm afraid."

"I don't know what to do, sir. I'm trying. Last time, the

Red Masque almost burned down my home. Now they've returned and no one believes me."

"I know the feeling, kid. This is not a simple fight. The blasted Red Masque are more than mere treasure thieves. Strange powers are working unseen in the Crown, Peter, and the city needs you."

"But I'm only thirteen!"

Rory shrugged. "It's not about *age*, kid, it's about *who you are*."

"Shouldn't we...I don't know, find the *real* Phantom? He's been reincarnated or something, right? Or she. Is that how it works?"

Rory smothered a cough. "Keep your voice down and eat your food, pipsqueak. No, we don't 'find him.' That ain't how it works. New York City chooses a new protector."

"Yeah but...huh?"

Rory leaned forward, his face looking younger and animated. "You think the Phantom's just some guy? Some weirdo wearing pajamas? No, kid. It's an ancient tradition, older than New York. You've felt it. The Crown feels alive, right?"

"Yes sir," whispered Peter.

"That's because it *is*. The land itself chooses a protector. And then *helps* the protector."

"I didn't know that."

"No one does."

"How?" asked Peter.

"I have no idea. It's magic."

"But Dot said each Phantom names his successor. Like Ollie gets to pick."

Rory shook his head. "She's wrong. It's the city doing the choosing. Cypress trained me, but only after I was brought to him. Shame I wasn't strong enough."

"What happened?"

"Like I said, story for another day," growled Rory.

"Was Ollie chosen?"

"*No.* That was a blasted disaster. And Dot hasn't been chosen either," he said. "Those hidden treasures are part of this, though I'm not exactly sure how. You've got to find them, Peter."

"I don't even know what I'm looking for, though," Peter said in a frustrated sputter. "Do you?"

"Wish I did. Trouble is, everything we once knew is gone. The line of Phantoms was broken and now...all is forgotten. I know this—Cypress Fitzgerald believed powerful treasures were here, in the Crown. Or at least one of them was, maybe more. He remained here to protect them. Ghosts stick around for a reason, you know."

"Is there anyone who knows about them? Who can tell me what to look for?"

Rory sat back in his chair, looking old again. He coughed into the crook of his elbow. "You'd have to ask a historian. Someone attentive to gossip and myths. Cypress never got a chance to tell me, but maybe others listened to the whispers."

"I think I know *where* the artifacts are," Peter said, "but I don't know *what* to look for."

"Where?"

"There's a place under the Crown where no one goes. Dad called it the Caves and I think—"

Rory held up his hand. "Not now. We don't know who's eavesdropping. We'll talk about this next time. Okay, pipsqueak?"

"But—"

"Peter?" asked Caroline Crawford. Peter felt like a spell'd

been broken and he blinked stupidly at her before remembering where he was.

"Oh...h-hi, Caroline," he said.

"You ordered the rigotoncini bolognese? I did too, but I think the tomatoes are a little over ripe. That's what my mother said."

"I think it's delicious."

"Would you like to come sit with us? Your friends all left."

"But Rory's..." Peter said and he was surprised to find Rory's chair empty; he'd slipped away. Rory must've been a good Phantom—the man was sneaky.

"Rory? Is he the elder gentleman? Are you related to him?"

"We're just friends. They moved in a few weeks ago," replied Peter.

Caroline made a tsk'ing sound as the waiter brought the check for the meal. "Your friends left you the bill. It'll be hundreds of dollars."

"Hundreds...?" repeated Peter, the blood draining from his face. He stared in horror at the slip of paper, afraid to pick it up. "They must've forgot."

"I'll take this," she said and neatly plucked the bill off the table. "And tell your *friends* that Caroline says they need to be more considerate."

"Caroline! You can't pay that."

"Watch me." She gave him one of her dazzling, heart-stopping smiles and said, "But next time you're here, Peter Constantine, you better be sitting at my table."

9

REVELATIONS

Dot was waiting for Peter the next morning as he left apartment 201, his arms full of books. "Peter, guess what!" she cried, surprising him so much he spilled school supplies across the hallway. "You're a clumsy kid, aren't you."

Peter got on all-fours, gathered his belongings, and grumbled, "It's too early to be shouting, you know."

"I've been up all night."

"Up all night? Is something wrong?" He looked curiously at the bags under her eyes and her ragged hair—she was a fright.

"I followed the men from the circus. Remember? The bald guy with a bushy mustache? I found it, Peter! I found the underground lair where the artifacts are hidden. At least, I assume that's where they're hidden because that's where the circus is searching."

"You mean the Caves?" asked Peter.

"You *knew* about them?"

"Only found out recently. Dad told me no one goes down there anymore. But I don't know how to get in."

Dot rubbed her red eyes, looking exhausted. "I followed

them and found the door and searched all night, because that's what the Phantom would do."

Peter opened his mouth to reply but thought better of it. Rory obviously didn't believe Dot was the next Phantom, but was it Peter's place to correct her? Probably not. Besides, what if Rory was wrong? Maybe Dot *was* the Phantom. After all, she'd discovered the long forgotten Caves.

She said, "Grandpa Ollie will be so pleased. He desperately wants to get his hands on one of the treasures."

"Where's the entrance?" asked Peter curiously.

"That's what's so sneaky. The circus built the animal cage in the garage to cover the entrance. It's a pair of doors they forced open."

Peter's pulse quickened. "Then they've been searching for weeks already."

"Definitely."

"Did you go in?"

"Of course I did," she said with a half snort. "I'm not afraid. Phantoms feel no fear. It's a disaster in there. There are no working lights so I didn't get far, and the circus is searching several floors below."

"I bet they're being clever and leaving no evidence," said Peter. "So even if I tell Dad, he won't believe me."

"We don't need him," she said through an enormous yawn. "We have me. The Phantom will handle it."

"Yeah," muttered Peter, unable to disguise the doubt in his voice. "Maybe. But I think we need help. We're outnumbered. Because if the circus built the animal cage specifically to disguise the door, then *someone* knew the door was there. Someone in charge is working with the Red Masque. And I bet it's Lino Kang."

Dot swayed on her feet and her eyes closed. She

teetered, wobbled to the verge of falling, and bonked her forehead on the wall before Peter could catch her.

"Huh! Wha—! Oh, sorry Peter, I think I drifted off. *Ouch.* What...what were you saying?"

"Jeez, Dot. You should go to bed," replied Peter in disbelief. It was astonishing she'd drifted off while standing up and talking.

"Ollie falls asleep all the time," she murmured. "But you're right. Such a smart guy, Pete. I'm going now. So sleepy. Maybe eat some bologna first, who knows." She staggered to the golden elevators, followed closely by Peter for fear she might knock herself unconscious. She stumbled inside and said, "Kay, bye Parker," as the doors whooshed closed.

Peter found an empty chair in the Nook and fell into it. Neither Joey nor Hawkins, both reading books nearby, noticed anything amiss until thirty minutes passed without him moving a muscle. Finally Hawkins pushed back his pageboy cap and asked, "Peter? What's up, my man? You look all weird and goofy."

"Yeah," he said. He was dumbstruck, his mind spinning too quickly to form a coherent response. The Caves, he kept thinking. The Red Masque was in the Caves.

Joey picked up a pencil and paper and began making notes for her upcoming history test. "Don't mind him, Hawkins. Peter's often up in the clouds like this, and he never tells me what's wrong."

"But he looks goofier than usual," replied Hawkins, who had an impressive array of Christmas-themed iced danishes spread across the coffee table. "Hey Peter, we're your friends, you know? You can tell us stuff."

"I dunno. It's a long story," said Peter doubtfully. Could he tell them? Probably not; they'd assume he'd gone bonkers. He'd have to start at the very beginning, going all the way back to the night his family fled The Evil Treasure Hunter. Most of the past fifteen months was a total secret from everyone. He didn't dare...

On the other hand, it'd be a relief to have friends to confide in. Moreover he'd recently told Dot they were outnumbered. What would Cypress Fitzgerald do?

"It's no use," said Joey, loftily shaking her head. "I've tried and tried."

"It's kinda a secret," Peter said reluctantly. "I'm not sure if I'm allowed to tell."

"Someone said you can't?"

"Well...no. Not really."

Hawkins laughed, "Then what's the problem?"

"You promise not to repeat this?"

Joey snapped her book closed and sat up straighter, though still skeptical.

Hawkins suggested, "Let's move to the corner." He jerked his chin, indicating Joey's sister Lela, lazily reading a magazine, or at least trying to, at the nearby coffee table. "Away from any eavesdroppers, know what I mean? We won't tell a soul."

The three friends left their schoolwork and moved to the farthest group of red overstuffed reading chairs. They hunched together like secret spies. Peter said, "This is nuts, guys. You won't believe me."

"Don't be silly, Peter," said Joey. "Of course we will."

"I promise everything I'm going to say is true," Peter said in a whisper.

Joey and Hawkins nodded solemnly.

He started by telling them about the first awful morning he woke in the Crown. About how his family had to leave their house because a scary man he called The Evil Treasure Hunter was after them. They arrived in New York City just as the Red Masque began robbing banks—and thanks to Manos, the treasure hunter, Gordie Abaddon, was forced into hiding. Hawkins and Joey both howled with laughter when Peter admitted stealing Atticus's key the night they fought in the snow and how that started the Phantom rumors again, and they gasped when Peter told them how in January The Evil Treasure Hunter himself had suddenly appeared in the Crown's Lobby, looking for Manos.

Peter felt relieved as he related the events, like a valve releasing steam. Surprisingly enough, neither of his friends expressed any doubt when Peter told them about his encounters with Cypress Fitzgerald, the ghost on the tenth floor. Joey already knew a little bit of the story, but she accepted the rest without comment. He explained how Cypress vanished after giving him a key and predicting Peter would need to protect the Crown. And about the terrible fire later that night, and how the fireman mistakenly assumed he was the Phantom, but in reality it was Peter covered in soot and wearing a scarf-mask. That night was when Peter had confronted The Evil Treasure Hunter inside Caroline Crawford's fiery living room and he'd seen the Red Masque disappearing into the dark.

The only interruption was when Hawkins held up his hand and said, "So the mouse, it helped you escape through the dumbwaiter shaft. The mouse knew the opening was behind that big wooden furniture? How?"

"I have no idea," admitted Peter.

"Where's the freaky mouse now?"

"Hangs out in my room, usually. You can meet it later."

Peter carried on, telling them about the moaning ghost in his bedroom, about the note leading him to the Hotel Chelsea, the dusty underground lair, the broken history of the Phantom, the circus and his suspicions about the Red

Masque and the secret treasure, about Ollie and Dot and Rory, the dreadful shadow he felt hanging over him, and finally about the sinister search going on inside the Caves.

He finished the story and his friends stared at him with enormous eyes. He cringed, praying they wouldn't burst into laughter.

"So..." said Hawkins slowly. He'd taken off his pageboy cap and fiddled with it. "The syndicate could be in the Caves right now? Looking for the powerful artifacts?"

"I think they do it mostly at night. Less chance of being discovered."

"I can't believe you've been doing this alone," marveled Joey. "That's such a boy thing. Why didn't you tell us?"

"My dad doesn't believe me. I didn't think you would either."

"Of *course* we'd believe you! You're my best friend, Peter," cried Hawkins passionately.

"According to Cypress, the Phantom wasn't just one guy," said Joey. "The Phantom is like...the head chef at a restaurant. When he's done, another takes his place. Right?"

"Correct, that's what he told me."

"And we've heard the prophecy," said Hawkins excitedly. "Dude said he was coming back!"

"How does it work?" asked Joey.

"I got no idea," Peter admitted. "New York City picks a protector, whatever the means. But I dunno how."

"I think Cypress is right." She was nodding with a far off look in her eyes. "I think you're the Phantom."

"That's insane, Joey. I'm thirteen."

"But it's so obvious! It's like the Crown has been *training* you. No one's offered to teach ME boxing or how to sword fight or do magic. Everything changed when you arrived. I mean, you have a supernatural mouse!"

Hawkins nodded in total agreement, studying Peter with renewed respect.

She continued, "You told me when you first arrived that the hotel felt alive. Do you remember?"

"I remember. I still feel that way."

"See? This is destiny."

"Do you have Cypress's key?" asked Hawkins. Peter pulled it from his pocket and dropped it into Hawkins's hands. "Huh. Looks weird, don't it. You think this is one of the hidden artifacts or whatever?"

Peter replied, "Doesn't seem special to me. All it's done is unlock the secret door under the Chelsea."

"What happens if the Red Masque finds these powerful things?" Joey asked.

"I don't know. Can't be good, right?"

"We need to know what the artifacts look like," said Hawkins. "You know? Otherwise, how do we know what we're searching for? Are you sure Rory or Ollie never saw them?"

"Never," Peter confirmed. Inwardly his heart began to glow, noting Hawkins said "we." His friends didn't think he was crazy after all, and now he had allies.

Joey plucked the key from Hawkins palm and said, "This isn't normal. A proper key has a shoulder, notches, and teeth. This key's bizarre. It's all black and swirly."

"We need a book 'bout this stuff. I love books. Books got everything."

Peter snapped his fingers. "Hey! That's a good idea," he said. "The Librarian!"

"She got books about this?" asked Hawkins.

"No, but she knows everything. C'mon!"

Peter, Joey, and Hawkins raced up the stairwell to the fourth floor. The Library was one of those beautiful and hushed rooms with gleaming oak bookshelves and soft Tiffany lamps. The sliding ladders had been decorated with silver ribbon. It was empty except for the Librarian, an ancient woman with short blue hair. She smiled pleasantly behind her desk and said, "Well, my favorite youngsters, come to visit an old woman. You're here early."

"Good morning, ma'am. Can we ask you some questions?"

"Oh dear me. About the Red Masque again?"

"Yes ma'am. And the Phantom."

She pursed her lips. "Him again, Mr. Constantine? I thought we decided the Phantom was history."

Hawkins said, "No way! He's back!"

"You're referring to Ms. Drake's article about the ghost, young man?"

"*Yes*," said Peter, giving Hawkins a hard and meaningful poke in the ribs. "That's what he's talking about, the ghost."

"So. You believe the prophecy?" the Librarian asked with a twinkle in her eyes. "That the Captain of the Night will return?"

"The who?" asked Joey.

"The Phantom. That's his nickname," said Peter. "Yes ma'am, I do. *We* do."

"Good. I was hoping you'd be a believer."

Peter said, "We heard a rumor about him."

"And which rumor is that, my dear?"

"Um. Well. We heard the Phantom used to have power-ful...stuff...which, you know...did stuff."

"Perhaps you could be more specific."

Joey interjected, "What Peter's *trying* to say is that we're wondering if it's true the Phantom had magical tools or weapons, and they might still be in the Crown. But we don't know what they are or even how to ask about them."

"That's what I said, basically," protested Peter.

The Librarian laid her hands together on the desk and she gave them a mysterious smile. "Do you know, I've worked here for seventy years. And you're the first to ask that question."

Hawkins's eyes grew wide. "*Seventy?*"

"You've heard that rumor," said Peter. "You told me you listen to the whispers. That it's your job to sift through information."

"That *is* my job. And yes, eager youngsters, I've heard the rumor that the Phantom possessed powerful weapons. Though I've not heard it mentioned for over fifty years, mind you."

"Do you know what they were? His weapons?"

"I do."

Peter felt butterflies take flight in his stomach. "What were they?"

"It's important to remember, dears, when last the Phantom was active. Years and years ago. It was a different time. A different era. A culture far removed from today. When the Crown was first built, there was no elevator. No lightbulbs, even. The Edison Electric Company couldn't convince the owners that electricity would change everything. It was a more civilized time, and the Phantom's weapons reflect that."

"What do you mean?" asked Hawkins.

"They are the weapons of a gentleman. They aren't some crude bomb or technological terror. The Phantom was civilized and so were his tools. Or so the rumors claim."

"Do you know what they were?" Peter asked.

"Before I answer that, I am curious. Are you worried about the Red Masque? That the syndicate is looking for these weapons?"

"Yes ma'am, we are."

She gave Peter a crisp nod. "*Good*. I am too. So. The Phantom had three weapons or tools, as you called them."

"Three," whispered Joey, who looked as excited as Peter felt.

"So the rumors go. You know the first one, I assume."

"We do?"

"His sword," she said as if it was obvious, and all three kids deflated with slumping shoulders.

"That's it? A sword?" Peter asked dejectedly.

Hawkins said, "Guy who lives in a tent near me has a sword and he's loony."

"Not just any sword, young man. The Phantom's was supposedly supernatural."

"Oh yeah?" said Peter, perking up. "How so?"

"Eyewitnesses claim to have seen it on fire."

"A *fiery* sword, that's so wicked!" cried Hawkins and he leapt across the thick carpet making violent slashing motions.

Peter thought back to his time in the lair under the Hotel Chelsea. He hadn't seen any sword that looked magical or fiery; in fact most of them looked eaten through with rust. He asked, "Where is the sword now?"

The Librarian spread her hands like, who knows? "That is a great mystery, isn't it? Treasure hunters searched for years. Even if the Phantom's sword wasn't magical, even if it was an ordinary blade, it would still be quite valuable because of its mythology."

Hawkins was running around bookshelves pretending to chop things with an invisible sword. Joey said, "What's the second weapon? Or tool?"

"The second one is particularly interesting to us, which I'll explain in a moment, dears. But first, you should understand that less is known about this particular tool of the Phantom's—a mystical gateway. Legend has it that the Phantom was able to enter into a magical world from the gateway and emerge elsewhere in the city. Quite silly, isn't it? Another source claims the Phantom wore a powerful ring that allowed access through the gateway. Only the ring wearer was permitted to enter."

Hawkins quit slashing and listened raptly to the Librarian. "A powerful ring," he whispered. "Like Frodo."

"Who?" asked Joey blankly.

The Librarian smiled kindly. "Frodo Baggins, my dear. You simply must read *Lord of the Rings* soon. Hawkins finished it in a week."

"So, a ring," Peter said thoughtfully. "Which led to a magical world. Sounds far fetched."

"It is. And as I said, this legend probably isn't true. However, it's of particular interest to us because one of the entrances to the magical world was supposedly inside the Crown itself."

"WHAT!" cried Hawkins. "Where?"

Peter felt as though someone rang his entire body with a hammer. He shivered with tingles and heard faint chimes between his ears. Could the secret treasure be a mystical gateway? Was that why Cypress Fitzgerald's ghost remained?

"No one knows, dear," answered the Librarian. "It's probably pure fantasy."

Maybe, thought Peter. And maybe not.

"A sword. A magical portal or ring," said Joey, ticking off her fingers. "What's the third thing?"

"The third tool is an old superstition. It is said that when New York City began to build modern towers and sewers in the early 1900s, the city planners wanted a way to access, well, everything. In other words, with the city expanding out of control the master builders wanted the ability the open any door. The solution of course was to design every lock so it could be opened by the city planners and police if need be."

Joey said, "But if they did that, every New Yorker would be able to open each other's door. The locks would be worthless."

But Peter knew what she was getting at. "Not every lock could be opened by every key. The rumor isn't about the locks, it's about the key. A master key."

"Precisely, my dear," the Librarian said. "And that was supposedly the Phantom's final tool. The last remaining master key, capable of opening any lock in the city."

Peter, Joey, and Hawkins stayed quiet a long time, trying not to look at each other. Inside Peter's pocket, the black key grew warm.

"Try it," said Joey, indicating door 202. Her door.

"I'm freaked out. I'm so freaked out." Hawkins's fists were clenched over his head, crushing his hat and hair.

Peter held the weird black key in his palm. "Joey, the master key—if this is even it—opened doors a hundred years ago. Not locks made recently. It won't work."

"You're scared," she said with an upward tilt to her chin.

"Of course I am! What if it doesn't work? Or even worse, what if it *does?*"

"Know what I believe, Peter?" asked Hawkins. "That *is* the Phantom's key, but it wasn't built by New York's city planners. That might just be the legend surrounding it. Because that doesn't look like a key built by humans. I believe it's magical."

"Hawkins—"

"Try it!"

"I *am*. Don't rush me." Cautiously he raised the key to the lock. Both his friends took an involuntary step backwards. "Look, see, it's a different shape. It won't fit, I can tell."

"Why're you so negative?" asked Joey, planting her fists on her hips. "You don't have any faith at all. Maybe it works, maybe it doesn't, but stop ruining the fun."

She was right, Peter knew. He was terrified that it might be true, terrified it might not be, and so he was far too pessimistic. He took a deep breath, held it, and shoved the key forward. The strange black metal twisted like a liquid and slid neatly into the lock. There was a soft pulse of light and the door clicked open.

"Shut UP!" cried Hawkins, jumping a foot into the air. "Shut up right now! Holy smokes!"

Joey paled and her fists slid off her hips. "Ohmygosh."

Peter yanked it out and hurried to his own door, apartment 201. The key fit and the door opened.

"I think you're right, Hawkins," Peter breathed. "Did you see? This isn't a simple master key. The metal—it moves. The legend is just a story trying to explain something magic."

"It's *totally* magical," Hawkins agreed. "It was the Phantom's. And you're the Phantom."

"Having a magic key doesn't make me the Phantom," Peter argued. "He could have given it to anyone."

"Yeah but he didn't. He gave it to you, Peter!"

From down the hall there came a sudden and angry shout. Peter shoved the key into his front pocket and they rushed into the Nook. Max the Magician stood in the middle of the room, glaring at Adolfo the strongman and Bruno the knife thrower. Behind them was a tall thin man wearing purple robes. His face was angular and pointy, just like his beard.

"What's going on?" asked Peter. Two butlers emerged from their rooms to inspect the commotion, and so did Mrs. Love, the concierge director.

"Ah! There is boy," said Bruno. For once he wore a shirt, though his bushy beard covered most of it. "Boy named Peter comes with Bruno."

Max Freeman was dressed in a tuxedo and for the first time since Peter'd known him he wasn't smiling. "These scoundrels have been asking about you, Peter. I told them they couldn't go to your room."

The giant Adolfo glared silently. The Nook had a tall ceiling, but his head seemed about to touch it.

Bruno pounded on his chest and said, "What is problem? I teach boy to throw knife. Boy is good."

"No knife-toting circus freak is getting past me to where the children sleep," snarled Max.

"What business is it of yours anyway?" asked the tall and robed man. He spoke in a theatrical hiss. "You half-rate trickster."

"*Trickster?*" Max nearly choked, his eyes bulging. "You're a two-bit charlatan! The forgettable sixth act of a circus! You entertain popcorn-munching children while they wait for elephants. While I alone draw crowds of twenty-five thousand in Las Vegas! I've seen toddlers perform more impressive magic than you, Shaman."

"I am a master wizard of the highest order! Conjurer of spirits and spells you cannot imagine! Don't you dare talk down to me, you mere showman. You're an entertainer, a con artist at best," the man named Shaman spat.

"This is a wizard rivalry," whispered Peter. "Max told me they hate each other."

"I love this hotel so much," replied Hawkins. Joey's mouth was hanging open.

Max laughed, though his eyes were hard and icy. "A novice like you couldn't conjure a cold!"

"Can't conjure a cold?" the pointy man sputtered. He waved his arms dramatically, smoke billowing from his robes, and suddenly he was holding a green snake. It coiled around his hand, stared at Max, and flicked a small red tongue. "How about a game of catch, trickster!"

Bruno released a high-pitched scream. "Bruno *hate* snakes!"

Mrs. Love clutched the arm of the nearest butler.

The Shaman and Max moved at the same time. Shaman swung his robed-arm like pitching a softball and launched the serpent into the air. Max stretched out his arm and playing cards erupted forth. The cards sliced through the air, cutting the snake into small pieces.

POOF.

The serpent vanished into a thin trail of smoke, slowly wafting upwards.

Max laughed. "Hah! The old snake trick used by *novices*."

"Where'd it go?" whispered Joey, peeking behind the couch. "I won't allow it to remain here."

"Don't worry kids," said Max haughtily. "This'll be over...*in a snap*." The magician snapped his fingers and an orange flame appeared over his palm, hovered a moment, and extinguished.

"That's it?" scoffed the Shaman. "Haha! What, petty showman, you forgot to refill your lighter fluid?"

Max grinned. "Not exactly."

At that moment Bruno cried out again and pointed at

Shaman's cowl. The purple robes were smoking and small tendrils of fire fluttered along the fabric. "Shaman! Shaman is on fire!" he roared and whacked the frail man on the back. Adolfo and Bruno knocked him over in heavy-handed attempts to snuff out the flames. The butlers ran to the kitchen for pitchers of water. Within the confusion and screams, Shaman vanished. No sign of him.

"Hey, where..." muttered Hawkins, looking thoroughly spooked. "...where'd the freaky guy go?"

"HERE!" Shaman cried, appearing with a swirl of purple directly behind Max. "Capable of moving unseen in the physical world is no small feat! Your feeble powers were unable to detect me. What do you say to *that,* trickster?"

"I say you're capable of using a distraction, which any simpleton can do. But can you move *through* the physical world, you bony fraud?" Max moved quickly, throwing something against the floor. There was a tremendous crash of light and everyone winced. Peter's vision was temporarily ruined—pulsing orange bursts were all he could see.

Slowly their eyesight returned and Max was gone.

"Oh heck. He's gone too," said Hawkins.

"No!" cried Joey, pointing at the giant window. "There he is!"

Max the Magician was on the other side of the glass. No tricks, no illusions, he was *outside.* His arms were spread wide like 'Ta da!' and he laughed without sound. Was he levitating? Peter and Joey and Hawkins rushed to the window as Max was swallowed by a ball of white flame and then he was gone. No matter how hard they pressed their faces to look up and down, they found nothing except empty 58th Street.

Peter grinned and said, "Max is the coolest."

Hawkins turned to Shaman and asked, "But mister, how'd he do *that?*"

Shaman narrowed his eyes and stomped out of the room, trailed by a spiraling plume of smoke from his cowl. He'd been defeated in the wizard's duel, apparently.

Bruno pointed at Peter and said, "Okay, was fun. Party over. You throw knives now?"

The door to the stairwell banged open and Manos appeared. His hair was messy and his handsome face was pale. Peter'd never seen him look so upset.

"Dad? What's wrong?"

"We have an emergency," said Manos in a shaky voice. "Everyone return to their rooms. And stay there."

"Why?"

"Tandra, the lioness—she's missing."

"WHAT!" the children cried.

"Everyone, hurry! Except you, Peter. You need to come with me."

10

LIONS AND CAVES

Peter and Manos stepped into the hotel's surveillance office and closed the door behind them. The small room was devoid of furniture (except for a swivel chair) but it was hot and crowded. Marlowe Blodgett was there, as was Mr. Banks and Mr. Conrad and a stern-looking security officer, a man so big he could barely reach the keyboard over his stomach. His tie had Santa on it.

"It's zee boy! Peter!" cried Marlowe. "He can clear zis zing up."

Mr. Banks, the hotel's majority share holder, arched a cold eyebrow at him and said, "Peter Constantine. You have some explaining to do."

Peter tried to gulp but couldn't; his throat was too dry. All the adults loomed over him, looking angry. He knew that was only his imagination, but that's what it felt like. "Y-yes sir."

Manos said softly, "Peter, we don't think you did anything wrong. But before we continue, where were you this morning?"

"Umm...uh, with Joey and Hawkins in the Nook. And then we went to the Library."

The Crown's manager, Mr. Conrad, nodded happily. "Then he has alibis. We'll check with the librarian. I never suspected him for a moment."

Mr. Banks, as always, was dressed in a tailored khaki sports jacket. He snapped, "Show Peter the tape."

The security officer indicated a screen and played a surveillance video in fast forward. On it, three boys snuck through the back doors of the Crown, hurried up the seldom-used utility staircase, and snuck into room 1919, Lino Kang's room. The security officer said, "These videos were taken an hour ago, while the circus was at breakfast."

"Tell me, Peter," said Mr. Banks. "Who *are* these boys?"

"I don't know, sir. Their faces are blurry."

The security officer nodded knowingly, a motion which caused his chin to vanish into his neck. "Kids wearing masks made out of pantyhose. Blurs the features."

The silent video continued. Soon the boys came out of 1919, carrying a lion cub and leaving the door open. A moment later, Tandra the lioness appeared in the hallway looking furious.

Peter gasped. "They *stole* a lion cub? And then Tandra got away?"

"I thought I instructed you not to let your *hooligans* at the park interfere with our hotel," said Mr. Banks nastily.

"It wasn't zee boy! It's as plain as day!" cried Marlow. "Zats not him on zee screen."

"It was his friends, Mr. Blodgett. They recently vandalized a nearby hotel and now *this*."

"It's not the Raiders, sir. Look." Peter pointed at the screen, which had paused. The boys were clearly visible, retreating down the stairs, and Peter indicated their shoes. "Those guys have cuffed khakis and nice loafers. My friends at the park never wear that kind of stuff. They have no money."

"Then who, may I ask, do you think stole the lion cub?"

"The Ritz kids," replied Peter immediately. "Has to be."

"The who? The what?" asked Mr. Conrad, rubbing his bald head.

"The mean kids who live at the Ritz Carlton. They're awful."

"Couldn't be," blubbered Mr. Banks. "The Ritz Carlton is a fine establishment. They would never."

"I know zis kid," said Marlowe Blodgett, bending towards the screen. "He looks familiar. Zis one here. He lives here at zee Crown. Does he not?"

Mr. Conrad stooped in for a closer look. "Huh. Looks like Atticus Snyder."

"Couldn't be! Not possible." Mr. Banks shook his head and crossed his arms defiantly. "The Snyders are upstanding Crown residents. Under no circumstances will we accuse the Snyder boy of a *felony*."

Peter and Manos shared a knowing look. It was definitely Atticus. Peter recognized the smirk through the mask.

"Hmm," said Mr. Conrad, squinting at the screen. "You might be right, sir, but the resemblance is strong."

Manos set his hand on Peter's shoulder. "I think we've proven Peter is innocent. None of his friends dress like the children on screen. The question is, what do we do now? Should I call the manager of the Ritz?"

"No!" shouted Mr. Banks, startling them all. "Heavens no. That's the last thing I want, a war of accusations between hotels. It'd be an absolute zoo in the papers."

"Zee lion cub is worth millions," said Marlowe. "I must

insist all resources be used to find her. As well as Tandra, zee lioness. As well as zee troublesome boys!"

Peter asked, "Did your cameras track Tandra? Or the cubs?"

The security officer grunted, "Tandra went into the stairwell and never came out. But, funny thing is, she ain't there no more. And the boys split up. I'm looking through video. Could take a while."

Mr. Banks's voice came out like a whip, "Work *faster*, you overgrown toadstool."

Mr. Conrad took a deep and shaky breath, and said, "Mr. Banks, in my role as Crown manager...I need to alert the authorities."

"The police! Have you gone *mad?*"

"And animal control."

Peter looked back and forth between the hotel's owner and the hotel's manager.

Mr. Banks tried to pace but there was no room. "Absolutely not! Not until we've tried to solve this problem in-house. Good grief, think of the fallout!"

"Sir, if someone gets hurt and we didn't—"

"No one will get hurt!"

Mr. Conrad rubbed furiously at his bald head. "There's no way this will be kept a secret, sir. I mean, for heaven's sake, it's a *lion*. On the loose!"

Manos grabbed Peter by the arm and pulled him from the room, saying, "No reason for you to listen to old men argue, eh?"

They walked upstairs to room 201, scrutinizing every abandoned hallway and corner along the way. No sign of lions. "What's gonna happen, Dad?"

"We'll find Tandra. And her cub."

"How do you know you'll find them?" asked Peter,.

As he said the words, he felt a shadow fall across his heart. The anxious feeling had returned.

"Because we have to," said Manos.

"Dad, do you feel anxious for no reason? Like super stressed?"

"I do right now." Manos grinned, but Peter knew his father had no clue what he meant. He didn't experience the same shadow, the same certainty that the Crown was in peril. Manos opened the door. "I'm going to help with the search. "

"Where's Mom?"

"Locked in the Laundry with her coworkers. Back later, okay?"

Peter went inside and shut the door. Through the walls he heard Joey and Hawkins talking in the neighboring apartment.

"About time, pipsqueak," said Rory, sitting at the small kitchen table.

"Augh! How'd you get in here?" cried Peter. He jumped and held up his fists as Arthur Graves had taught him.

"Think you're the only one who can get into rooms?"

"Do you have a magical key too?"

"I met your mouse," Rory said with a slight cough. He pointed to the kitchen counter, where the fat white rodent sat unusually still. "She belonged to Cypress, didn't she."

"It's a *she*? How'd you know?"

"You got a lot to learn, kid. Let me ask you something. How do you feel right now?"

Peter shrugged. "Ummm. The lion is missing. So I guess...a little upset?"

"No! Not that. In your heart. Tell me how you *feel*."

"Awful. I'm anxious, like there's a shadow."

Rory clapped his old gnarled hands, and said, "Bingo. You got the gift, kid."

"Doesn't feel like a gift," Peter muttered unhappily, rubbing his chest. "You feel it too?"

Rory nodded.

"Does it feel like it's coming from below us?" asked Peter.

"A'course," said Rory and he coughed into his handkerchief. "That's where the trouble is. And you need to investigate."

"*Me?*"

"It's you, kid. Gotta be."

"Can you come too?"

Rory shook his head. "No, Peter. Coming here to talk with you has taken all my strength."

"I don't want to go into the Caves alone," he admitted.

"Take the mouse."

"What good would that do?"

"She's more important than you realize." Rory smiled but ended up coughing into his handkerchief. "If nothing else, she'll watch your back."

"Mouse watching my back. Yeah, that'll help," muttered Peter. He scribbled a note for his parents in case they returned first.

I'll be back soon. I'm safe. - Peter

At least I hope I am, he thought. This is ridiculous.

He held out his hand, and the mouse jumped on and climbed to his shoulder.

In the hallway, Peter said, "Sure you don't want to go with me? Could be an adventure. And I'm terrified."

Rory waved the question away. "I'm ready for my adventure to be over."

"Wish me luck," Peter said, staring at the floor between his feet, trying to pinpoint the source of his distress.

"You don't need it, kid. You've got the heart and the strength."

The Crown felt especially empty with all the residents and guests sent to their rooms. Mr. Conrad was right—there was no way to keep this disaster a secret from the outside world. Dozens of calls had probably already been placed to 911. He hustled down the staircase, following some sort of intuition. He knew exactly where to go.

He emerged inside the Crown's garage. This level, which was three floors below the street, had been converted into a headquarters for the Circus of Doom. The circus kept extra tents and hay bales and ropes and nets and all manner of supplies here. Much of the space was dedicated to a massive cage used to give their bears a minor vacation from the spotlight. The floors of the cage had been covered with dirt and hay. There was a large brown bear inside pacing back and forth. Peter was no expert, but it looked upset.

"There," he said, pointing at a set of double-doors partially hidden behind the bear. "The entrance to the Caves. That's where we have to go."

The mouse made a sound that Peter took for approval.

"Where is everyone?" he wondered, peering around the thick support post they were hidding behind. "Shouldn't the animal be supervised?"

Even though he knew the bear was tame, and even though it did nothing more than glare suspiciously at them, still he broke a sweat edging around the cage's heavy bars. The animal smelled like stale fruit and Peter held his breath.

One of the doors to the Caves had been left partially cracked. Slowly he pushed it, and cool musty air spilled out like an open mouth exhaling. Inside all was black. The feeling of dread had increased, like Peter was getting closer.

Flashlights were set beside the doorway and Peter snatched one.

"Ready?" he whispered, and he pretended his voice didn't tremble.

The mouse nodded.

Peter clicked on the light and stepped inside.

The room looked like a warehouse for ancient furniture. He swept the flashlight's beam across hundreds of old beds and wooden dressers and tables. Scattered mirrors caught the light and send ricocheting bursts in all directions. The darkness spread as far as he could see, as if the room ran to infinity. No lions. No Red Masque.

"Dad said the Crown used the Caves as storage. They filled it up with old stuff and then forgot about it," whispered Peter, creeping forward through the tangle of furniture legs. There was no straight path and they wound their way as if in a maze. "I guess no one comes down here anymore. It's too full and no one wants to clean it out. If the Red Masque knew what they were looking for then—"

The mouse squeaked quietly, like, *Quiet! Don't prattle because you're nervous.*

How on earth did Rory know she was a girl mouse? The man was full of surprises and wisdom. Too bad he was so old. Peter could use a partner, one who wasn't a mouse. He could never ask Joey or Hawkins to hunt lions with him.

Figures jumped from the darkness and Peter froze, but it was only his light falling on statues. Greasy faces appeared and faded as they passed oil paintings.

For ten minutes he tiptoed deeper into the labyrinth, expecting monsters and villains around every turn. Though he couldn't be sure, this felt more expansive than a simple Crown basement. Surely at this point he was below one of the adjacent hotels. At the far end of the room he and the mouse reached a wide staircase plunging into lower levels like a pit. Peter knew if he hesitated then he'd never gather enough courage to continue. Scary things must be conquered, his dad told him, so he refused to pause before descending the steps, straining his ears for strange noises.

Could the magical portal be down here? The Librarian said legend claimed the Phantom could enter a magical world and one of the doorways was in the Crown. Peter had believed her instantly, because every other legend or myth he'd heard during the past year was turning into hard reality. All the stories were true, so why shouldn't this one be? But what did a magical portal look like? And what about the ring she mentioned?

The second level was even darker and mustier, the floor littered with boxes of old kitchen utensils. There were pots and pans and trays and champagne glasses and bowls, and even rusty stoves and ovens and mixers. Boxes stretched in every direction, often stacked higher than his head. The syndicate could be down here and he might never see them. Soon he was passing wooden crates, spray painted with details such as, "TWIN MATTRESSES" and "CANDLES" and "CHRISTMAS GARLAND" and "SILK PILLOW CASES." Like stalking the Grand Canyon covered in graffiti.

Onward he walked, guided only by the impression that he should.

"I need a weapon," he whispered to the mouse. "What am I supposed to do, punch the Red Masque? They're adults and I'm only thirteen."

Shush, the mouse seemed to say. She had no problem being alone this far underground, but Peter felt the isolation acutely, like abandonment.

After a long and winding walk, he was brought back to

the staircase having found nothing. The magic portal could have been under his nose for all he knew.

Through the walls he detected a faint roar and the floor vibrated. The roar approached, lasted for thirty seconds, and then faded. Though he'd never ridden one, he recognized it as a subterranean subway passing nearby.

The third floor was the bottom—the stairs descend no further. This level was dedicated to metal machinery. Elevator motors, heat radiators, cooling coils, fans, broken dumbwaiter doors, ice machines, duct work. The air tasted of oil and copper. It was here that Peter finally found traces of the treasure syndicate's search. The dusty floor was crisscrossed with bootprints and chunks of metal had been moved and disassembled.

"Are they looking for the magic doorway?" he wondered. His whispers echoed in the black distance. "Or maybe the sword?"

Or the key? But they wouldn't find that down here.

Based on scuff marks, Peter guessed the Red Masque had almost finished searching the third floor. Would they move on to the second? Had they found anything?

He was close to the source of his anxiety. He felt it as though walking towards an open furnace. The Crown was groaning like a living thing.

The gigantic room ended at a wall, as rooms usually do. Unlike the other walls in the Caves, this one had heavy iron doors at the center. Three of them. Old and rusty and secured with a bar so they couldn't be opened from the other side. Except for the door on the right—that door was open.

Heart pounding, he crept closer. This was it. The Crown's angry and open wound. Someone had removed the bar and pried the door loose. Vaguely he recalled talking with his father about secret tunnels running through the city. It was possible to travel from building to building through these passages, but they were usually locked at both ends.

He shined his light inside but the tunnel was so black that the air seemed to swallow up his flashlight's power. The passage ran somewhere into the distance he couldn't see.

"Intruders are getting into the Caves from the outside," Peter whispered. "For weeks, I bet."

The dark tunnel filled him with fear, as though evil was seeping out. He pushed the door but nothing happened, other than orange dust caking his palm. The mouse sniffed. He clamped the flashlight in his teeth, placed both hands on the door and leaned with all his weight. There was a screech of twisting metal and the door slammed closed with a thunderous BOOM. The sound echoed and bounced off the walls over and over, Peter wincing each time. He hefted the bar, almost too weighty for him, and dropped it in place, effectively locking the door from this side.

Immediately the Crown seemed to breathe a sigh of relief. The shadow lifted from his heart and his back straightened. The anxiety was gone.

He removed the flashlight from his teeth and said, "Well, mouse, I don't know how long it'll last. But that's the best I can do right now."

In response, the mouse snarled. A deep and guttural sound. Peter nearly dropped his light, glancing with fright at his mouse. But it wasn't her.

It was Tandra the lioness, stalking out of the shadows. She was crouched close to the floor, barring her shocking fangs. Her eyes caught and reflected the light. She was even larger up close.

"Holy *smokes*," breathed Peter, going cold. "Nice kitty..."

At the moment, Tandra didn't look nice. She looked like her baby was missing and she suspected Peter.

"Tandra," Peter said, backing up. "Tandra? How'd you get down here, Tandra?" He moved so an old broken toilet was between them. His knees shook. "Are you looking for your baby? Down here? Let's go back upstairs, Tandra."

She came around the toilet, her shoulder muscles bunching and clenching.

"I didn't take your baby," he reasoned, trying not to panic. "...but I bet I'm the same height as the guys who did... I'm gonna kill Atticus," he muttered.

Tandra gathered for a pounce.

RUN! the mouse squeaked.

Peter ran. He was quite a good leaper and he cleared a three-foot-high boiler, landing in stride. Based on his mouse's frightened noises, so did Tandra. He swerved around fans and water heaters, cutting corners and going over obstacles, wondering what he'd done to deserve such rotten luck. Without obstacles to keep between him and the lion, he'd be dead. Tandra was so close he could smell her. He pumped his arms, the cone from his flashlight swinging wildly, plunging every other step into darkness.

"HELP!" he shouted. "Tandra's down HERE!"

As he neared the staircase, his beam fell on someone. A big man, bald and angry, with a mustache. It was the mysterious man Dot had followed to the Caves! He was only there for a second and gone again, but it was enough to distract Peter. His foot caught an old fan blade. He sprawled face first across the dusty floor and his flashlight broke. Though he could no longer see the lioness, he could hear her. He curled into a ball, knowing he was doomed.

"TANDRA!" cried a voice. A man with a flashlight came leaping down the stairs. "Tandra, no! Easy girl!"

Marlowe Blodgett slid to a stop next to Peter, placing himself between Peter and the crouching predator.

"Tandra," he panted. "Tandra, sweetheart, don't hurt zee boy. Okay, girl? You are scared and angry down here, but don't hurt zee boy."

"Mr. Blodgett," wheezed Peter. "J-just in time. There's s-someone else." He pointed into the dark towards the bald man, but he was gone. The man, Peter realized, would already be hidden in the maze. They'd never find him.

The lion gave Peter a final angry leer and turned away. Marlowe held out his hand and Tandra pressed her nose into it. "I don't see anyone, Peter. What is zis place? I saw zee upset bear and zee open door and...what are you doing down here?"

"I...I was looking for...I can't remember, now," replied Peter truthfully. His wits had been completely scattered by the chase.

"A young boy can't go looking for lions on his own! What is zee matter with you? You could have died!"

A radio crackled at Marlowe's hip. Though the voice was distorted, they heard enough. "*Marlowe? ...arlowe, can you read? ...cub has been found. Repeat, cub...found. Some girl...white leather jacket...calls herself Dot. ...arlowe? You copy?*"

"Hooray, zee cub is found!" cried Marlowe. "And who is zis Dot, Peter? What kind of name is Dot? You know her? But oh no, look," he said, carefully lifting Peter's shoulder. "I zink when you fell you have squished a mouse."

11

IT'S A PARTY, PETER

News of the lost lions indeed reached the outside world, but not before the animals had been found again. As a result, instead of the story being one of horror and outrage, it was one of a brave rescue by a girl named Dot who'd discovered three unknown kids trying to sneak out with the cub. She'd taken the baby lion and driven them away. The Circus of Doom was throwing an impromptu party on Christmas night to celebrate the halfway point in their stay at the Crown and to recognize Dot for her heroics.

No one was celebrating Peter. He and Marlowe thought it best not to disclose how Tandra had been found for fear it might give his parents a heart attack. Peter did tell his father about the open door in the basement, so Manos secured the doors to the Caves with a padlock. Little good it would do, thought Peter, if the Red Masque wanted to get in. What, the treasure syndicate couldn't buy a pair of bolt cutters?

His mouse was indeed squished, but not dead. More like dazed and indignant. By the following day, she showed no residual damage other than a limp. She stayed under Peter's pillow and ate an impressive amount of cheddar cheese.

Christmas Eve arrived and so did the annual observation
of Phantom, a game of hide-n-seek that took place inside the
Crown from floors one to fifteen. Peter, Joey, Hawkins, Lela,
Leo, Grover Ivory, Atticus, Marcellus, Caroline and her
brother, and the other kids gathered in the Lobby for the
declaration of rules and the Phantom selection.

At the last minute, a slightly apprehensive Dot joined
the crowd and was immediately selected by the Crown's
desk clerk to be the first Phantom. Dot had become a minor
celebrity after finding the lost cub and the gamers greeted
this decision with cheers and applause. She blushed and
her ever-present frown dissolved into an embarrassed smile.

She began counting and the kids scattered to the far
corners of the Crown. Peter chased after Caroline Crawford
but his entire body ached from boxing and fencing lessons
earlier. He didn't like practicing both in one day, but Dot
had insisted (she'd become a much better sword fighter,
though still inferior to Peter) and now he could barely move.

Caroline turned, noticed him following, and said, "Peter
Constantine! Why are you wincing?"

He grinned. "Long day."

"Come hide with me?"

They found a good spot near the daycare center on the
third floor. By cramming together, they fit nicely behind an
ice machine, a tight situation neither minded. She smelled
like flowers and icing or something that made him feel like
he could fly. Smushed as they were, their hands kept
brushing.

"Why did you have a long day?" she whispered.

"Lots to do. Don't you have long days sometimes?"

She said, "I think you're the hardest working person I
know, Peter. I heard a rumor that you're taking sword
fighting lessons."

"I have no idea what I'm doing, so it's more like awkward sword swishing, instead of lessons."

"Isn't that fun? Trying new things with friends?"

Peter chuckled. He didn't know where to look, because her blue eyes were so bright they'd melt him. "Yes. Until I make a mistake and it hurts. Like whacking a wall."

"I think that sounds quite exciting. Have you been injured?"

"Just scrapes and bruises. Want to try?" he asked.

"You'd teach me?"

Peter swallowed what felt like a bowling ball in his throat. "I don't know what I'm doing, to be honest."

"You're better than you think, I imagine. You're taller and stronger than me. I probably couldn't lift the sword." They both laughed at the idea of her struggling to pick up her weapon. "What if you hurt me?"

"I'd never do that."

She nodded and her silky blonde hair brushed his arm. "I believe you. But I imagine it wouldn't suit my strengths. Mother has me practicing piano and painting."

"Do you enjoy it?"

"No, but she says they're proper pursuits for young ladies. All she does is play on her phone, so I'm not sure what qualifies her to say that. Do you know what I enjoy most?"

"What?" asked Peter.

"Jogging in the Park. Isn't that odd? Father doesn't let me go without my brother but it makes me feel alive."

"Doesn't sound odd."

She gave a slight shrug. "It's the only time I don't have adults watching. Complete freedom, but it rarely happens."

"I'm exactly the other way," said Peter. "I have complete freedom and little adult supervision."

"We're opposites, aren't we? A little like Romeo and Juliet. But...you know, without the...love part. Thanks for hiding with me, Peter."

"GOTCHA!" cried Dot, springing into their vision. They were so startled they both jumped and laughed.

Dot was excellent at Phantom and won the game in under thirty minutes. As they gathered again in the Lobby, she found Peter and poked him in the ribs. "Not bad, eh?"

"That was quick."

"Not for the *real* Phantom," said Dot, shooting him a knowing look. "You made it easy on me, hiding with your girlfriend."

"She's not...keep your voice down," whispered Peter, and his face reddened.

"Why not? She's gorgeous."

"Just...shush."

The next Phantom was chosen. It was Lino Kang's son Marcellus, and Joey beamed at him (she thought the exotic circus boy outrageously attractive). The children bolted from the Lobby. Peter jogged past his previous hiding spot, hoping for more time smashed behind the ice machine with Caroline but she'd gone elsewhere.

On the fourth floor he discovered Atticus Snyder trying to break into the Library. A boy who looked familiar was with him.

"Library's off limits," Peter told them.

"Look who it is. Peter Nobody, aren't you, chum," the boy called. It was Capulet, the handsome and broad-shouldered teenager from the Ritz. "You're the boy from the alley, the mole person. I hear Atticus smacks you around at boxing lessons."

"You're a Ritz kid. This game is only for Crown kids," snapped Peter.

"Oh?" Capulet smirked. "Are you just a boring do-gooder, always following the rules?"

Atticus made a *shoo* motion with the back of his hand. "Run along, Peter. Capulet and I have no trash to give you, chum."

"They know it was you, Atticus," said Peter, his hands balling into fists. He hated bullies. "They have you on film taking Tandra's cub."

"Oh yeah? Then how come I haven't been accused? Stupid little Peter. They can't touch me. My family and I are the most important residents in this decrepit hotel."

Capulet rubbed a hand along one of the original posts at the Library's entrance. "Could do with a new paint job, at the very least. This place smells ancient."

"No it doesn't! This is the best hotel in the city."

"Too bad you won't get to live here much longer. It's no secret Mr. Banks wants your family out," said Atticus with a sneer.

"That's not true."

"Like I said, poor stupid little Peter, the ignorant trash boy."

"Just leave Tandra and her cubs alone, Atticus," growled Peter.

"Why should he?" Capulet crossed his muscular arms and chuckled. "What's it to you, chum?"

"Why would you take them?"

"Why not? Great fun, you know."

Both the boys's faces froze, staring beyond Peter. Marcellus Kang had been eavesdropping and he came cautiously around the corner. He was a slight boy, looking upset. "*You?* You stole the cub?"

"No no," laughed Atticus, hitting Capulet on the arm.

"Just having fun, old boy. Pay no attention. Say, aren't you the Phantom? We better run!"

"It was you," repeated Marcellus.

"No it *wasn't*. Besides, you can't prove a thing. Nobody would believe the word of a circus carnie against me and Capulet."

Marcellus looked so livid that he was trembling.

"C'mon, Cap. I'm tired of this stupid game," said Atticus and he turned for the golden elevators.

"See you round, Peter," called Capulet. "Gonna have fun with you, chum!"

Marcellus waited until they'd left and he asked, "Why are they so cruel?"

Peter sighed. "I'm not sure. Sometimes the wealthy invent ways to keep entertained."

"I don't understand."

"Me neither. Maybe being rich isn't all it's cracked up to be, so they're still looking."

Marcellus said, "I don't think I will play this game any longer. Will you be the Phantom?"

"Sure. And...I'm sorry about them, Marcellus. I'll try to keep Atticus away from your lions," said Peter.

"Thank you, Peter. You're a good friend. Good luck being the Phantom."

Peter watched him go with a heavy heart. Suddenly the game seemed a lot less fun.

THE FOLLOWING MORNING WAS CHRISTMAS. The Constantine family and Hawkins ate waffles and drank orange juice and opened presents—Hawkins received a new jacket and Peter got sneakers. He'd been scavenging lost coins from the Park and the Crown, allowing him to purchase his parents a small gift certificate to the thirteenth floor lounge, bringing his mother to tears. Hawkins gave the family new luxurious silk pillow cases, purchased from the store downstairs with "money I found in old wallets!" which they knew meant "stolen." The pillow cases were outrageously expensive. Max the Magician sent Peter a new deck of trick cards, Ernestine Parker gifted him a fancy pen and stationary, and Arthur Graves gave him his very own shiny set of red boxing gloves.

All the second-floor residents ate lunch together in the heavily decorated Nook, and it was the happiest Peter'd felt in months. There was no shadow weighing him down, no lessons that day, no homework, no Red Masque, and nothing needed fixing. He and Joey and Hawkins ate themselves sick on ham sandwiches and jello fruit salad and iced cookies and hot chocolate. The laughter was cheerily glazed over with anticipation for the evening's celebration and the circus's promised entertainment.

As the hour drew near, the invitees retreated to their apartments to prepare. Peter's mother put on earrings and a sparkly dress that made Hawkins stare and his father comment, "Wow, honey, you look twenty-five again. But better." With his parents' permission, the two boys raided the Laundry's lost-and-found for Hawkins and took khakis and a vest. (Hawkins nabbed a watch too, while Peter's back was turned. Could never have too many of those.) Peter planned on wearing his cashmere turtleneck but upon returning from the Laundry he discovered a gift sent from Mrs. Ivey, the manager of King's Furnishings on the first floor—brown slacks and a blue sports jacket.

There was a note:

Only a loan, Mr. Constantine.

Enjoy yourself!

Say hello to Ms. Crawford for me.

-Mrs. Ivey

THE CELEBRATION, or gala, was held in the ballroom on the main floor and every person in the Crown attended, including the desk clerks, who took turns popping in. Lino Kang and Marlowe Blodgett, dressed in exotic tuxedos, personally greeted each guest at the wide entrance, shaking and kissing hands. Christmas party music pumped from the speakers and the tables were pushed back for dancing. Jugglers threw torches in the corners and Adolfo the strongman picked up the women and Shaman performed conjuring tricks and Bruno threw knives.

The hotel guests and staff had never seen Peter's mother wearing anything other than her Laundry garb and she caused quite the sensation. She danced with Mr. Banks and Mr. Conrad and Lino Kang, while Manos drank bubbly champagne with friends and enjoyed himself.

Max Freeman and his fiancé danced too, as did Ernestine Parker and crazy old Mr. Hayes.

"Peter!" Caroline Crawford materialized from the throng. She wore a red evening gown.

"Hello Caroline," he said, racking his brain to remember Ms. Parker's lessons. He was supposed to comment on her dress, but it got jumbled coming out, "I like your...shoulder...sequin...trumpet...umm, that's not right, hang on—"

"Don't be silly. C'mon!" She gripped his hand and pulled him onto the dance floor, where her brother Brian was dancing with Lela.

"I've forgotten how," he stammered, staring at his feet as though seeing them for the first time.

"I don't want to dance because I'm good at it, Peter.

Besides I've forgotten how too!" Caroline was wearing heels and they stood nearly eye-to-eye, and together they swayed and bumped and lurched until settling into an awkward rhythm. "Peter. Your mother is a knockout."

"That's weird. She's...just my mom."

"Not many woman can wear that dress. I bet my mother is green with envy. You get your lashes from her, you know."

"I got...huh?" His lashes? What was he supposed to say to that? He mumbled something stupid. Then he accidentally stepped on her toe.

This was going dismally. He could make neither his mouth nor his feet work, and soon Caroline would grow tired of him and wander off. He just knew it. If *only* he was could remember his lessons. If only he was smoother, like Cypress had been.

What would the Phantom do?

He would have courage and confidence. He'd laugh and be cool under pressure. Kinda like his own father was, he thought.

As Peter watched, Manos walked onto the dance floor and grabbed Jovanna by the hand and pulled her close. They smiled and swayed and the other jealous men were forced to wait their turn.

I can do this, he thought.

So Peter held his breath, clutched Caroline by the hand, and pulled her as near as he dared (which really wasn't very close). Suddenly he remembered the steps to the dance and he laughed with relief.

"What's funny?" she asked, her eyes widening.

"Nothing special, Caroline. It's only that I'm having a great time." He removed his jacket and slung it across a chair's backrest, and they danced for three more songs. Ernestine Parker saw them and nodded her approval.

Eventually Caroline started fanning herself and she said, "You don't look as warm as I feel."

"Should we get some punch? I bet those heels are murder."

"Definitely," she replied. Secretly she marveled at Peter's transformation from terrified boy to confident gentleman. She worried he'd get bored with her and move on.

They found an empty table to sit at with their fruit punch, and soon they were joined by Leo and Joey and Hawkins, who'd been watching Shaman perform tricks.

"I feel like I swallowed an entire hot dog stand," groaned Hawkins. "Rich people eat more in one day than I do in a week."

Leo nodded knowingly. "In my country the citizens have more self-control. Few obese people."

"You calling me obese?" Hawkins grinned and he reached for his punch but gave up.

"Rich people eat so they won't be lonely," said Caroline. "That's what I've observed."

"How come you're so thin, then?" asked Hawkins curiously.

"I'm not lonely enough, I suppose."

"I only pig out when I play video games," said Leo. "But I play them all the time."

"It takes tremendous self-control to work in the bakery every day and not eat the sweets," said Joey softly. She looked a little uncomfortable at a gala with the powerful and wealthy guests. "Father says I have an iron will power."

"There's mean old Victor Webb," said Peter, indicated the man glaring at the hors d'oeuvres. "I'm surprised he left his smelly pit of a room."

"It smells?" asked Joey.

"Like onions. And possibly chicken livers."

"Arthur Graves is talking to him," Caroline noted. "Isn't he your boxing coach?"

"Yeah and he's a grump too. But I like him."

Leo made a whimpering sound. "Don't let him see me eating this cake. He'll make me do pushups."

"Don't you like boxing?" asked Joey.

"You are making a joke," said Leo. "It's torture."

"But you'll get big and strong like Peter, won't you?" Caroline asked. She said it matter-of-factly, as though discussing the weather.

"In my country that's not always good. The powerful people don't have to exercise. I don't know why my parents punish me," Leo replied miserably.

"Do you think I'm allowed to dance?" Joey asked. "I've never tried."

"Of course, Josephine!" said Caroline brightly.

"But I'm only a baker, and not even one of note."

"On my gosh, don't be absurd. Hawkins, you must take her to the dance floor. I insist."

Hawkins stood with an, "Ooooof," sound and followed a timid Joey. He held his stomach and said, "Maybe I'll work off all those cakes."

"Look, Darci Drake is sitting by herself," said Caroline, secretively pointed at the spiky-haired women in the corner, scribbling in her black notebook. "We should invite her over."

"Darci is on the lookout for the Phantom. And the treasure syndicate. She thinks the Red Masque is around every corner..." said Peter. That was when he noticed Dot. She stood near the doorway in her leather jacket, arms crossed.

Suddenly Peter felt as though cold water had been splashed over his head. Dot was doing what the Phantom should do. She was keeping watch. And what was Peter doing? Eating too much. She was alert and Peter was distracted. He'd forgotten all about the Red Masque and the imminent danger. Almost certainly the enemy was in this very room and he'd become too lazy to care, just like Rory had warned. He cast a quick glance around the room, searching for the scary bald man with the mustache—he wasn't here, which meant he was currently searching the Caves.

Peter's shoulders slumped. Dot had been the one to find the cub while Peter almost got eaten. She was the one who demanded they keep sword fighting. She found the entrance to the Caves by herself. She even won the Phantom game in record time.

Rory didn't believe she would fulfill the prophecy, but she was certainly closer to it than Peter was. She deserved the magic key. Not him. It was a sobering realization.

Where was Rory anyway? Ollie was on his fourth plate of food, happily swaying in the corner and looking astonishingly bloated.

"Peter?" asked Caroline. "Are you okay? You look like you've seen a ghost."

"I'm okay," he said quietly.

"Cheer up! It's a party, Peter."

"I'll be right back. Excuse me." He left the ballroom with a heavy heart. It was time for Dot to have the key. She'd earned it and he couldn't put it off for one more minute.

12

THE FAERY GIRL

Peter left the gala's noise and light, and jogged upstairs. The rest of the Crown was as quiet as a tomb, and he'd never felt more alone.

Peter let himself into the apartment and was surprised to find his parents there. He hadn't seen them leave the gala. "Mom? Dad? What're you doing?"

Jovanna looked a little embarrassed. She held up her shoes and giggled, "Broke my heel. Silly me. Your father walked me back. You should return to the party, sweetheart—"

She froze. So did Peter. There on the kitchen table between them was the fat white mouse, blinking happily at Peter.

"Mom," Peter said, holding up his hands. "Don't get crazy. I'll handle this."

But it was too late. His mother snatched a pot and brought the bottom crashing down on the unsuspecting mouse. "Yaaaaargh!" she shrieked.

Peter cried, "Mom! No!" His stomach flip-flopped, antici-pating a gooey crunch, a disgusting end to the poor mouse.

But instead of a crunch there was a poof of air, like she hit a sponge instead of an animal. There was a flash of light so brilliant it hurt Peter's eyes, and something like a firework erupted from under the pot and shot into Peter's room.

His mother cried, "I got it! Manos, I got the mouse! Come clean it up."

"What was *that*?" Peter gasped, blinking away the light burst in his vision.

"That, my beautiful boy, was a mouse. And I killed it, the fierce warrior that I am, a true New Yorker." Jovanna grinned proudly. "But your father has to clean it up. Yuck."

"No no, that flash of light!"

"Flash of light?" she asked. "What are you talking about?"

Manos got off the couch, straightened his tie, and said, "On the table, my love? Couldn't you have picked a better spot to execute the little guy?"

"When *you* are brave enough to kill a mouse then *you* can decide where to kill it, dear."

Peter gaped at his mother. "Mom, did you really not see it? It was like...an explosion!"

Manos carefully lifted the pot and looked underneath. "Hmmm. I hate to burst your bubble, fierce warrior, but I think you missed it."

"*What?*"

"See for yourself." He lifted the pot. Something was on the table but it wasn't a dead animal. It looked like sugar or flour. He brushed the bottom of the pan and proclaimed, "Looks more like you killed a dust bunny."

"No," Jovanna said, seizing the pot and turning it over and over. "No no. I killed it! I felt it, Manos."

"Mom, didn't you see the firework that shot into my room?" Peter asked, exasperated.

"Firework? Peter, now is not a good time to be silly. Your father is playing a joke on me."

"A joke?" Manos laughed. "What joke? You missed the mouse."

She growled, "I did not! The body must have...fallen onto the floor."

"Where? Show me, my love."

While his parents argued, Peter cautiously crept into his room. There *had* been an explosion and he *had* seen something rocket in here. "Hello?" he whispered. "Mouse? Are you alive?"

His eyes drew to the bed.

Something was on it.

The something looked like a kaleidoscope of color focused into a ball, and inside the crazy riot of light was a person. A tiny person, no bigger than an action figure. Peter'd never seen anything like it. The tiny person climbed to its feet and stretched. Or at least that's what it looked like, but Peter thought there was an excellent chance he was hallucinating. Maybe the fruit punch had been spiked.

The brilliant little figure cried, "The poor mouse perished decades ago, dearest Peter, but I'm FREEEEE!" The voice sounded like a song. Like Peter was listening to music instead of words. "Liberty at LAST!"

Peter stood frozen. Unable to move. Surely he was dreaming.

"Look at me!" the figure said. "I'm GORGEOUS! What a tremendous WASTE, beauty starved inside a mouse."

Peter's mouth worked silently as the figure jumped and flew in circles above his bed, singing.

Jovanna stormed into the room and said, "Peter, tell your father I killed the mouse! Tell him this instant!"

Peter looked at his mother. Then at the flying...thing. Then at his mother, and back to the flying thing.

"Mom," he whispered. "Can you...can't you...see it?"

"No! We can't find it anywhere!"

"But...but..." Peter stammered.

"I know, it's *so* weird! It's like the mouse was a ghost! I'm going back to the party," Jovanna said, and she stormed out and slammed his door.

The flying ball of sunlight was doing cartwheels and singing, "FLYING again! Oh I could soar to the heavens. Look at me, I'm Amelia Earhart!"

Peter pinched himself. It hurt. Did that mean he wasn't dreaming?

"Blessed pillow! I can FEEL it!" The sparkly thing landed and rolled across his pillow and his sheets. "I feel it with my skin, not with gross mouse fur. My stars, your new pillow case is DIVINE."

Peter cleared his throat and said, "Excuse me?"

It sang, "I should have permitted that crazy woman to murder me months ago. HAHA!" and it shot up into the air again.

Peter squinted his eyes and peered into the ball of light. The figure had arms and legs and a body and a face. A pretty face, in fact.

"You're a girl," Peter realized. "Rory was right."

"But poorest Peter!" The luminescent girl stopped fluttering and said, "No longer will you see me. That presents a problem. Especially because I'm so fond of you."

"Why won't I see you?" he asked.

"Because NO human can see me," she sighed. "Well, no human except babies."

"But I can."

"No you cannot, my dear," she replied. She laughed and it sounded like a harp. "That's absurd."

Peter was puzzled. "But...I see you right now."

"You *do*?"

"Of course. We're talking, aren't we?"

The flying girl shot off like a rocket again, bouncing around his walls, setting off rainbow detonations each time. "That's PREPOSTEROUS! Unbelievable!"

"Why is it unbelievable?" he asked, twirling in circles to keep up.

"You can hear me too!"

"You sound like a song."

"Miracle of miracles!" she cried. "Oh blessed marvelous day!"

"My mom, I don't think she saw you."

"Of course not, dearest Peter! No one can, except little children. And YOU, apparently, against all odds."

Peter rubbed at his eyes and cleaned out his ears, just to make sure. "Are you...are you the mouse's...ghost?"

"Don't be dense. Because ew and gross, Peter. I inhabited that mouse decades ago, so Cypress could see me."

Peter's legs were going wobbly and he sat heavily onto the bed. "I think I'm having a stroke or something."

"Think of the mouse as the jacket I wore for the past MANY unfortunate years. It was entirely made of dust, these days. Disgusting and uncomfortable."

"But...but..."

The girl was zooming in circles around his ceiling. "Why didn't I leave the mouse, you ask? Why did I stay inside, if it was so gross? A perfect question. I got stuck, for lack of a better phrase."

"You've been—"

"Stuck!"

"Since Cypress Fitzgerald?"

"QUITE SO!"

"Okay, but what are you?" asked Peter.

"The best way to describe it, Peter, is that I'm not human."

"Yeah I guessed that."

She stopped flying and landed on his bed post and twirled like a ballerina. "How divine it is to move. So, let's see. Humans are ALWAYS perplexed with us. Considering how large you are, your brains are miniscule. I'm a Wee Person. Throughout the ages we've been referred to as fairies and fair folk and other things. Personally I prefer the term sprite."

"Sprite? Like the soda?" he asked.

"I've been trapped in a mouse for a century. Remind me again, what's soda?"

"It's bubbly and fizzy and delicious."

"Then yes!" she cried and started zooming again. "I'm PRECISELY like soda!"

"Did you ever see Peter Pan?" he asked. "And Tinker Bell?"

"No, but my kind have often been called Tinkers."

Peter said, "You don't have wings."

"Neither do YOU, you know."

"But I'm human."

"Now you're starting to understand!" She laughed musically.

"No. I'm really not."

"Neither did Cypress, but I couldn't speak to him. I CAN speak to you! I'll explain everything. Right after my nap," she said, and she dove into one of his open clothing drawers. Her voice emerged from within, muffled. "Mind if I sleep in one of your clean stockings?"

"*Now?* Do you have to sleep right now?" Peter asked, kneeling beside the drawer and peering in. Sure enough, one of his socks was glowing.

"This is more talking and flying than I've managed in a century. It's not really a nap, not like you think of it. Remember, I'm NOT human."

Peter said, "I won't forget that, I promise. Do you have a name?"

"How rude of me, forgot to introduce myself." His sock yawned and the color dimmed. "Please call me Fara, and it's a pleasure to meet you properly, dearest Peter."

"Fara? FAIR-ra? Sounds a little like faery."

Her lyrical voice was softer now. "My real name is Tylwyth Faa Pulch of the Lenape."

"Wow, so yeah, I'll call you Fara. Fara the faery girl."

"I'm not usually so..." Another yawn. "...so.... The mouse was dreadfully uncomfortable. Now that I'm out...can't stay awake...Good night."

The sock giggled and the light winked out. Peter gently poked at it but nothing happened. He whispered, "Fara?"

No response.

"Okay. I guess, good night," said Peter, feeling like an idiot talking to a sock drawer.

PETER DREAMED that night about The Evil Treasure Hunter. The cruel man stalked the halls, searching for Manos. He rubbed his hands together and said, "The bears, the bears, I'm going to lock the traitor Manos in with the bears."

Peter woke with a start, his hair a sweaty mess. The covers were clenched in his fists.

"Just a dream," he mumbled, still heavy with sleep. He

was about to get out of bed when he noticed strange voices in his room.

"Shoo! Be gone!"

"Ye can't fool me, it's not him," a voice said savagely.

"You haven't the slightest notion of what you're saying. You NEVER have. Shoo!"

A pirate ghost was sitting on his dresser, fending off attacks from a sparkly ball of light. Fara was ramming and head-butting the ghost as hard as she could, grunting with the effort, and it swatted at her.

"Get out!" Fara shouted at the downcast spirit. "Get thee hence! Go go GO!"

"It's not him. Can't be," the ghost repeated unhappily. "Too good to be true."

Fara whirled around the room, as though getting a running start, and slammed into the unhappy spirit. A poof of smoke and suddenly they were alone. Fara ricocheted off the wall, sparkling like a diamond, and landed on the bed. She tottered unsteadily and sat down, holding her head. "Ooooooooh, I despise miserable ghouls."

"That was a ghost," gasped Peter stupidly, still a little slow from sleep. He pointed at the wall through which the ghost had vanished. "Right?"

"Indeed. A miserable old pirate captain feeling sorry for himself. PFAH! Good riddance."

"Pirate Captain? Why was he here?" he asked, wondering why his bedroom had become a hub of the supernatural.

"His name's Captain Kidd, and he's remained here for the same reason all ghosts do. He cannot move on. Can't or won't. He was like that ALIVE, too."

"Okay but why *my* room?"

Someone banged on the other side of his bedroom wall.

Peter heard Joey's voice, as if from a great distance. "Boy! Who are you talking to this early?"

"Banging on walls," sang Fara to herself happily. "Reminds me of old days. Cypress and Zelda used to squabble in that fashion."

Peter returned the banging and called, "Talking to myself! Go back to sleep." He climbed out of bed and limped into the bathroom, mumbling, "Maybe Tandra ate me and this is the afterlife. That would explain things."

Fara flew into the bathroom with him and said, "I've developed a THEORY."

"Hey! D'you mind? A little privacy, please!"

"Oh dear!" she cried and zoomed back out. "You humans. So peculiar. ANYWAY. As I was saying last night, only children can see me. Babies and the early baby walkers, mostly."

"You mean toddlers?" Peter asked.

"Whatever you call them. Most of the time, by age five or six, children have stopped paying attention. They FORGET about the magic they saw as babies and we fade from their vision. But YOU can see me! I've watched you for months, Peter, and I think Cypress was correct about you. You have a PURE heart. You're innocent and kind. You aren't corrupt yet, therefore you witness the good things, like me! Pure heart, pure eyes."

Peter finished washing and returned from the bathroom and sat on his bed. He scrubbed his face with his hands and thought of exactly zero good responses to that.

Fara said, "Do you know how many people strolled past Cypress in the hallway without seeing him? Thousands. Too preoccupied with themselves. They shivered, kept their heads down, and moved on. You're exceptionally rare, Peter."

"So...not to be rude, but, who *are* you? Why were you hanging out with Cypress Fitzgerald the ghost?" asked Peter. "And now me?"

"That's an EXTENSIVE story, Peter. And an ongoing one. The story of my entire existence, to be exact. What you need to know at this moment is, I'm on your side."

"What side is that?"

"The side of grace and courage and light."

Peter changed out of his pajamas and into jeans and a plain t-shirt. "Do you miss Cypress?"

Her sparkling turned a shade of blue. "Very much. We were together for a HUNDRED years. Much longer than usual."

"I bet Cypress couldn't see you, because he was an adult."

"Exactly, he was a rascal. That's why I appeared to him as a mouse. DISASTROUS mistake. And then he disappeared without saying goodbye."

Peter opened his drawer and pulled out the magical key. He'd strung it through the chain, and he let it dangle from his finger. "You interrupted me last night. I was about to give the key to Dot."

"PETER CONSTANTINE! Don't you DARE."

"Do you know what it does?" asked Peter, surprised at her outburst.

"Obviously! I MADE that key."

He regarded her suspiciously. "Liar."

"Sheriff Lewis Stegman persisted in getting locked out of rooms as the city grew. He'd taken one too many knocks to the head, the poor man. So I built the key."

"Sheriff who?"

"He died a hundred and fifty years ago. Not important." She landed on his finger and fondly examined the key. "The process took me a week and afterwards I slept an entire MONTH. Sheriff Stegman couldn't see me either and I had a horrible time convincing him to use it. Like I said, he'd gone a little bonkers by then."

"You've been in the city for a hundred and fifty years?"

"More like, over a THOUSAND years, Peter. Lenaphoking is my home."

"Lenny-ponky?"

Fara lifted off again and flew around the room. "Lenape-hoking. An ancient name of the land you call New York City. Perhaps it's been longer than a millennium. We don't experience time the same way, you know."

Peter's father entered, swinging open the door. WHACK. It connected solidly with Fara and swatted her against the wall as if she was a big bee. She issued a wheezing noise and dropped to the floor. "Morning Peter," Manos said.

"DAD! Careful!"

Manos was still wearing his tie from last night and he looked exhausted. He examined Peter carefully. "Beg your pardon?"

From the floor, Fara squeaked, "...I'm alive...ooooooo..."

"N-nothing," stammered Peter. "Just...you know, you startled me. Maybe open the door slower next time."

"You're turning into a proper teenager, I see. I'm heading to the nineteenth floor to answer a couple calls. Wanna come with?"

"N-no thanks, Dad. Still a little tired. Right?"

"Who've you been talking to? You're chatting up a storm."

"Oh. J-just...myself. You know, singing. And...stuff."

"Sure, kid. See you soon." He swung the door closed.

Peter dropped to his knees. "Fara! Are you okay?"

She sat up and held her head. "I'm not yet accustomed to flying. Gracious."

"Can I get you anything?"

"I'll miss cheese," she sighed. "Now that I'm not a mouse, I can't eat it."

He picked her up and set her on his shoulder. "I'm getting some cereal."

"Oh sure, rub it in."

In the kitchen, Peter prepared a bowl of Frosted Flakes. Fara rocketed around the room, disappearing from sight one minute and resting on the table the next. Peter crunched thoughtfully on a mouthful. He asked, "What will you do now that you're free?"

"Assist you, of course. It's my life's work."

"Assist me how?"

"I assume you're joking? Defeating the Red Masque, clearly."

Peter's spoon dropped into his cereal and he choked. He coughed until tears streamed down his cheeks. Fara sat crisscross on the table, rested her chin in her hands, and beamed. "I-I think..." he gagged and cleared his throat. "I think you're confused."

"Don't be obstinate, Peter. You HEARD what Cypress Fitzgerald said."

"He said I was the next Phantom. But only because he had no other options."

"That's NOT true!" Fara cried. "We waited a LONG time to find you, Peter."

"But haven't you met Dot?"

"Of course. I spied on her! But she's related to that walrus, Ollie. I could never pick her."

Peter shook his head. "I'm not him, Fara. I'm not the Phantom."

"But I don't understand." Fara's shoulders slumped, as though Peter had given her terrible news.

"I'm thirteen."

"SO? I'm a thousand. You cannot help how old you are."

Peter stammered, "I'm not even very strong."

"We're only as strong as the strength we give to others, Peter. And you have a servant's heart."

"I get scared. I couldn't walk to the Hotel Chelsea—I got there by accident. A lion nearly ate me. I can't drive a car, I don't have a weapon, I don't know what the Red Masque looks like, and I've never shaved."

"Let's go shave you this instant! I'll SCALP you, if you like."

"That's not the point," said Peter unhappily.

"Don't you remember the fire? You charged UPWARDS into a burning building! You ascended the laundry chute, rescued the Crawford kids, and stared down the Red Masque while the CEILING caved in! I was THERE!" she shrieked. "I couldn't believe it, Peter! You were so courageous!"

He set his spoon forcefully into the bowl. "That was a lucky accident, and I almost died. You need a grownup, Fara. Not a kid."

"It's not what's on the outside, Peter Constantine."

"I hate the Red Masque. I do. And I want to help. But I've been trying to do this alone and I can't. The syndicate has been in the hotel for weeks and I can't find them or stop them. We need someone else. A professional."

Fara listened quietly, no longer sparkling. "Who do you think we need?"

"I don't know. Rory told me the city usually chooses someone. Do you understand what he means?"

"I do," she said softly, and her light had nearly extinguished. Peter had trouble seeing her.

"Tell me."

"I can't. If you're not the Phantom then there are secrets which won't be revealed to you."

"The Red Masque is *here*, Fara. Right here, and I can't do a thing about it. We need the real Phantom."

"Very well. I'll find the right person, Peter. However, do me a favor. Hold onto the key until I do?"

"Absolutely."

"Wear it around your neck."

"I will," he said. "How will we know if the city chooses someone?"

"I'll know," replied Fara. "We need someone fearless. Someone who loves New York City. Someone willing to take risks, who hates villains and bullies, someone intelligent, strong, loyal, and hard-working. With a good heart."

"Okay!" Peter nodded enthusiastically, trying to remember everything she said. "That's a great list, we can find that person."

"It's more difficult than you realize." Then she mumbled, "For example you'd fit the description if you weren't so unbelievably stupid."

"What?"

"Nothing." Some of Fara's sparkle returned and she said, "In the meantime, Peter, the danger is greater than you know. Just because you cannot see the menace does not mean it's not real and terrible. The Red Masque cannot be permitted to search the Crown's basement any further. The city and the world is dependent on us."

"The Librarian told me there might be a magical doorway down there. Do you know if she's right?"

"I'm not permitted to discuss it except with the PHAN-TOM, Peter," she said with a pointed look.

"Not allowed? Who makes the rules?"

"I CANNOT tell you! PAY ATTENTION!" she shrieked.

"Have you heard of the Judge? Can you tell about him?"

"Yes, he's dreadful, but now's not the time. We HAVE to eject the Red Masque out from the basement."

"I have an idea," he said, grinning. "And it's gonna be great. And maybe get me killed."

"You have an idea to defeat the Red Masque, EVEN though you're not the Phantom?" she asked.

"Yes, exactly."

"I'm exhausted with you already, dearest Peter."

13

OPERATION PHANTOM

"Where'd you run off to last night?" demanded Joey when Peter emerged into the Nook. "I know one cute blonde princess who was very hurt."

"Personally I hoped you'd fallen into a huge pit of pooh," said Grover Ivory, who had returned to his chair in the corner. He wore socks but not shoes. "Or become trapped under something heavy."

Peter ignored him. "Where's Hawkins? We need to talk and he didn't sleep in my room last."

"Probably because your room smells like dead feet," muttered Grover.

"Hawkins said he needed to visit his other home for Christmas," replied Joey. "It was cold last night, so he must really be attached to that place, wherever it is. Probably underground. What do you want to talk about?"

"Let's wait and see if he shows up." Peter retrieved his novel from the coffee table drawer. He was reading the book for English class. "That way I don't have to explain it twice."

"You missed a good show," she said. "The circus performed loads of tricks. The best part, during the finale, Lino Kang announced that the entire Barclay's center was being reserved one night for the Crown next month. Can you imagine? An entire circus performance just for us!"

"All the Crown? At once?"

"Well don't look so unhappy about it," she said with a frown.

"He can't help it, Josephine. He's exceptionally ugly," contributed Grover.

Peter dropped into a chair, thinking. "The circus is trying to get all of us out of the building."

"You think it's about the..." She paused, her eyes flicking to Grover, who was listening intently. "...you-know-what, don't you?"

"Josephine," he whined. "You can tell me anything, you know. I'd never betray you, unlike Putrid Peter."

"Who's putrid?" demanded Peter.

"Grover," said Joey in a scathing voice. "Enough. I'm telling your mother if you keep acting nasty. You should have better manners than this."

Grover stood and closed his comic book. "I'm going upstairs," he announced with as much dignity as he could muster, but the truth was his feelings were hurt. Any slight from Joey stung. "Unless you'd like me to stay, that is, Josephine."

"Bye Grover," said Peter happily. "See you next time."

"Good bye, Putrid Peter. Your hair looks awful, by the way, but at least it covers your face." Grover stalked from the room.

Come to think of it, Peter couldn't remember his last haircut. He patted his shock of black hair experimentally.

Joey rolled her eyes. "Don't let him bother you, Peter. That's what he wants. But you've got to be nicer to him, even when he's awful. He can't go outside like the rest of us and he's gone crazy, cooped in here."

Fara came whizzing into the room, streaking over their heads and leaving a rainbow trail. "Look at me SOAR! The worst thing about mice? They cannot FLY!"

"Peter? Are you listening?" asked Joey.

Fara landed on Peter's open novel and said, "Ooooh a book. What is it you're reading? My favorites are the Grimm Brothers. They got stuff RIGHT, practically history books, from back when people believed."

He tried brushing her to the side but she snatched onto his finger and said, "Jules Verne! A classic. Stop it, I want to read too."

"Get off," he whispered, shaking his hand. "Leggo, leggo."

"Peter!" shouted Joey. "WHAT are you doing?"

Fara released and flew circles around Joey's head. "She cannot see me, Peter. See what I mean? You're unique. Hello Joey? HELLLLOOOOOOOO!"

Peter didn't know who to speak to, so he said, "Ummmm, sorry Joey... It was...a bug."

"A BUG?!" cried Fara.

"You're acting weird, Peter Constantine."

"Peter, you CANNOT tell her about me. It's one of the rules. No one can know," said Fara, hovering between Joey's angry eyes.

"Um...uh...okay, s-sorry, Joey." He lowered his head to the book so he could focus. Life had grown wildly out of control.

The morning passed. Butlers and parents came in for coffee, said hello, and filtered out. Finally, near lunch Hawkins appeared, shivering. Peter stood and snapped his book closed. "There you are!"

"H-hey, P-P-Peter."

"Hawkins! You look like an ice cube," cried Joey, touching his jacket. "What were you thinking?"

"Home is h-home." He grinned, teeth chattering. "Got my indep-p-pendence and a p-place no one can kick m-me out of."

Joey fetched him a steaming cup of hot chocolate and they gathered in the corner. Fara perched on Peter's shoulder. "I need your help," he whispered to his two friends. "I'm not the Phantom—"

"Y-yes you are," said Hawkins immediately.

"SEE?" Fara shouted.

"Just...shhh. I'm not the Phantom but hopefully he'll appear soon. In the meantime, we need to stop the Red Masque. I went into the Caves and discovered they're using secret underground tunnels to sneak into the Crown and search it. If they get their hands on that magic portal or whatever it is—"

"Or the key," said Hawkins.

"Or the sword," said Joey.

"Right. You get the idea. It'll be bad. They could destroy our home, or the entire city. And the adults don't believe us. But I have a plan. First, during tonight's Circus of Doom's performance, we break into their rooms and search, see what we can find."

Joey asked, "I don't like that. How would we even get in?"

"He's got a magic key, duh," said Hawkins.

Joey still didn't look happy.

Fara hovered above them and she said, "Here's my advice, Peter—do NOT include Ollie or Dot in your plans. I know you respect Dot and you believe she might be the next Phantom, but there's a REASON she wasn't chosen. She

yearns to be the Phantom, but she does NOT have the forti-
tude. She has desire but not the courage. Kay?"

Listening to Fara, Peter realized he'd missed Hawkins's
question. "Huh? Sorry, say it again?"

Hawkins said, "What if we find something we can
use?"

"If we find evidence then we can tell my dad and the
police. If not, we begin Operation Phantom," said Peter.

Their eyes grew round. "Wicked," Hawkins said passionately. "What's Operation Phantom?"

"This is the Red Masque we're talking about. Much of
their history has been spent fighting the Phantom, so they
have to be at least a little worried he'll return. Right? So
that's what we're gonna do—we'll bring him back and scare
the Red Masque away."

"Bring him back?" asked Joey skeptically. "How?"

"We're going to *become* him. All of us," said Peter and the
hairs on his arms raised and he heard faint chimes between
his ears. "We'll make them THINK the Phantom has
returned."

"OH!" cried Hawkins. "I'm reading this great book right
now called *The Phantom of the Opera*. Peter, it's so perfect.
This dude in a mask haunts a big building and freaks
everyone out!"

Fara whispered in Peter's ear, "OOOOOH, purchase a
copy of that book. Sounds intriguing."

"How's he do it?" asked Joey. "I don't want to get into
trouble."

"He hides behind mirrors and in the ceiling, and he
shouts and drops chandeliers, he leaves notes and makes
threats, and he kidnaps people—all cause he knows the
place so well."

Peter nodded knowingly. "That's exactly what we're

gonna do. The Phantom of the Crown, except we'll save it, not haunt it. And we start tonight."

THE USUAL FLEET of yellow taxis and Ubers shuttled the Circus of Doom troop off the Crown sidewalk and towards Barclays at precisely five o'clock. The circus had a show at eight-thirty that evening.

Peter, Joey, and Hawkins waited impatiently in the cozy Nook until the service elevator doors banged open at five-fifteen and Mr. Schwartz the butler exited. He was going off-duty from his position on the nineteenth floor and he would be replaced soon by another butler, but not immediately. Because the nineteenth floor emptied each evening for the show, the need for a butler wasn't pressing for the next five hours. As soon as Mr. Schwartz's apartment door closed, they dashed to the elevator and mashed the button marked 19.

"Ohmygosh, ohmygosh," said Joey, wringing her hands. "This is terrifying. I'm terrified now."

"This's great," gushed Hawkins, grinning. "We're straight up vigilantes, like Zorro."

"Vigilantes *die*," she reminded him pointedly. "Or worse, their parents find out."

Fara was perched on Peter's shoulder, unusually quiet.

The doors slid open and they cautiously ventured out into the golden hallway. Their ears detected harp music wafting from overhead speakers and their feet sank into the thick carpet. The corridors were empty. As they had planned, Hawkins snuck unseen to a spot under the hallway security camera and waited. Peter and Joey crept to the corner, hidden from camera view.

Joey pointed at door 1925 and asked quietly, "That one?"

"No. That room is clean. That's Bruno's. I'm in there a lot, throwing knives."

"Of course you are," she grumbled.

Peter whistled. Immediately Hawkins leapt to the security camera and planted a sticker on the lens. It stuck fast, blocking the device's view. He returned the whistle, and Peter and Joey bolted to room 1923, unseen by the camera. Peter's key melted into the lock and the door popped open.

"Amazing," Joey breathed.

As soon as they were in, Hawkins snatched the sticker off the camera. Even if the security guard monitoring the cameras from the main level had been vigilant enough to notice the disrupted video, it had lasted less than five seconds and he probably didn't even get out of his comfy swivel chair. Hawkins's friends were now safely inside and no one had seen a thing.

Joey and Peter practically ran through Adolfo's apartment, looking in the kitchen, searching the closet, and tossing the television room. They couldn't hunt through the entire nineteenth floor, but the strongman always struck them as extra scary. Turns out, Adolfo was a slob. His red underwear and socks were everywhere and he'd broken half the furniture plus two television remotes. His wife's side of the bed wasn't any cleaner.

"I imagine this woman doesn't require many suitcases," Fara noted, speaking for the first time. She was hovering in the closet. "Her clothes are TINY. Although I'd look particularly darling in this sequined dress..."

Joey snatched up a pillow from the couch, gasped, and muffled a scream. Under the pillow lay a thick green python. Joey made a noise that sounded like, "FFF-HHHHH-HH-HHHHH!!"

The snake began a lazy climb up the cushion.

"There's nothing here," whispered Peter. "Joey, c'mon." He cracked the door and whistled.

Hawkins planted the sticker on the camera again and repeated the signal. Peter and Joey darted from room 1923 to 1919, the gigantic suite where the heads of circus stayed.

Tandra the lioness rose from her den as Peter closed the heavy double doors behind them. Her golden eyes flashed. She snarled dangerously at Peter, but relaxed when she saw Joey.

"Hi sweetie," cooed Joey, walking to the bars across Tandra's bedroom/den. "Hi Tandra, girl. How're the babies?"

"Joey!" whispered Peter. "Don't talk to the dangerous monster!"

"Monster? I'm here fixing the cage every few days and Tandra is as gentle as a lamb, silly boy."

"A man-eating lamb, maybe," muttered Peter, experiencing an awful flashback from their encounter in the Caves.

1919 was shared by Lino Kang, Marcellus his son, Marlowe Blodgett, and Keith. The majestic rooms just kept going and going the farther Peter explored. There was even a fountain in the second kitchen. Unlike Adolfo's apartment, these rooms were clean and organized. In the third television room, on the coffee table, Peter found a stack of papers. Within there was a full map of the Crown with scrawls across the page. A black marker had been used to scratch off individual rooms and entire sections of the hotel.

"Joey!" he called. Even though the suite was empty, he felt like an intruder about to be discovered any moment. "Look at this. I bet this is a map of where they've hunted. They search a section and then cross it off."

"Do you think this will convince your dad?"

"No." Peter ground his teeth in frustration. "He'll just say Lino's keeping track of residents who've had a personal performance from the circus, as he said they would."

"He might be right."

"Doubt it. Let's keep looking."

It took them the better part of an hour to rifle through every drawer, every suitcase, every cabinet, and to scan each piece of paper. In the end, they decided, there was nothing to convince the police of a nefarious plan to steal magical artifacts.

Fara fluttered close to Peter and said, "Tandra wants to know what you're doing."

"Huh? You can speak to animals?"

"Of COURSE I can. Don't be dense."

"Umm. Tell her...we're cleaning," offered Peter.

"I'll try, but she's an intuitive lion."

A moment later, Joey entered the room. "It's useless," she said, fists on her hips.

Peter nodded. "Then it's time to begin Operation Phantom." He pulled a red magic marker from his pocket and proceeded into a bathroom. On the gigantic mirror, in blocky letters, he drew a message.

YOU WON'T FIND
    WHAT YOU'RE LOOKING
    FOR. NOT IF I
    CAN HELP IT!
    BE GONE FROM
    THE CROWN!!
    SINCERELY,
    -THE PHANTOM

                        . . .

HE FINISHED, stepped back, and proclaimed, "We've begun the war! Someone inside the circus is working with the Red Masque. I think it's Lino Kang. But even if if it's not Lino, the rest of the circus will hear about the message on the mirror. And they'll know their time is up."

Joey screwed up her nose skeptically. "But...'sincerely?' That's what the Phantom would write?"

"I don't know, I didn't get a chance to ask him. Cause he's dead," retorted Peter.

Fara mumbled on his shoulder, "Remind me, dearest Peter, WHY won't you be the Phantom? You even sign your notes with his name."

"Oh gosh. This will change everything, you know," said Joey nervously. "Are we positive?"

Peter nodded, a dangerous glint in his eye. "This is what the Phantom would do, I think, so that's what we'll do."

"But—"

"I'm not sitting around anymore, Joey. I won't grow fat and lazy while the Red Masque pilfers the Caves. If the Phantom won't stop them, we will. And I'll never put you in danger."

"We should go," she said. "I bet Hawkins is wondering if we got eaten."

They returned to the entrance and Peter whistled through the cracked door. A moment later the whistle was returned and they rushed out. Back at the elevator, Hawkins demanded, "What took so long? A maid almost called security on me."

"That place is huge," said Joey. "So big we probably missed places."

"Well? What'd you find?"

"Nothing," replied Peter, mashing the button for the

second floor. "So we left a note on the mirror, like we planned."

Hawkins stared at the closing doors thoughtfully. "Oh man. The Crown's about to get crazy."

"Now what?"

"Now we wait and we watch," said Peter. "And we plan the next phase of Operation Phantom. We're going to make the Red Masque's life miserable."

That night, as Peter was falling asleep on the floor (Hawkins had the bed for the night), Fara hunkered down nearby inside a clean sock he set out for her. Peter squinted and he was able to see through her aura of light and detect facial features. She was smiling with eyes closed. "Where do you go, Fara?" he asked softly.

Hawkins made a violent snorting noise and rolled over, murmuring about hot dogs.

Fara yawned. "What do you mean?"

"You're not always here. You leave for much of the day, you know? I see you in bursts."

"Remember, Peter. I'm NOT human."

"I remember." He smiled sleepily.

"I don't exist in your world all day. Remaining visible requires energy. It drains me, so I leave. Even in the mouse, I often wasn't there."

"Where do you go?"

"It's a secret. If you were the PHANTOM, I could tell you."

"How many Phantoms have you known?" asked Peter curiously. His eyes were getting heavy and Fara was turning into a blur.

"Far too many. I wish humans lived longer. You silly people keep dying."

Peter shifted on the floor, getting more comfortable.

Sleep was close...so close... "I asked you this before, but... the Librarian told me about someone named the Judge. The leader of the Red Masque. Is he real?"

"I wish he wasn't, but...he's real," whispered Fara, and her light dimmed. "And he's terrible."

"Do you know where he is?" asked Peter, on the cusp of unconsciousness.

"I do not. Nor do I know WHO he is, at the moment," she said. "The Phantom is a responsibility handed down from one person to another, and that's how the Judge operates too. One power-hungry and devious MONSTER passes the title down to the next, for centuries. It takes a remarkable person to resist him. A special person." Fara paused a moment, staring at the ceiling. "Don't you feel it, Peter? Each little boy is born with the belief that he's destined for greatness, that life is an adventure and he's the hero. It's not fair that your adventure is so perilous, but that's the story you're in. You're the hero and our need is great and so is the danger. I know you believe you're not worthy of the task, that someone HAS to be better equipped. But we desperately need you, Peter. I need you to believe me. ...Okay? ...Peter?"

But Peter was already snoring.

14

THREE LITTLE INSURGENTS

Day two of the insurgence dawned. Joey left early for the bakery. She wanted to keep an eye on the Windsor Restaurant to monitor the circus at breakfast and report back if performers looked worried or suspicious.

Peter and Hawkins jogged down the steps to the garage with the intention of spying on the Caves. Manos had attached a padlock, but Peter held a sinking suspicion it'd done little good.

Despite industrial heaters, the garage remained slightly chilly. The circus bears had been taken to Barclays, leaving the cage empty. Yet there was another animal tethered near the entrance to the Caves, and it stopped the boys in their tracks.

"Peter, look!" gasped Hawkins and he pointed. "Elephas maximus indicus!"

"Do you mean the elephant?" whispered Peter, staring awestruck at the animal. The elephant wasn't fully mature, only a little taller than Peter, but it was thick and powerful. It's eyes swiveled toward Hawkins and Peter as it scooped hay with it's trunk.

"An Indian elephant! See the ears? Smaller than an African elephant."

"You got a good eye, boy," said a man, unnoticed on the far side of the elephant. He came around, patting the animal's gray rump. It was the bald man Peter suspected of being in the Red Masque. The hairs on Peter's arm raised. "His name's Aggy, short for Agamemnon, and he isn't fully grown. Only a few years old but already strong enough to crush little boys if they get in his way," he grumbled, stroking his mustache. The man had a gruff voice and big jaw. His black eyes were hard, and they seemed to bore into Peter's brain.

"Can I pet him?" asked Hawkins.

"Not my fault if he squishes you," the big man grunted. Up close, he looked exhausted. Possibly from searching the Caves all night.

Peter followed Hawkins, pretending he wanted to touch the elephant. To his surprise Aggy smelled sweet—sweet enough to cover the scent of rotten hay from the nearby cage. The entrance to the Caves was on the far side of the elephant, almost like it was being used as a shield. Peter walked around to get a better view...

Relief flooded through him; the padlock Manos had used to secure the Caves was still in place, snapped through the...but wait, was it? As Peter drew near he noticed the shackle was neatly sawed in half, undetectable from a distance.

Someone had cut the lock.

"I knew it," he whispered. At that moment his foot caught on something and he stumbled. The elephant shuffled in alarm.

"Watch yourself, boy," barked the man, angrily knuckling his mustache. "Maybe it's time you brats ran home. Shouldn't be down here in the first place."

"What's this?" wondered Peter, examining the rope he'd tripped on. One end was tied to the elephant's ankle, the other end to a cinderblock.

"Aggy's tether. Holds him in place."

"That?" hooted Hawkins. "That little rope and a cinderblock? No way, Aggy weighs over a ton. He could run off whenever he wants."

"He *could*. But he doesn't. Aggy's strong but doesn't know it," replied the bald man. "He was trained as a calf with a heavier rope. He learned he couldn't break it. Now he's older and could snap the rope easily, but he never tries. He's held back by the memory."

Hawkins scratched Aggy's ear affectionately. "Doesn't know how strong he is. Poor Aggy."

"You had your look, now run along," the man ordered.

"Yes sir," said Peter. "C'mon, Hawkins."

"Okay, okay. Bye Aggy."

Back in the stairwell, Peter whispered, "Did you notice the lock?"

"Sorry Peter. I got distracted. How great is that elephant! Do you think we should sneak down and ride him?"

"Focus, Hawkins. The lock's been cut. The Red Masque's still in the Caves."

"Those rats! Your dad should kick 'em out."

Peter agreed. "Yeah, but he won't. A cut lock isn't enough. Mr. Banks is protecting them."

"Why's he doing that?"

"Good question."

Back in the Nook, after several hours of homework, Joey reappeared from the Windsor bakery covered in flour. She announced, "Something's got them stirred up. Lino Kang came to breakfast in a foul mood. He was snapping at everyone and even made his server cry."

"Hah!" said Hawkins, grinning. "Big ol' baby. Wait till we're through with him!"

"I need to see something," said Peter, standing from his homework. "Wait here, I'll be back in a minute." He hopped into the elevator, rode to the nineteenth floor and walked around the corner, whistling innocently.

Keith stood in front of 1919. His arms were crossed and he leaned against the doorframe, like a guard.

"G'morning, Keith. How're things?"

Keith offered a curt nod and watched Peter suspiciously. "What do you want?"

"On my way to 1925. Anything I can help with? You look upset."

"Not upset," snapped Keith. "Nobody's upset! Just a weird night, is all."

"Okay. Well. Ring if you need anything." Peter stopped at 1925 and knocked.

Bruno threw open the door and roared, "It's boy! Peter! What have I broke? You come to fix?"

"No sir. I was nearby and thought maybe you'd like to practice throwing knives?"

"Ah! A good idea, but not today. Boss is upset. Maybe tomorrow Bruno will teach you," he said, pounding his chest with a heavy fist.

"Sure, sounds great. Is anything wrong?"

"I do not know for sure. Boss tells Bruno nothing, but Bruno isn't blind. Something bad happened."

"Uh oh. Was it last night's performance?" asked Peter.

"No no! Circus was great, best yet."

"Which boss is upset? Maybe I could help."

The big man scratched his bushy beard thoughtfully. "Well. Probably, most angry is—"

"HEY! Bruno!" called Keith. "No more. Keep that big yap of yours shut. We solve our own problems, understand?"

"Sorry, Peter. Tomorrow we throw knives, if all is well," said Bruno and he closed the door.

Keith glared at Peter all the way back to the service elevator.

Peter rode the noisy car down and leapt into the Nook. "They're rattled! Bruno said the boss is upset. Dunno which is the boss, though."

"Probably Lino Kang," said Hawkins thoughtfully. "Dude's terrifying, right?"

Peter silently wondered if the bald man was the boss. He got the feeling that man somehow in charge.

"But if Lino Kang was in the Red Masque, wouldn't he try to look less terrifying?" asked Joey. "Guilty people try to look innocent."

"We're giving them another scare tonight," said Peter. "I bet they'll be prepared, but I've got a plan."

"I was really hoping once would be enough to drive them away," said Joey, tightly clutching the arms of her chair. "Last night stressed me out."

"They cut the lock to the Caves, Joey. They're still searching."

"WHAT are you little kids *talking* about?" asked Lela, Joey's older sister. She stood at one of the Nook's entrances, her mouth hanging open. She resembled a giraffe, tall and thin. "Cause you sound *weird*."

"Nothing, Lela. Go away!" shouted Joey irritably.

"You were talking about *strange* stuff," drawled Lela.

"Oh man," whispered Hawkins. "We're busted. I'm going to jail."

"You're being *stupid*, and I'm telling mother, Josephine. I don't know what you said, but I know it's *bad*."

"Hey Lela," said Peter. "Do you want a brownie?"

"No I don't want a *brownie*. Brownie's have *carbs*."

Peter walked towards her. "But you have one in your ear."

"No I don't." Lela cautiously backed away. "Peter, don't do your magic stuff, you know that *freaks* me out. I don't have a brownie in my ear. Do I?"

"Let me get it," said Peter, waving his hands like Max the magician did. "It's riiiiiight...here..."

"Peter, *don't!*"

Peter tugged on Lela's earlobe and held up a brownie for her to see. "See? I got it. No big deal. Were you saving it for later?"

Lela didn't want to smile but she did anyway. "That was *not* in my ear! Was it? Okay, do it again."

Peter waved his hands again theatrically. "You have something in your other ear..."

"Another brownie, I bet. That's *lame*. Pick something better, Peter."

"Uh oh."

"Huh? What's *uh oh*?" Her smile vanished. "What is it? What's wrong?"

"In your ear," said Peter softly. "Oh no..."

"Peter, *what?*"

"It's a snake."

Lela turned pale and her mouth worked soundlessly.

Peter said, "A little black one, slithering out...here, let me..."

Lela released an ear-splitting scream. She bolted from the Nook, hopping and smacking at her ear. Her apartment door slammed but they still heard her voice.

Joey sighed. "Gosh she's dumb. Nice job, Peter."

"Maybe she'll forget what she overhead," he said, returning to the table.

"Peter, my man, that was too great. She was all blah blah blah...and then you were all *taadaaaa*...how'd you do that?"

"I didn't really have a snake, Hawkins."

"I know, but the brownie thing?"

"Diversion and slight of hand."

Hawkins frowned. "Got to get me a book on magic."

"So tonight," said Peter, leaning closer to his friends to guard against eavesdroppers. "We're going back to 1919. But I bet they'll leave a guard. Maybe Keith, because he's not a performer."

"The little person? The Phantom can totally defeat him!" said Hawkins.

"We don't want to defeat just Keith, we want to scare them all. Like in your *Phantom of the Opera* book, we want them to think their room is haunted. Besides, maybe Keith isn't in the Red Masque. Maybe he's just doing what he's told."

Joey asked, "What do we do?"

Peter grinned. "You know this hotel backwards and forwards, Joey. Think you could cut the electricity to that room?"

THAT EVENING AFTER DINNER, Peter dressed in his black cashmere turtleneck and black pants. He stuffed his black ski mask into his pocket, and he and Hawkins walked to a supply closet on the eleventh floor, smiling pleasantly to the guests. When the coast was clear, they slipped inside.

Hawkins weaved through the custodian's vacuums and

cleaning supplies to a forgotten dumbwaiter portal at the back. "Smells line Pine-Sol," he noted. He shoved open the dumbwaiter doors. "You're telling me, a long time ago the butlers used this to send supplies up to the wealthier residents?"

Peter nodded. "It's like a miniature elevator they operated by hand until electricity was installed. It was perfect for sending up food and medicine."

"Rich people had elevators even before there *were* elevators. Why'd they quit using them?"

"Dunno."

Hawkins's face looked doubtful. "It's not very big. You sure you fit?"

"I used it before. Saved my life." Peter checked his watch —he had thirty minutes. By contorting his body, he was able to slide inside the shaft and stand up. Fara came inside too, but her light didn't cast out the darkness—Peter could see her glow but somehow it didn't reach the rest of the world. He said, "Remember, Hawkins—give me twenty minutes. If I haven't called that means I reached the top and I'm ready to go. Then wait ten minutes and tell Joey to cut the power. Right?"

"My job's easy, Peter. It's you I'm worried about."

"Nah." Peter grinned with nervous energy. "This'll be fun." He peered up the vertical shaft. "Hope there's no spiders."

"Even if you're not the Phantom, you're the bravest kid I know. Good luck," Hawkins said.

Peter pressed his sneaker onto the wooden slat and began to climb. Because the framework was exposed, it acted as a ladder. He fumbled his hand upward in the dark, located the next rung, and pushed off the slat below. He ascended the shaft in pitch black, quietly whispering each time he passed a set of doors. "Floor twelve...floor thirteen."

By the fifteenth, his shoulders ached. At seventeen his legs did too, so he temporarily rested, his elbow hooked around a wooden board.

"Fara?" he panted.

"Yes Peter?"

"Remind me next time to wear glasses and a mask. I'm getting dust in my eyes and mouth," he said, and he coughed into his shirt to muffle the sound.

"Are you nervous? About the height of your ascent?" she asked.

"Not really. Heights don't bother me. Besides," he said, staring downwards, "I can't see a thing."

She fluttered upward and circled the tiny shaft. "That's precisely the sort of brave quip Cypress would've said."

"Do you think this is a good idea?"

"Being the Phantom is NOT about making safe choices. It's about doing what you must, often without having good options, and without having time to plan. Needs must when the devil drives, you know."

"I have no idea what that means."

"The Phantom—"

"I'm not the Phantom though," Peter pointed out.

"I know," she replied, a bit irritated. "Yet you certainly BEHAVE like him."

"Wouldn't the real Phantom just kick their door down, grab the Red Masque by the ear, and throw them out of the Crown?"

"Possibly," she muttered. "But perhaps that's why they keep DYING, doing foolhardy stuff like THAT."

"Two more floors," he said, gazing upwards into the

black. "Let's go." His muscles had tightened during the rest and he grunted with the effort of moving again.

Floor eighteen, and then...

He stopped at the nineteenth floor and wiped his forehead. On the other side of the sliding dumbwaiter door was suite 1919. He checked his glow-in-the-dark watch—three minutes to go, and then Hawkins would understand that he'd reached the top without trouble and he'd alert Joey, who waited ready at the electrical box.

"Fara," he whispered. "Do you understand how human night vision works?"

"Without bright lights, your human eyeballs grow accustomed to the dark and your vision improves. What fascinating creatures you are."

"Yeah, well, you're ruining my night vision. Turn off your butt...or whatever it is."

"Oh. Many apologies." Her light dimmed and she flew into his pocket. "Better?"

"Much." From his other pocket he withdrew his ski mask and plopped it atop his head. No use pulling it on now, it'd only make him hotter. He also withdrew his snow gloves and tugged them on. Careful not to make a sound, he tested the dumbwaiter doors—they were stuck, so he decided to wait. No reason to create unnecessary noise yet; he didn't know exactly where this door opened into.

Time ticked by slowly. By now Hawkins had left to meet Joey, but Peter still had six minutes to wait. He pressed his ear against the dumbwaiter door and concentrated. Eventually he heard movement, like someone opening and closing a refrigerator.

Just as he suspected, a guard had been posted inside 1919. The note on the mirror had *definitely* spooked them.

Suddenly there was a loud SNAP and the shaft grew a shade darker. He heard a crash inside 1919 and someone cried out in surprise. Joey, reliable as ever, had killed the power.

Using the surprised cry to his advantage, Peter shoved open the dumbwaiter door. It protested for a half-second and then crashed wide. The dumbwaiter portal was inside a closet directly behind a big water heater. By holding his breath he was able to slither out from the shaft, over the tank, and fall face-first onto the floor.

Peter scrambled to his feet and cautiously opened the closet door. Thanks to his night vision and the ambient city light streaming through the big windows he could see perfectly well.

Keith, however, could not. He was the guard left behind and he stumbled around blindly, waving his arms, trying to locate his phone. When the power'd been cut, Keith had dropped his bowl of spaghetti onto the floor, creating a terrific mess.

Fara snickered from Peter's pocket. "Look at that dewdropper! Good luck, Peter."

Peter filled his lungs and pitched his voice low. "Keeeeeeeeith," he called in a deep and spooky tone. "KEEEEEIIIIIITTHH!!"

"Augh!" Keith cried. "No! No no no! It's not me, it's not me!" He turned and sprinted in the direction he thought was the front door, running smack into the kitchen wall. "OOOOPH!" he groaned, falling to the floor. "Please no! It's not me, Mr. Phantom, sir!"

Peter pressed his glove tightly to his mouth to stifle laughter. Keith got up, banged his shin on the coffee table, and toppled over again, directly into his spaghetti.

"KEITH!" Peter shouted again, loud as he could. "THE PHANTOM COMES FOR YOOOOOU!"

"NO! Please no!" he shouted, staggering to his feet. Keith made it to the front door, yanked it open, and bolted out. "Heeeeeelp!" he called and the door slammed behind him.

"I can't believe how well that worked," marveled Peter.

"HURRY! You don't have long," warned Fara.

Tandra made unhappy coughing growls from her den.

Peter dashed into the darkened kitchen and fetched a knife. Using the sharp tip, he scratched a big letter P into the bathroom door. He repeated the strokes, carving deeper and deeper.

"Just like Zorro used to do," said Peter with grim satisfaction.

"P for Peter?" asked Fara.

"P for Phantom." He ran into the master bedroom, which he assumed belonged to Lino Kang. He gashed the wall, spelling GET OUT, and signing it again with letter P. "There! That ought to give them another sleepless night."

"Gotta admit, Peter," said Fara, perched on his shoulder again. "This is QUITE clever. Using your brain instead of your brawn.""

As Peter returned the knife to the kitchen, a loud crash came from the front door. His blood ran cold. Keith was back and he cried, "See? See, Manos! I'm not crazy, the power's out, and the Phantom did it! Your stupid hotel is haunted!"

"Hmmm," came a more calm-sounding voice. "You're right, the power is out. Let's see..."

It was Peter's father, possibly the last person on earth Peter wanted to walk through the door!

"Holy smokes," he hissed. "How'd he get here so quickly!" His mask had been perched uselessly around the crown of his head, but now he tugged it down over his face. Not much good it'd do, though, because his dad had seen him wear the mask before. He dashed to the closet and silently closed the door behind him.

"I believe your father must be quite good at his profession," noted Fara. "His response time to complaints is astonishing! I'm impressed."

Just then, the lights snapped back on. Joey had waited the predetermined four minutes and restored power.

Peter leaped onto the big water tank and slid as quietly and as frantically as he could over the back, aiming his feet down through the open dumbwaiter doors. The squeeze was so tight that the door scrapped his back, tugging at his shirt. His sneakers kicked wildly for a foothold inside the shaft but found nothing. Fara flew in and called, "A little more. Keep going, Peter! A liiiiiittle farther..." He let himself slither until he held the water tank with only his fingertips, but finally his feet connected with a wooden slat. "Whew!" she called. His whole body folded into the shaft. He quietly closed the dumbwaiter doors and ripped off the hot mask.

"Oh my gosh," he panted. "Can't *believe* Dad was there."

"The previous Phantoms never had THAT problem!"

"Let's get out of here," he whispered and began the long climb down.

Thirty grueling minutes later, Peter arrived in the Nook. His heart had resumed normal rhythm and he'd stopped sweating. Joey and Hawkins kept their eyes fixed woodenly on the books they pretended to read. Two butlers were sitting in chairs at the big window watching the evening pedestrians, and Mrs. Love knitted in the corner, pleasantly oblivious to Peter's recent drama. Lela and one of her friends snapped pages of magazines at the adjacent coffee table. Peter sat down and grabbed his book.

Without looking up or moving his lips, Hawkins whispered, "How'd it go?"

"Operation Phantom in full effect," replied Peter, equally soft. "Scared the daylights out of Keith. Nearly knocked himself unconscious before running for help."

Joey and Hawkins clamped their mouths closed and quaked with laughter. Tears streamed down their cheeks.

Lela watched them suspiciously and said, "I *know* you're up to something, little twerps. Once I find out what, I'll—"

The service elevator doors slid open and out walked Manos. He stopped when he noticed the three kids, and he inspected them like they were guilty of something.

With exaggerated innocence, Joey asked, "Hello Mr. Constantine, is there trouble?"

"I'm not sure yet, Josephine."

"Anything I can help with?"

Manos shook his head, both exhausted and frustrated, and replied, "Going for my tools. Nothing I can't handle."

"Hey Dad," called Peter. "I forgot to tell you. The Caves need a new padlock."

"What happened to the one I installed?"

"Someone cut it."

Manos didn't reply for a long time. Peter bet he was having increasing suspicion about Mr. Banks allowing the circus to remain. Finally he said, "Thanks, Peter. This evening is getting stranger by the minute."

Manos trudged towards 201 and out of view. The three friends grinned at one another, though Peter felt a pang of guilt; he wished Operation Phantom wouldn't cause his father extra work.

Hawkins waved his novel, *The Phantom of the Opera*, and whispered, "I know *exactly* what we're doing next!"

15

DARCI DRAKE'S ARTICLE

Over the next week, the Circus of Doom began receiving mysterious letters. LOTS of letters. On day one, three envelopes were delivered to room 1919, labeled in blocky letters,

CIRCUS

ROOM 1919

THE CROWN

The next day, 1919 received three more and so did room 1923. On the third day, every room occupied by the circus received at least one such envelope, and room 1919 got thirteen. On the fourth day, over a *hundred* were delivered.

A simple note was stuffed inside each envelope.

THE RED MASQUE MUST LEAVE

IMMEDIATELY

OR THINGS WILL GET WORSE!

-PHANTOM

Lino Kang, in a state of outrage, ordered the hotel to cease delivering their mail, but not before the damage was done—every member of the circus looked as though they'd seen a ghost. He demanded a full investigation, but what could be done? The mail originated from around the city with no way of tracking the senders.

Little did he know his tormentors were Peter, Hawkins, and Joey, sitting at a table in the corner of the Nook, steadily churning out the spooky stationary and looking for all the world like studious children doing homework. When they had another day's batch prepared, Joey would visit the offices near the Lobby and steal a stack of blank envelopes and stamps. At first she felt guilty about the pilfered supplies, but she noticed the stamps had been sitting in drawers long enough to be covered in dust. And besides, they were acting in the Crown's best interest. Each member of the Phantom insurgence would stuff their envelopes and then wander outside to various mailboxes, drop them in, and wait for mayhem to be delivered the following day.

In the midst of the madness, Peter and his father Manos returned to the Caves. Both brandishing a flashlight, they made the long trek through the dark labyrinth to the secret tunnels on the third floor and discovered the heavy door wide open again, as Peter predicted.

"See, Dad? Believe me *now*? The Red Masque is in the hotel!" said Peter as they shoved the door closed and dropped the bar across. Even with his father by his side, the secret tunnel terrified him.

Manos didn't respond, but Peter saw it in his eyes—his father was worried.

On the way back, Peter pointed out scuff marks in the dust, and other obvious indications that a massive search was underway and it had reached the second floor of the Caves.

"They're searching, Dad. I know they are," Peter said, his voice echoing in the black distance.

"For what, son?"

"They believe ancient and powerful artifacts, or weapons, are down here. Look at this old water tank. It's been disassembled and they didn't even bother to put it back together correctly. And look! There are pry bars and flashlights in the corner."

Once again, Manos didn't respond to Peter's allegations. But he did snap TWO padlocks onto the outside door and arrange for a security guard to swing by the entrance several times a day.

Upon hearing the news that Lino Kang halted the mail deliveries, Hawkins looked relieved. "Thank goodness. Thought my hand was about to fall off, you know? My fingers cramped up all night!"

"Yeah but what do we do now?" asked Joey. "The circus hasn't left."

Fortunately, the famous writer Darci Drake answered the question for her. With only two weeks remaining before the Circus of Doom's final performance (which was being held for the Crown residents only, thereby removing all obstacles for a massive, all-encompassing treasure hunt), Darci published an exposé in the New York Times.

Joey snagged a copy, dashed into the Nook, and shoved it in front of Peter's face. Hawkins read over his shoulder.

The Phantom Returns to Haunt the Crown: - Circus of Doom Spooked

-In case you haven't heard the rumors—he's back, the infamous Phantom of New York, and he's set his sights squarely on the fabled Circus of Doom, current residents of the Crown Hotel. As this writer can tell you, because she is also a resident, the Phantom is creating quite the stir...

. . .

IN THE ARTICLE, Darci Drake outlined details about the first warning note left on the mirror, and she included photographs of the carving Peter had scraped into the door and wall of 1919.

Joey stared with shock at the newspaper. "How'd she get a camera inside Lino Kang's room? And so quickly!"

"She's a reporter," replied Hawkins wisely. "They know everything."

Peter skimmed to the bottom.

...IS THE PHANTOM CORRECT? Is the Circus up to no good at the Crown? And what does he think they're searching for?

This writer doesn't know.

Yet.

"THIS IS BAD," Joey said worriedly. "This is so bad. If we're caught...oh my gosh, I can't even think about it!"

The guest elevator chimed and Marcellus Kang stepped out, timidly waving at them. "I have homework," said the boy "Is this where you do yours?"

"Yes! You should join us," said Joey, going slightly red in her cheeks. "I was about to start...um...*something*," she said, quickly rifling through her school supplies for something to do.

Hawkins was confused. "But you said you were done for the—"

"No I didn't," she replied too quickly. "Besides, I still have...to...copy my history notes, you know."

Marcellus sat down, his outfit of white linen making Peter's jeans and hoodie look grubby. He held up a novel. "I am reading *The Life of Pi*. It's about a tiger and a circus, you know."

Hawkins nodded in appreciation. "Read it. Loved it."

Out of habit, Peter leaned back in his chair, took aim with a pencil, and chucked it at the trashcan in the corner. He didn't have a knife, so he'd taken to throwing pencils. His teacher Bruno could tell if Peter hadn't been practicing. It irked Joey to no end.

"A nice shot," Marcellus told him. He indicated Joey's pen and asked, "May I borrow?"

"Yes, of course, certainly," she said. "We love to practice throwing our writing utensils. Do it all the time. I'll fetch some more!"

Hawkins, befuddled, said, "But you always yell at Peter when—"

"No I don't, and hush up," she said in savage undertones.

Hawkins shrugged and slid the newspaper across to Marcellus. Careful to watch any reaction, he said, "Say, circus boy. Have you read this yet?"

Marcellus glanced at the paper and his face paled. He stood and gripped the paper in trembling fingers. "Oh dear. My father...oh dear. He will not handle this well. Please forgive me, I must go." He hurried to the elevator and was whisked away as quickly as he'd arrived.

Joey glared at Hawkins. "You could have waited a few more minutes!"

"Why, so you could throw your writing utensils?"

Peter said, "That article came out today. I bet Lino's already seen it. We better brace ourselves."

The article acted like a bomb going off in the Crown. According to Darci Drake, the *Red Masque* might be in the Crown. Calls flooded the front desk, scared guests checked out early, and brave new arrivals booked every room with the hope of spotting a ghost. Lino Kang could be heard roaring from two floor away, directing his anger at Mr. Conrad and Mr. Banks, and demanding Darci Drake be ejected from the hotel immediately. The performers were unnerved and they had several bad performances in a row.

Peter enjoyed the insanity, hoping it might drive out the evil treasure syndicate. At least, he enjoyed it until Darci seized his arm at the end of the week as he passed through the sparkling Lobby. Her short hair was gathered into a kind of a half bun and she wore sunglasses, as she always did. She tugged him to her table near the coffee shop and pressed a bowl of ice cream into his hands.

"Dearest Mowgli, it's been too long since our last chat! You like cookies'n'cream, yes? I have a good memory for details." She used her most charming voice.

"Ummm...yes ma'am, I do. But—"

"Sweet boy, I have to tell you—I'm simply *obsessed* with the Phantom." To prove her point, she laid her black notebook flat on the table and opened it. On those two pages alone Peter saw the word Phantom at least a dozen times. "He could be the biggest story in the decade, in my professional opinion."

"But what's that have to do with me?" asked Peter nervously. He set his ice cream down untouched.

"Why don't you answer that question yourself?" Her smile was devious. She tucked her feet under and sat on them, looking like a cheshire cat. "I've taken the liberty of researching more about the curious life of Peter Constantine."

Peter gulped. "And?"

"And I learned the most *marvelous* things. Listen, handsome, I told you once I didn't care about the Red Masque. A thousand apologies, I was wrong. This Phantom extravaganza has made me rethink everything, and it all started with you."

"No it didn't," cried Peter. He tried to get up but she yanked him back.

"Don't forget, Mowgli, that I know your secret! That night, a year ago, in the snow? You fought poor Atticus Snyder and started the Phantom rumors again."

"Oh," stammered Peter. "Okay, yeah, you're right, although I wouldn't feel too badly for Atticus. I forgot you knew. But remember, you promised never to write anything without my permission."

"I won't forget, love." She stopped talking when she spotted a man approaching, carrying her latest book. The man had a goofy smile on his face and a pen in his hand—an autograph seeker. "No!" she cried. "Not right now, be gone!" She snatched a spoon from the table and threw it at him. "Come back later, ta-ta! Hugs and kisses, now go!"

The man, like a wounded dog, whimpered and slumped away.

"Sorry, Peter, where were we?" she asked, instantly returning to her endearing self.

"I was just leaving."

"Oh yes, now I remember! You started the Phantom rumors again."

"But not on purpose—"

"And then I did a little more digging, and caught wind of additional gossip. There is a belief held by some in the Crown that you SAW the ghost on the tenth floor."

Peter began to sweat. "Well, even if that's true, didn't a lot of people see the ghost?"

"I think the Phantom has returned, as he promised," she said, dropping her voice to a conspiratorial whisper. "Like I said in the article, he's now a ghost. The ghost from the tenth floor, Cypress Fitzgerald. Do you know what that means?"

"Ummm...that you forgot to take your medicine?" asked Peter, making a feeble attempt at a joke.

"It means, dear Mowgli, that you have seen and spoken to the actual Phantom!" Peter had to give her credit—she wasn't exactly right, but she was far closer to the truth than anyone else. "And I need to know *everything*."

She paused as crazy old Mr. Hayes tottered by. The man waved happily at Peter, mumbling something about checkers and Alexia, before moving on.

"Why *does* he call you Alexia?" Darci asked. "Never mind, I don't care. Tell me about the Phantom."

"What makes you think I spoke to the ghost on the tenth floor?" he asked.

"A reliable source."

"Who?"

"Sweet Peter, have you seen the response to my article? It's huge. MONUMENTAL. My inbox is flooded. People are dying for more, and who am I to withhold the story? I won't! Plus, the illustrious buffoon Lino Kang is out for my head, and I need more information."

"Okay, but who told you?" he persisted.

"A writer never reveals her sources," said Darci with false dignity, closing her eyes.

"Then I'm not telling you anything."

"Fine, it was Marlowe Blodgett."

That made sense. Marlowe loved ghost stories and Joey had blurted on the elevator all those months ago that Peter had spoken to the ghost. And, like a fool, Peter had given him some details, which apparently had now been passed on to Darci Drake.

"Peter, my love," she said, picking up her notebook and her pen. "*Spill.*"

Peter wracked his brain, sorting through his many secrets. Was there anything he could tell her which wouldn't cause more problems? Probably not. Not even Ollie and Dot knew he had spoken to Cypress Fitzgerald. Rory knew, and he would advise Peter to keep his blasted yap shut.

Speaking of Rory, where *was* he? Peter hadn't seen him in over a week, maybe longer.

"Oh dear," groaned Darci, and she sucked irritably at her teeth. "Speak of the devil and he shall appear."

"Huh?" asked Peter. She pointed across the bustling Lobby to the entrance doors, through which Marlowe Blodgett was striding, dressed as usual like a swashbuckler. "Don't you like Mr. Blodgett? I think he's very nice."

"Perhaps *too* nice," she said wryly. "Marlowe's become a little sweet on me, the poor man."

"What's wrong with that? He's great!"

Darci stood and packed her things in a desperate rush. "Not for me, Mowgli. He's too obsessed with ghosts, a bizarre fascination. Also, no man of mine wears eye liner. We'll continue this conversation later, my dear. Cheers!"

She dashed out of sight, leaving Peter a little breathless and his head spinning, like a tornado had just passed through.

PETER ATTENDED his boxing lesson that afternoon at Arthur Grave's sparsely decorated apartment. His new gloves had fresh padding, much squishier than Arthur's old pair, and his knuckles ached less. He pounded the heavy dummy and it sounded like thunder compared to the softer thumping of Atticus's fists and the pitter-patter of Leo's.

Near the end of practice, Atticus was too exhausted to hold up the mitts and withstand Peter's barrage of punches, too tired to even sneer effectively. So Arthur Graves himself slipped on a pair of mitts and held up targets for Peter to punish, and when they finished he cried, "Daggum, Pete! Got them quick hands! Strong shoulders too, like it's supposed to be. Must be hard working, same as Manos." Arthur jerked a thumb towards Leo (who lay gasping like a fish on the floor) and Atticus (who was whimpering as he took off his gloves). "Look at these two. Video games never made a man strong. Neither did wealth. Hard work is what it takes. Sweat and grit and pain."

"Pain and...and... sweat," groaned Leo. "I have those...sir."

"Not but twice a week, boy! Need to work hard every day. Every *dang* day."

"There's more than one type of strength, I'm sure you realize," interjected Atticus. His pale red hair was plastered to his forehead. "Or perhaps you don't. The Snyders, we have mental strength, attending the finest educational institutions in the country. We also have financial power and a robust portfolio, including beach houses on three continents. We—"

"We? Talking 'bout *you*, boy. Not your papa. Money don't make the man, Snyder," barked Graves. "True strength and character ain't something you *inherit* in a will. Gotta want it! Gotta work for it."

"I don't need character," scoffed Atticus. He packed his bag to leave, refusing to look at them. Peter thought he might start crying. "I have a trust fund."

"You ain't learned nothing this past year." Arthur sadly shook his head. "Listened to not a word."

"I don't HAVE to listen!" Atticus roared, suddenly fuming and indignant. "I'm in line to take over Snyder Industries! Don't you get it? The most POWERFUL robotics manufacturer in the WORLD. What does Peter get? What will Peter take over? A mop! A tiny apartment he won't even own! That's IT. What's so special about Peter? I CAN'T understand this hotel's bizarre fascination with the GARBAGE boy. You and Max and the Crawfords and Ernestine Parker...it's like you all adopted him. You know why he punches hard? He carries TRASH every day!"

"So?" asked Arthur quietly. Peter was too stunned by the outburst to comment. Leo looked like he wanted to disappear.

"So EVERYTHING! Why do you even let him in here with me and Leo? It makes no sense."

Arthur kept using the soft tone of voice. "I started out delivering papers before school when I was a kid. Think less of me, Snyder? I was born with nothing. Given nothing. Didn't go to no college. I was good at one thing—hittin' people. So that's what I did. In a boxing ring. Think less of me?"

"Boxing is the sweet science, Mr. Graves, an honorable sport, but—"

"Maybe I look beyond the physical, Snyder. Maybe I see what's inside." Arthur waved his hand at Peter. "You see a boy named Pete who wasn't given as much as you. But me, I see a champion."

Atticus snatched his bag and stomped to the door. "Our station in life *matters*. Who we are *matters*."

"Who you are has nothing to do with money, kid."

"I'm a Snyder. And that's got everything to do with

money," Atticus said with a sniveling smile. He threw open the door and left, muttering about living in a stupid hotel.

Leo said goodbye and hurried home, afraid Arthur might turn on him next. In the sudden silence, Peter helped put away the heavy dummies and punching mitts, his ears burning. He didn't have a bag to pack, only the gloves. On his way out, he said, "Thank you, sir. For the kind words."

"Wasn't kind words, Peter. Was accurate words. I worry about what Snyder might become one day," Arthur replied gruffly, standing beside the door.

"He's just a kid though, sir. He'll grow up."

"Just a kid? What's age matter? So long, Pete." Arthur closed the door and Peter turned down the hall.

"Peter Constantine!" Dot shouted, startling him so badly he dropped the gloves. She was marching towards Arthur's room looking displeased. She still wore all white, but recently she'd started wearing a white long-sleeve t-shirt instead of the leather jacket. The white sunglasses were perched on her head, holding her short blonde hair back.

"Stop doing that," he muttered, retrieving his gloves. "Just say hello in a soft voice like normal people."

"We need to talk. Follow me," she demanded, and she led him to the golden elevators. Peter would really rather not, tired and sweaty as he was, but Dot seemed determined. In the elevator, she asked, "What's got Atticus so upset?"

"An argument with Arthur Graves. How do you know Atticus?"

"He's an interesting kid. I've eaten with him at the Windsor a couple times."

"Interesting kid?" Peter blinked stupidly, wondering if he'd heard right. "Perhaps we're talking about different guys."

"Atticus Snyder. Well dressed, rich, intelligent, about your age?"

"Atticus Snyder, pompous, spoiled, about my age, and a *bully*," he corrected her.

"Well, I like the guy. Said he's going to introduce me to some of his friends at the Ritz. Said they'd like me," Dot announced defensively.

Peter had a retort prepared but he recalled something Rory once said—Dot had been cooped in the basement much of her life without having a chance to really live. Perhaps making new friends, even ghastly friends like Atticus and the Ritz kids, was important to her. So Peter held his tongue..

Dot marched directly to 1010, Cypress's old room, pushed inside, and tossed him a sword. Without warning, she launched into an attack, one Peter easily knocked aside.

"I saw the article in the paper," she snapped, jabbing at him. "Darci Drake's report."

Peter casually deflected a few more of her sword thrusts. "Yeah, me too. It's got the place crazy upset, huh?"

"Crazy upset," she said, glaring. "Nice phrasing."

Fara the faery girl burst from the fireplace with an explosion of sparkles. "Ah HAH. Found you, Peter! You're a difficult guy to locate."

"That's you, isn't it?" Dot was asking. "The Phantom in the article? You're the one pulling the juvenile pranks on the circus?"

"Uh oh." Fara's aura turned a shade of blue. "Someone's grumpy."

"They aren't juvenile," protested Peter. "And they're not pranks. I'm trying to drive the Red Masque out before they find whatever it is they're looking for."

"You should have told me," Dot said furiously. "I should have been included!"

"But we're on the same team, aren't we? You've been fighting against the Red Masque without letting *me* know, I assume," Peter said, although he wouldn't be surprised to learn otherwise. She and Ollie had shown a tendency to let their attention wander. "Why do I need to run my plans by you?"

"Because I'm the REAL Phantom!" Dot flung herself at him, hacking and swinging like a girl possessed. Peter deflected her attacks, ducked out of the way, and nicked her on the back of her thigh. "And you're—ouch!—you're just some kid."

"She's NOT the real Phantom," shouted Fara. "Don't heed her, Peter. And my HEAVENS, you're quite talented with a sword."

"Just some kid?" asked Peter, confused and hurt. "But I'm helping. I'm the one who found your secret lair under the Chelsea, the one who alerted your family about the circus. Last year in the fire, I helped—"

"Doesn't matter, Peter." She swung with her all her might, putting both hands on the sword's hilt, so viciously her sunglasses fell off. Peter jerked backwards and the tip of her blade thudded into the carpet, getting caught. She tugged angrily. "My grandfather was the Phantom! So was my great grandfather. It's in my blood. Which means, I get to be next!"

"I'm not sure it works that way."

"It DOESN'T," agreed Fara. "But, seriously Peter, when did you get so adept at swordplay?"

Dot yanked her sword free and swung at Peter's head. He ducked and this time her blade lodged deeply into the wall.

Peter was shocked to see a tear leak out of her eye. Why was everyone crying today?

"Dot, I'm confused. What's going on?"

"I should have been included," she seethed. She wiped at her eyes. "You shouldn't be driving away the Red Masque; *I* should be."

"Who's stopping you?"

"But you're already winning!" She yanked at her sword but it was stuck fast. If she had connected with Peter's head it would've *really* hurt.

"Wining what?"

"What if Ollie finds out it's you? What if he finds out the rumors swirling around the Crown are about YOU? And not me, his granddaughter?"

"It doesn't matter who gets the credit."

"YES it does!" She quit pulling on the sword and turned away from him. "Dumb sword...doesn't even work right...I gave you the better one, anyway."

"You did?" asked Peter, looking curiously at his rusty old blade. "What's the difference?"

"There's no difference, Peter," answered Fara. "Hush now. She's depressed."

Dot spoke so low Peter almost didn't hear. "If I'm not the Phantom, then what am I?" She paused. "I need someone to teach me. Show me what to do. And how to do it."

"But that's the problem, isn't it?" asked Peter. "There is no one. We just have to...figure it out. Make it up as we go."

Fara perched on Peter's shoulder. "That's right. Being the Phantom isn't something you DO, it's something you ARE. He or she is a servant and guardian. If someone has to teach you WHAT to do...then you're not the Phantom."

Somehow, while he'd been listening to Fara, Dot had gotten closer. A LOT closer. Peter was surprised to discover he was a little taller than her, and even more startled when she rested her head on his shoulder. "I'm sorry, Peter...for yelling. This is more difficult than I thought it'd be," she said, sniffing.

Dumbfounded, Peter stared at Fara and mouthed, *What just happened? What do I do?*

"She's crying, Peter," Fara scolded him. "Put your arm around her, you great oaf."

Hesitant and awkward, Peter placed his clammy hand on her shoulder. After a moment's indecision he gave her a gentle squeeze, though he wasn't quite sure why he was required to comfort someone who'd been trying to jam a sword into his neck.

"Ahh, blast it," said a voice behind them. It was Rory, limping into the room. He crossed his arms and watched them with a sad expression on his face. "I knew this would crush her."

"I don't know what to do," Dot said, her voice muffled in Peter's shirt.

Rory caught Peter's eye. "Being the Phantom ain't that much fun, is it, kid?"

"It's not me," protested Peter.

Dot made a snorting noise. "Obviously. If I can't figure it out, there's no way *you* could."

The three of them stood there a long time, a deeply confused and unhappy group. Eventually Fara flew to Dot's sword, still stuck in the wall. She landed on the quivering hilt and said, "It's time we acquire you a weapon, Peter. A REAL one."

DESPERATE TIMES CALLING

"Only four more days," said Hawkins gloomily. "And then the city's doomed."

It was a chilly January day. The three insurgents stood on the lagoon's bridge in Central Park, staring back at the Crown Hotel, glittering pink and silver in the sunlight. The forest had long since lost its leaves, except for scattered pines.

Hawkins didn't have to remind them what happened in four days—the entire hotel planned on attending the Circus's final performance—even the front desk would close for a few hours. The building would be completely empty, and the Red Masque was going to tear it apart and find the powerful artifacts, or weapons, or whatever they were. Fara had admitted something was hidden in the Caves—something she didn't want the Red Masque to find—but she wouldn't tell Peter what it was. She would only tell the Phantom, and since Peter denied it was him...

Joey asked, "What's the name of the guy who's after your dad?"

"Gordie Abaddon," Peter answered. "The Evil Treasure Hunter."

"Do you think he's in there?" She pointed at their hotel.

"He's around. I get this awful feeling when I think about him." But then again, Peter had an awful feeling most all the time. The lurking dread never faded these days.

"How come we haven't seen him?" asked Hawkins.

"I dunno. I dunno anything, it seems. And we're getting desperate."

"Shouldn't you know what to do? Aren't you the Phantom?" asked Joey.

"No."

Hawkins exclaimed, "Yes you are, Peter."

"No I'm *not.*"

Hawkins said, "But Cypress the ghost thought you were. Right? How's it work?"

"I don't really know. But it's not me."

"Cause you're too OBSTINATE and headstrong," groaned Fara, flying circles around the group, leaving a rainbow trail. "Now hurry up, I need to show you something."

Joey shivered and zipped her jacket higher. "Any ideas? We're running out of time."

"I have an idea," said Peter. "But it's nuts."

"Yes!" Hawkins's breath created a cloud of fog. "I like crazy. What's the plan?"

"First, I need you two to make a map of the nineteenth floor hallways. Specifically of where the laundry chutes are, and also where the security cameras point."

"Easy," said Joey. "That's all?"

"You'll have to be sneaky. The circus has a guard patrolling the level and he can't know what you're up to. I also need to know what the guard is doing. Let's meet in the Nook in an hour—"

"More time! THREE hours!" shouted Fara.

"Umm...I mean, three hours. We'll look at the map and I'll share my idea."

"What are you gonna do?" asked Hawkins.

"I need to run a few errands."

"Around the city?" He glared at Peter, suspiciously. "Maybe I should go too, you know? You'll get lost."

"No I won't!"

"I know you. You're kinda hopeless out here."

Joey nodded knowingly. "I agree. A total disaster."

"Like a baby kitten, Peter."

"Actually, a baby kitten might have a better chance of not getting lost," mused Joey.

"Hey, both of you, hush up!" shouted Peter.

Fara tugged on the collar of his jacket. "Come ON!"

"I'll see you in three hours." Peter followed Fara off Gapstow Bridge and through Hallett Nature Sanctuary, the grass crunching beneath his sneakers. Because of the frigid temperature, the pathways were empty of pedestrians. "Where are we going?"

"Returning to the Chelsea, of course! You brought the key, yes?"

"I got it," said Peter and his stomach twisted in a knot. The last time he'd gone to the Chelsea he'd gotten lost and ended up pushed around by the Ritz kids. But that was before he had a faery guide. They headed down 7th Avenue, weaving through the heavily dressed New Yorkers and hustling past Times Square. Thirty minutes later Fara cut through the chaos of 23rd Street, and the majesty of the scarlet Chelsea surprised him once again.

"Is the Chelsea a magic hotel?" he asked, panting from the race through the frosty air.

"Of COURSE! Just LOOK at it."

Peter's key slid smoothly into the brick lock and emitted a pulse of light. The door swung inwards and they descend the steep staircase.

"I haven't been here in YEARS," Fara uttered in the darkness. "Cypress hated this dungeon."

Peter shoved open the inner door and fumbled for the pull-string for the overhead lightbulb. It buzzed to life, illuminating the dusty workshop.

"What a MESS!" she shrieked. "Don't those ogres have any PRIDE? Nothing's changed in fifty years. Or maybe longer!"

Peter cupped his hands and blew into them. The heat had been turned off, and his teeth chattered. "What are we looking for?"

"A sword." Fara flitted across the room and peered into moldy boxes.

"That's it? Dot has a couple of those at the Crown."

"Not just any sword, Peter. THE sword."

Peter gasped. "Cypress's sword? The one he had in the paintings?"

"Yes! Although it's not Cypress's sword. It's name is Dyrnwyn, an ancient and powerful blade, far older than him."

"Durrwhat?"

"Dyrnwyn! Came over with the pilgrims centuries ago. Think of it as a faery sword," came her reply from underneath a table.

Peter walked to the mannequin of the Phantom, the one with the huge black jacket once worn by Ollie. At the waist was buckled a gold sword. Peter drew the blade out from the jewel-encrusted scabbard. "Is this it?"

"Heavens NO," she cried, flying over. She snorted with laughter. "That's a short sword intended for costumes! I'm not surprised Ollie chose it, the great blubbering monkey. Who would ever wield a sword made of GOLD?" She landed on Peter's shoulder. "Peter! Your skin! It's like you're an ice statue. Are you cold?"

"Very."

"I noticed Rory's old jacket...here...somewhere..." she muttered, returning to the tables of nicknacks. "Ah HAH. Here! Don the uniform, Peter! You're approximately Rory's size. He was a compact man, and you're more substantial than most youths your age."

Peter held up a dusty leather jacket. "Fara, it's kinda awesome!"

"His jacket used to be quite stylish, I believe. Now it's VINTAGE. I envy you humans your clothes. Phantoms ALWAYS wear great jackets, you know. Part of the ensemble."

Peter slid into it, admiring the buttons and rubbing the soft brown material. "I don't know if I'm cool enough to wear it."

"Rory was dashing, back in his day! Of course, I was trapped in a MOUSE at the time..."

"What happened to Rory? He won't tell me, but it sounded like his time as the Phantom ended poorly."

"It's not my place to tell," she said, but Peter noted her light dimmed. He wished he hadn't asked.

From the bizarre collection of Phantom gear, Peter picked up a thin silver disk, quite hard, about the size of a tire. "Did this belong to Cypress?"

"No, I don't recognize that contraption."

"Possibly a shield."

"Makes sense. Ollie'd want something to hide behind," she scoffed. "Most likely *his* invention."

"Like Captain America."

"Who?"

"The comic book hero. He throws a shield and it always comes back," explained Peter, inspecting the disc.

"How does it return? Magic?"

"Don't think so. He's in the military."

"Maybe a WIZARD military!"

"Let's try, find out if it returns." Peter drew his arm back and chucked the heavy disc like a frisbee. It arced straight into a stack of old metal helmets and sent them cascading across the concrete floor. CRASH! Such a clamor Peter had never heard, and the noise nearly burst his ears before the disc clattered to a stop.

"Peter! I insist you do NOT do that again. You OBVIOUSLY don't know how to operate Sergeant America's magic shield."

"It's *Captain* America," he corrected her, holding his ears.

"He's an officer and all he gets is a *shield*?"

"Never mind, forget I said anything." Peter found a collection of rusty swords near the radios. "Are you looking for one of these? They're so old."

Fara hovered near his shoulder and smiled fondly. "Cypress's collection! He loved swords. Just like George Washington once did. George used Dyrnwyn too."

"George *Washington?* You're kidding! You knew him?"

"Of course. A brave but SMELLY fellow. I remember what he said as he crossed the Delaware. It was freezing and nobody felt like heroes that day—wait, THERE!"

"What? Where?"

"Isn't it BEAUTIFUL!" she cried, landing on an old blade

and patting it lovingly. "I'd forgotten how elegant it is! I
wonder why it's tossed haphazardly in with the others?"

"This one?" Tentatively, Peter stretched a reverent hand
to grasp the Fara's weapon by the cracked leather hilt. His
fingers closely comfortably around it...and although he
hadn't expected a shaft of light from heaven or an angelic
choir, the moment felt strangely anticlimactic. He raised the
sword, dubiously inspecting the nicked blade. "*This* is Dyrnwyn?" It looked like all the others—a thin saber that once
had been sharp. "The faery sword, you're sure?"

"Of COURSE! See how it's slightly darker in color?"
Balancing on the sword's dull tip, Fara asked, "Can you not
feel it's power?"

"It's ancient. There's no marking or anything. I think it
might crack in half."

"Don't focus on the outside, Peter. Look beneath the
surface."

He held it closer to his face. Under the rust and the
scratches Peter detected a stylish and well balanced saber,
but it had seen far better days, a long LONG time ago. In
truth, the blade looked in worse shape than most.

"I dunno, Fara," he said. "What's so special about it?"

"To begin with, Dyrnwyn burns anyone who wields it
for evil purposes. Sears their hand. Also, it can turn the tide
of a battle—just ask General John Wool, who brought it to
New York City where it remained."

"General who?"

"Are you sure you don't feel *anything?*" she asked
worriedly.

"No. What's it supposed to do?" He gave it an experi-
mental swish.

"It shall come alive, in the right hands."

"It didn't burn me, though. So I guess I'm not evil, right?"

He gave a half chuckle, wondering if Fara's long residence in the mouse had addled her memory. Both of Dot's swords were nicer and newer than this. He suggested, "Maybe it'll come alive once you find the real Phantom?" Though to be honest, Peter thought, it looked more ready for a a museum or perhaps a recycling bin, rather than actual combat.

"We should return," said Fara glumly. She landed on a sheath. "Here, slide it in this scabbard. In that manner you can carry it and no one will think you strange."

Peter rammed the sword into the sheath and said, "People will DEFINITELY think I'm strange carrying this around." He found an old blanket and wrapped it up so the weapon was completely covered. "Should I put Rory's jacket back?"

"No no, keep it. It's handsome on you," she said with a sigh. "You look just like him. Like Cypress, I mean."

Peter grinned, swelling with pride. He looked down at himself. "Like Cypress? I think he and I are related."

"Absolutely, without question. You two have the same courage and spirit. Everyone who met Cypress loved him, just like you. I know for CERTAIN Caroline Crawford will think you look dashing in that jacket."

"Well, what are we waiting for?" Peter asked with a laugh and he race up the stairs to the exit.

Fara watched him go, the brave and handsome boy wearing Cypress's key around his neck, carrying the faery sword in his fists, dressed in the Phantom's jacket, and bent on destroying the Red Masque. "What a frustrating boy," she grumbled and launched herself after him. "But what a Phantom he'll be!"

~

JOEY UNROLLED the baker's parchment paper across the table. She'd sketched the nineteenth floor on it. Hawkins pinned the four corners with books. "Okay, here it is," she said.

"Wow, this is great, Joey," gushed Peter, admiring the straight lines and perfect corners of the maze. Her cheeks turned pink. They were alone at Peter's kitchen table.

"Here are the four laundry chutes." She gestured to four faint circles on the inner walls. "And these marks here are the security cameras. I drew arrows to indicate the direction they face."

"The cameras don't vacillate," interjected Hawkins.

"What's that mean?" asked Peter.

"You know, twist back and forth. I guess what I mean is, they don't swivel or rotate."

"Whatever," grumbled Joey. "Use smaller words."

Peter pulled thoughtfully at his lip, examining the map, his eyes darting from the laundry chutes to the cameras. "Here," he said, jamming a finger at the northern most chute. "This is where we'll strike. There aren't enough cameras to watch the entire floor, which we already knew. And this laundry hatch isn't monitored."

"Tell us the plan," said Joey. "We don't know what we're doing."

"Okay, but first, what about the guard?"

"It was Keith," replied Hawkins. "You know, the little person? He was walking in circles around the whole floor, glaring at everyone. He made a circuit every six and a half minutes."

"How'd you know how long it takes him?" asked Joey suspiciously.

"I timed him! Didn't you?"

"No, cause I'm not weird."

"Six minutes is plenty of time," said Peter.

"For what?"

"Six minutes is enough time to leave a message for the guard and escape. I'm going to paint the note onto the wall. With red paint," said Peter.

Joey's eyes almost popped out. "Paint the *wall*?"

Hawkins asked, "But how will you get in and out without the cameras spotting you? The guard will make it wicked difficult to blind out the camera."

"I'll climb out from the laundry chute, obviously."

They stared at him with blank expressions.

Peter asked, "What's wrong?"

"Are you trying to be funny?" Joey crossed her arms and sat back in her chair.

"Peter, my man, you lost your mind. How would you get into the chute in the first place?"

"I enter from a lower level. It's easy, I've done it before," replied Peter.

"Wha...who...WHY?" burst Joey.

Hawkins said, "Peter, the dumbwaiter shaft had wooden ladder rungs, kinda. It was *easy* to climb. But how you gonna climb up a laundry chute? It's a smooth drop, right?" said Hawkins.

"I dunno, I just kinda...scoot."

Joey threw her hands into the air. "Peter! WHAT are you talking about? You've always been an infuriating boy, but that's madness. You could fall nineteen floors!"

"I won't! And even if I do, there's always mountains of soft laundry below."

Hawkins asked, "You want us to go up the chute with you? Cause, I'm not so great with heights."

"No way, it's too dangerous."

"But you just said—"

"I need one of you in the Laundry, in case I need to drop supplies down the chute. Probably you, Joey, because they know you. And I need Hawkins to wait for me on the floor below, to let me know when the coast is clear so I can climb out."

Joey said critically, "I don't like it. You could get hurt."

"We're out of time, Joey! The final performance is on Friday. In case you haven't noticed, nothing we've done has driven them away. If there is some kind of mystic portal in the Caves, and if the terrorists get their hands on it...who knows what'll happen."

"Or if they get the sword," Hawkins reminded him. "Don't forget that one. I bet it's wicked awesome."

"Yeah, that's right," said Peter hastily, though he knew the sword was under his bed. Moreover, it was a rusty old piece of junk.

"Let's do it," exclaimed Hawkins. "I love New York and I want to bust the Red Masque."

Joey groaned.

Peter rubbed his hands together. "The circus usually rolls out before dinner. Let's go at seven. I'll enter the laundry chute on floor fourteen. Fewer butlers on that level. Joey, think you can find a can of spray paint?"

"Yes," she said reluctantly. "But you're definitely going to die."

"Hah! The Phantom feels no fear."

"You said you're not him," she pointed out.

"Errr, that's right. I'm not. I was joking," he said, though in truth he'd gotten carried away for a moment. He'd almost started to believe.

∾

THAT EVENING IN HIS BEDROOM, Peter dressed in sneakers, jeans, and his black turtleneck. The shirt was made from expensive material and he knew it wouldn't last long if he kept climbing laundry chutes and dumbwaiter shafts. So he pulled on the brown leather jacket for protection and he examined himself in the mirror.

Hawkins proclaimed, "Peter, that jacket is the coolest thing I've ever seen. You look like...like..."

"Like who?"

"I dunno. Someone awesome. Han Solo, maybe?" Hawkins screwed up his face in concentration.

"I thought he wore a vest."

"Yeah but he wears a coat in Empire Strikes Back. No!" Hawkins snapped his fingers. "You know who it is? Indiana Jones. That's his leather jacket."

"That movie's PG-13. Mom and Dad won't let me watch," admitted Peter.

"You're about to climb up a laundry chute to defeat an evil terrorist group, but you can't watch Indiana Jones yet," muttered Hawkins, shaking his head. "I don't get white people." He shoved a can of red spray paint into a pillow case and tied it to Peter's belt.

Fara fluttered nearby and she asked, "Are you taking Dyrnwyn?"

"No, it'll clang too much in the chute."

"The spray paint will clang? You think?" asked Hawkins.

Peter winced. "No, ummm...sorry, Hawkins. The can's fine in the pillow case, you're right."

"You need a mask," mused Fara.

"No, it gets too hot," protested Peter.

"What does?" asked Hawkins, confused.

"Ahhh...the mask. It's a heavy ski mask, and I get hot. Sorry, Hawkins, I'm talking to myself too much, huh."

"Then take this one," the faery girl suggested, landing on the box in his closet where Peter kept his old costumes.

He grabbed the black domino mask and turned it over. "This one? It's from a cheap Robin outfit. Doesn't cover my mouth."

"Who is Robin?" she asked.

"Batman's side-kick."

"A bat allied with a robin? That's an unusual partnership," she commented.

"Dude, I know who Robin is." Hawkins watched Peter funnily. "You're acting weird. And that mask is fine, but no one should see you anyway."

"Better safe than sorry, Peter," Fara told him.

"Fine," he grumbled, shoving it into his jacket pocket. Talking to two people at once was tricky.

While his parents watched television, the boys snuck from the apartment and stole up the service stairwell to the fourteenth floor. Hawkins checked to make sure the coast was clear. He whispered for Peter and the boys opened the laundry hatch.

"Holy smokes," whispered Hawkins, and his voice echoed inside the black shaft. "If you fall, you'll land in the Laundry going ninety miles an hour, Peter."

"How'd you know that?"

"Simple math. Way too fast for sheets to stop you. Gotta be careful, my man."

Peter checked his watch. Joey should be in place. He got his leg over the hatch and slid in. It was an extremely tight fit, much more cramped than the dumbwaiter climb. With his sneakers pressed into one wall of the chute, his back was pushed firmly into the opposite side. "Wish me luck."

"I'm too scared," said Hawkins. "I think I'll pray instead."

Peter gave him a half wave and inched upward into the

gloom. Hawkins closed the door, just as he had a few nights ago, and once again Peter was cast into total darkness. Fara was a soft ball of light hovering above him, but she intentionally stayed dim. During his last climb, he'd traveled eight floors in twenty minutes. Tonight's travel progressed much slower because he was squished and because he wanted to move as silently as possible. He counted the floors, going from fourteen to nineteen in thirty-five minutes. By the time he reached his destination his thighs were cramping and his calve muscles shook with exhaustion.

He paused to wait and catch his breath outside the nineteenth-floor hatch, the outline glowing with faint light. As he rested, he pushed open the hatch a quarter of an inch, enough for Fara to sneak out and keep watch.

Light suddenly blazed from the level above—someone was opening the laundry hatch on twenty. Peter held his breath. The hatch slammed closed, thank goodness, but he detected a strange whooshing sound. A bag of dirty laundry landed directly onto his upturned face with a heavy SPLAT. Someone had dropped the bag, unaware a boy was crouched inside the chute.

"OOOF!" he wheezed, nearly losing his footing. He sputtered and shoved the bag between his knees, pushing and prodding until it slid free and fell below him. "That was gross."

He detected a faint knocking on the hatch. He pushed it open and Fara zoomed in. "It's about TIME! I started knocking twenty seconds ago!"

"You weren't very loud."

"It's quite difficult! Now c'mon, you're just SITTING there! The guard walked past half a minute ago!"

Peter scrambled out, half jumping and half falling onto

the thickly carpeted hallway. The nineteenth floor smelled like flowers, and harp music played from the speakers.

"I'll stand guard!" She zoomed out of sight. He retrieved the can of red paint from his pillow case, shook it, and sprayed a message on the wall. He moved slowly to make it red and thick, and then he traced over each letter.

THIS IS YOUR LAST WARNING!
     BE GONE!
     -Phantom

"HURRY! HE'S RETURNING!" cried Fara, flying into view from around the corner.

"Already?"

"It's not Keith, it's a big guy who walks faster! The frightening one."

Peter yanked open the hatch and dove in head first. It was such a tight fit that he caught himself quickly with hard pressure on the walls, but the can of spray paint tumbled free. He heard it ricocheting far below. Joey would have a heart attack.

He righted himself and inched back to the hatch so he could eavesdrop, although he wasn't sure he would hear anything over his thundering heart.

Nevertheless, he heard a man gasp in the hallway.

"Impossible!" came a deep rumble. "It cannot be."

"This guy gives me the CREEPS," said Fara.

Peter pressed the hatch open a fraction of an inch and peered out.

The bald giant with a mustache was in the hallway, glaring at Peter's message. Peter's blood ran hot—he hated this guy. The man ran a thick finger through the paint. "Has to be a trick," the bald man grunted to himself. "The Phantom's been gone fifty years."

Instead of hastily retreating down the chute, Peter snapped his black mask into place across his face, and clenched his fists. His blood boiled.

"Peter? Shouldn't you retreat? Remember the plan," said Fara worriedly.

"The plan's changed."

In a fit of rage, the bald guy smacked the wall, smearing the message and flinging wet paint everywhere. "If he truly returned then he'll be destroyed again. I'll do it myself!" he snarled and stormed down the hallway.

Acting on some hidden reckless instinct, Peter shot upwards though the hatch, landing on the carpet with more grace and power than he would've thought possible. The bald man stiffened, detecting noise behind, but Peter had already leapt on him. In a flash Peter had the empty pillowcase wrapped around the man's face, and the two crashed to the floor.

"I WON'T be destroyed so easily," Peter growled. He was seething, blind to danger. The man tried to stand but Peter had him pinned, a position Peter could only hold for another second or two. The bald man was enormously strong. "This is your final warning!"

"PETER! Run!" screamed Fara.

The man twisted and swung a gigantic fist but Peter dashed away. Escaping down the laundry chute would take too long, and possibly he'd be trapped, so he bolted to the nearest stairwell.

Fara hovered above the door, shining brilliantly with energy and light. She looked like the sun!

Peter frantically contrived a plan. Instead of jumping

down the stairs, he raced upward. He sprinted to the twentieth floor and reached the roof just as echoes of pursuit reached his ears. The bald man howled with rage, and began thundering DOWNWARDS. Peter had guessed correctly, throwing the villain off his trail.

He whipped off the mask and shrugged out of the jacket, carrying it in his arms. As casually as possible, he strolled from the stairwell and into the chilly night air. If any swimmers at the pool noticed him, they showed no sign.

"Calm down, Peter," he whispered, willing his heart to resume a normal rhythm. "Calm down. He can't catch you now."

Fara hovered nearby. "What WAS that? You nearly got caught."

"I dunno, I just hate that guy."

"You HAVE to master your emotions! I used to scream that at Cypress but he couldn't understand."

"Did you hear that man? He practically admitted it. He's part of the Red Masque," said Peter.

"I heard, yes. Not much has changed in a hundred years. Except maybe the goons have swelled in proportions!"

Peter pressed the button calling for the service elevator. "How did you glow so brightly back there? You were almost blinding."

"It requires ENORMOUS energy to impart myself onto your world in a visible way. But I can do it in emergencies!"

Peter shivered all the way down, unwilling to slip back into his coat. Somewhere inside the Crown a very unhappy and dangerous man was looking for him, and the jacket might be a giveaway. He snuck past the Nook to his apartment, but Joey intercepted him in the hallway.

"Quick, gimme your jacket!" she whispered urgently. She

snatched it and ran inside her own apartment just as Manos came out from 201.

"Hey Dad," Peter said nonchalantly. "Where you going?"

"Where else?" Manos sighed. "The nineteenth floor of course. Guests are complaining of shouting and spray paint."

"Ugh. Crazy circus people," groaned Peter.

17

REVENGE OF THE PASTRIES

Manos shook Peter awake the following morning. "Morning, kid. I need your help."

"Mmmm?" Peter sat up and groggily rubbed his eyes. "Something broken?"

"I've got pancakes ready and after that we're going to the security office," replied Manos.

"What for? What's wrong?"

"The security guard called. He identified our prankster, caught on video last night. Mr. Conrad asked us to meet him in the video room in ten minutes."

"Oh." Peter's heart dropped into his stomach. "O-okay." He'd been spotted. Surely his family would be kicked out of the hotel for this stunt. He dressed numbly, careful not to step on Hawkins. They ate a silent breakfast, Peter barely able to breathe.

They walked to the main floor and knocked on the security office. Mr. Conrad opened the door and they shuffled inside the cramped room. "We meet again," said Mr. Conrad without a smile.

"At least this time no one stole a lion," offered Manos.

"I thought we should talk without Mr. Banks, the owner. He's been acting...peculiar, especially about the Circus of Doom," Mr. Conrad said. "We have video footage from last night and I want Peter to see it."

"S-sure." Peter was on the verge of panic.

The security guard said, "Lemme show you what I got." He reached over his large stomach and pressed buttons with a fat finger. "This is from last night. The nineteenth floor, around eight o'clock."

The screen showed a vacant hallway, nothing happening. All of a sudden, a bright light flared, causing the lens's contrast and focus to go wonky. Behind the bright flare, Peter saw movement. First a small figure darted past, and then a big one.

"See that?" the guard asked.

Manos said, "Yep. What happened?"

"I dunno really. We know someone spray painted the wall last night around this time. Then the camera glitches, you see, and two people run into the stairwell."

Relief flooded Peter. The camera *glitched?* That had to be him, fleeing from the bald man directly under the camera, so why couldn't he be seen? A coincidence?

No! It was Fara. He remembered. She had been hovering above the doorway. Blazing like the sun, distracting the camera and preventing his identification.

"Pretty impressive, huh?" whispered Fara into his ear, causing him to jump. When had she arrived? "I'm more than just an outrageously gorgeous face. You're welcome, Peter. I saved your bacon."

"But, lookie here," the guard continued, freezing the video. "It's the best image we got."

Peter's face was frozen on screen. If he didn't know beforehand, he would never guess it was himself. The focus was wrong and the flare too bright. But clearly visible was a mask and a jacket.

Mr. Conrad gawked. "You know who that looks like?"

"Heck yeah I do." The guard chuckled. "Looks like the Phantom of New York, that's who it looks like."

Manos peered more closely at the screen and said, "Huh. Kinda does."

Peter tried not to grin. Not even his own father recognized him.

"There's another dude," said the guard. "Running after the Phantom, but I can't get a good image of him."

Mr. Conrad looked a little woozy and he held onto the chair for support. "Surely that's not...the Phantom's not even real.

"Looks real to me."

"Didn't you say you had two videos to show us? And that Peter needed to be here?" said Mr. Conrad.

"Lemme show you the other video." The guard punched a few more buttons. "Same floor, nineteen. But this video is from the middle of the night, maybe three o'clock."

The screen switched to a different hallway. A figure tiptoed into view, and Peter nearly groaned. It was Dot, dressed in a black cape and mask. Her blonde hair was held back by the mask and the white sunglasses she'd forgotten to remove. She inexpertly tried carving something into a door using the dull tip of her sword. Dot evidently heard a noise because she jumped and ran off.

"I checked the door," remarked the guard. "No damage done. Girl don't know how to use that thing."

"That's not the same person," said Mr. Conrad. "In the previous video, the Phantom had brown hair. This is a young woman with blonde hair. Wearing a cape."

"I hate to say 'I told you so,' Peter," chirped Fara musically from her perch on his shoulder. "But a Phantom she is NOT."

"You right, Mr. Conrad," said the guard. "Different people. My guess? She's a copycat. Trying to mimic the real thing."

"The *real* thing?" Mr. Conrad rubbed his bald head irritably.

"You know, the ghost! The one Ms. Drake wrote about, haunting the circus. Maybe that's why the video went weird, you know, cause the real Phantom's a ghost."

Mr. Conrad looked woozy again.

Peter grinned. This whole thing felt ludicrous.

Manos asked, "So why'd you call Peter?"

"I seen Peter talking with this girl a couple times." The guard tapped the screen. "Helping her and her grandpa carry luggage and stuff. Thought maybe he could identify her. You know? Make sure we got the right girl before we call the cops."

"Don't call the police!" said Peter instinctively. "We don't know for sure who that is."

"I dunno, Peter," the guard said, pointing at the frozen Dot. "Looks an awful lot like that girl on the tenth floor. I tried to find her on video afterward, see which room she went to, but she was smart enough to stay hidden."

"Maybe," said Peter cautiously. "It might be her. But...I can't be sure."

"What about the other dude? The one with dark hair and the jacket."

"The Phantom? I've never met him before," said Peter. "I don't know who he is."

Fara snickered happily.

"That's NOT the Phantom!" Mr. Conrad wiped his forehead with a handkerchief. "He doesn't exist! This small room is too hot! I'm glad we didn't include the owner. I think it's better if I handle this myself."

"What will you do?" asked Peter.

"I believe that's Ollie Franklin's granddaughter. He's a very nice man. Seems reasonable. I'll show them the video and insist there be no more shenanigans. The Crown has grown too wild without pretend vigilantes causing more trouble."

Peter winced. He was a pretend vigilante causing trouble.

"Let me know if I can help," offered Manos.

Mr. Conrad gave them a weak smile. "Thank you for coming down. Hopefully this is the last time you'll be summoned to the video room."

Out of curiosity, Peter asked the guard, "Are you going to the circus Friday night?"

"Oh yeah. We all going. Mr. Banks even got me two seats, so I can spread out."

"Every employee will be there, even the security team," responded Mr. Conrad with a frustrated roll of his eyes. "By order of our owner. The Crown will be so empty that I'm locking the front doors for two hours—a first in the history of the hotel."

THURSDAY AFTERNOON, the three friends sat glumly in the Nook, a wealth of pastries piled uneaten on the table between them. They had no appetite— they had failed. Tomorrow the hotel would empty for the circus's final performance, and the Red Masque was going to tear apart the Caves and all of the Crown with no one to stop them. Both Peter and Joey had warned their parents, and each had begged permission to skip the performance to no avail. Even Fara looked stumped, sitting crosslegged on a raspberry cupcake.

"We could call the police?" suggested Hawkins. "From Barclays?"

Joey said, "They wouldn't believe us. What would we say? 'Hey police, we're at Barclays but we're positive something bad is happening at the Crown, even though we can't see it and we have no proof'?"

Peter drummed his fingers on the table, deep in thought. Grover Ivory, watching from a nearby chair, snorted with laughter. "Lookit Peter, banging on the table like a monkey! Maybe I should get him a banana."

Hawkins muttered, "One of these days I'm going to throw that skinny kid outside and let him sizzle."

The golden elevator dinged and out walked Caroline Crawford. "Hello Peter Constantine!" she said brightly. "And Joey and Hawkins."

Peter stood and pulled out a chair for her.

Grover gawked. "Caroline! What are *you* doing down here?"

"I came to see my friends."

"You're friends with PETER?" gasped Grover. "But...but..."

"But what, Grover?"

"But he doesn't shower. Look at that hair, it's like he cuts it in the kitchen blender," cried Grover, waving emphatically.

Peter glared. "I shower!"

"I like his hair very much. If you can't be kind then you should leave," Caroline told him primly, and she sat at the table. With a huff, Grover faced the other way, crossing his arms. Caroline told the crew, "I haven't seen you three in weeks. You're never at the Park anymore. And Hawkins, do you still attend Trinity?"

"Yeah." He gave her an embarrassed shrug, fiddling with his cap. "We've been too busy, I guess. Right, Peter?"

Peter nodded. "There's a lot going on. Sorry, I've been preoccupied."

"I wish sometimes you'd include me," she said, turning a little pink in her cheeks. "Isn't that what friends do? It gets dull on the fourteenth floor, all alone. You could do your homework in my kitchen."

"You'd let us in?" asked Joey in bewilderment. "Just to... hang out?"

"Certainly. It'd be great fun."

Fara chirped from her spot on a cupcake, "I advise you to include Caroline, Peter. I perceive that she's got a good heart."

Caroline's attention was drawn to the mountain of pastries on the table.

Joey, embarrassed, said, "We're not going to eat all this, so you know. The Windsor had a surplus. Took me two trips to carry it all."

Fara gestured towards Caroline. "Another reason you should include her, Peter? She's ALMOST as fabulous as me, your favorite faery girl."

"Did you hear that?" asked Caroline, and she placed her hand on Peter's arm. "It sounds like...music."

Peter's eyes widened, darting from Fara and back.

"Hear what?" asked Joey. She looked at Hawkins. "Did you hear something?"

"Maybe it's Grover's breathing."

Caroline reached out her hand towards the cupcake, waving her fingers. "I thought I saw...and...it sounds like chimes. Do you hear it too, Peter?"

"Oh my HEAVENS," cried Fara, floating upwards. "PETER! She sees me!"

Caroline's pressure on Peter's arm increased. "Tell me you hear that."

"Uhhh," said Peter, frozen with indecision.

Fara rocketed upwards and zoomed around the room. "TWO people see me! What are the odds? Astronomical, I can tell you, dearest Peter! You and Caroline Crawford are MADE for one another, very star-crossed lovers and all that. How DELIGHTFUL!"

"I don't see it anymore." Caroline sounded a bit sheepish. "Sorry, ignore me. Must be my imagination." But she kept squinting at the pastries.

To change the subject, Peter asked, "Caroline, if we reveal what we've been doing, do you promise not to tell?"

"Cross my heart." Her hand was still on Peter's arm.

Hawkins leaned forward, conspiratorially. "Gotta whisper, so Grover don't hear. We think the Red Masque is in the hotel."

"Oh absolutely," said Caroline at once, nodding. "A portion of the Circus of Doom is acting extremely suspicious."

Peter was stunned. "I thought we'd have to convince you."

Caroline continued, "My father thinks so too. But he highly suspects everyone, especially the Snyders."

"I wouldn't be shocked, those twits," whispered Joey. "Atticus irks me to no end."

"Did you know it was Atticus's father who demanded Mr. Banks let the circus stay here? That's a piece of juicy gossip we only heard recently," said Caroline. "Mr. Banks has wanted to evict them but his most powerful residents, the Snyders, won't let him."

"That makes SO much sense!" said Peter. "I always wondered about that family."

Hawkins, still bent over the table partially to whisper and partially because he liked the way Caroline smelled, said, "We think the Red Masque is searching for something, like a secret treasure. And tomorrow night while we're at the performance they'll bring in extra help and find it. It won't matter how much noise they make or how much damage they do, because no one will hear them."

Joey contributed, "The Red Masque enters through underground tunnels. Very clever, you ask me."

"That makes perfect sense," said Caroline. "What should we do?"

"Our parents don't believe us," admitted Peter. "They're forcing us to attend the circus."

"What would you do if you stayed?" she asked.

"Keep watch and call the police the instant we see trouble. Otherwise the Crown will be empty and they'll have several hours to search."

"I have a solution," Caroline offered, finally letting go of Peter and folding her hands nervously on the table. "But it would involve lying, which I don't enjoy."

"I'm all ears," said Peter.

"Ask your parents if you can ride with my family and sit with us at the performance. We were given spectacular box seats. That way, your parents will *think* you're at Barclays, but you'll really be here, waiting for the police."

Joey gasped. Hawkins eyes grew round, and he slowly nodded.

"That's brilliant, Caroline!" said Peter. "And I bet it'll work."

"Gorgeous AND intelligent, just like Joey and myself,"

Fara remarked from his shoulder, near his ear. "You're a lucky rogue, Peter."

Caroline's attention snapped onto Peter's shoulder and she examined him suspiciously. Fara clamped a hand over her mouth.

Grover startled them all, speaking loudly from just beyond Caroline. "I didn't hear *all* that, but what I heard is *highly* suspicious! You jerks are about to cause mischief, and get my precious Josephine into trouble."

"Grover," groaned Joey. "Go upstairs."

Grover made a defiant 'hmpf' noise. "Not until you dweebs explain what's going on. But not you, Peter. You don't talk; I imagine your breath reeks of old hamburger."

The golden elevators dinged, and the group was surprised to see Bruno the knife-thrower, Adolfo the strongman, and Shaman the magician step out. Bruno had knives tucked into his belt, while Shaman moved like gliding on a cloud. The strongman had to duck his head to exit the elevator.

"Is boy! Peter! We must talk," roared Bruno with a toothy smile barely visible under his beard.

"*No*, you bushy impaler, you mustn't." Shaman cut his narrow eyes toward Peter. "You must get back on the elevator with me, Bruno."

"Oh, take hike, wizard! Peter is good boy. Bruno say he will talk to Peter and so he does," said Bruno.

Adolfo frowned unhappily.

Peter got the impression the group of three performers had been arguing for quite a while.

"What's going on, Bruno?" asked Peter nervously.

They approached Peter's table. Bruno slammed an object onto the surface, causing the mountain of assorted pastries to quake. Peter and his friends scooted backward, worried it might be a snake or worse. But it wasn't a snake—on the table lay a shiny silver throwing knife.

"Is gift! For Peter," said Bruno, beaming. "Boy is good student."

"Of course he is," muttered Joey under her breath.

"Wow, oh my gosh," said Peter excitedly. He plucked it from the table and inspected the glinting blade. His name had been etched into the side. "It's got my name on it."

"Peter will become great impalement artist!"

"Thanks so much, Bruno."

"Now," said Shaman, seething and pulling Bruno towards the elevators. "Shall we go, then?"

Adolfo nodded, emphatic and silent.

"No! Will talk to boy," growled Bruno.

"It's *not* his business, you hairy imbecile."

From Peter's side, Caroline Crawford asked, "What's not his business?"

"Peter, you talk to ghost!" blurted Bruno. "Talk to ghost, keep us safe!"

Peter said, "Huh? I don't get it."

"Big surprise," muttered Grover from beyond the squishy chair. He was hiding and peering fearfully at Adolfo.

Shaman, his face hidden inside the purple robes, addressed the friends icily. "Bruno here believes the nonsense about the Crown's haunting. Pay him no attention, my little dimwits."

"Bruno hears rumor; Peter talks to Phantom ghost," said the bearded man. "You help circus before he comes back. Bruno hate ghosts!"

"You want me to make the ghost leave you alone?" asked Peter.

Hawkins eyes bulged with the effort of suppressing laughter.

"Circus is haunted!" cried Bruno.

Adolfo gave a white-faced nod before catching himself. Apparently the giant was afraid of ghosts too.

"Bruno, you'd be wise to shut your mouth," snapped Shaman, "before someone else has to do it for you."

"I can't tell the Phantom to stop," said Peter, catching all their attention. "If the Phantom wants you to leave, you should go."

Bruno was on the cusp of bolting for the nearest train out of town. He and Adolfo clutched each other by the arm.

"And what does a little boy like you know about the Phantom?" asked Shaman suspiciously.

"I know the Phantom was real. I know he promised to return. And I know he hates the Red Masque," said Peter, and Shaman flinched.

"But Phantom haunts *us*," Bruno pointed out. "We aren't Red Masque! We are circus only!"

Caroline glared at Shaman. "Maybe not all of you."

Shaman pushed thick folds of his sleeves away from his hands, like clearing room for a spell. "You little pipsqueaks are meddling with dangerous forces far beyond your imagination. Perhaps a demonstration of power would quiet you down."

Joey whispered, "If he starts a fire, I'm going for the extinguisher under the sink."

"I'll protect you, my love!" called Grover, now on all-fours behind the chair, only his eyes visible.

"No magic!" called Bruno. "Bruno just wants ghost gone."

A ding came from the elevator bank. Lino Kang and his son Marcellus strolled into view. Lino frowned, his black-lined eyes taking in the scene. The circus master growled, "I, Lino Kang, wondered where my three star performers had gone, and *here* I find them. Mingling with scullions when they *should* be preparing for tonight's performance!"

"Scullions?" scoffed Hawkins.

"I am Lino Kang! And I demand to know what you little children are doing, distracting the Circus of Doom!"

Marcellus gave Peter a wave, looking humiliated by his father's antics, as usual.

"Distracting?" Caroline was unimpressed by Lino. "They came *here*."

"Silence! You do not speak to Lino Kang in such a way!" he roared.

Peter stiffened.

"Ring Master, these children are frightening Bruno with ghost stories," simpered Shaman, bowing his head. "They claim to have knowledge of the Phantom."

"Is that so?" asked Lino darkly.

"No we don't!" shouted Hawkins. "All Peter said was that the Phantom hates the Red Masque, and everyone knows that!"

"You children will come with me," said Lino in a soft, dangerous voice. "And we'll speak with the Crown's owner about your knowledge of the Phantom hoax."

"We're not going anywhere." Caroline crossed her arms and gave an imperial tilt to her chin. "And you're no longer welcome on this level."

"Will you come willingly?" asked Lino. "Or will you be dragged?"

Peter glared at him. "We're staying."

"Adolfo!" said Lino Kang. "Grab them."

Marcellus tugged Lino's shirt. "Father, you should not do this."

Adolfo stepped forward.

Peter set himself between the strongman and Caroline. "Not a chance."

Then something happened. Something no one expected.

A chocolate-frosted cupcake streaked over their heads and detonated against Lino Kang's face with a gooey SMACK. The ring master gasped in surprise, inhaling a sizable chunk of cake. He doubled over, coughing.

Crazy old Mr. Hayes had materialized unnoticed behind them. He stood at the table full of pastries like a man ready to wage war. He cried, "Alexia, DUCK!"

Peter breathed, "Uh oh."

Delicious baked missiles launched across the room, a shocking barrage of pastry violence. Joey dove for cover. Hawkins, who'd never experienced a bombing from Mr. Hayes, received a lemon tart up his nose so forcefully his sinuses clogged. Peter tossed Caroline on the couch and draped himself protectively over her against the rain of sugar.

Shaman raised his hand like a shield, but a doughnut frisbee'd straight down his sleeve, splattering against his armpit. A second doughnut, a Boston creme, exploded thickly on his forehead.

Chocolate bonbons shattered like doughy firecrackers against Adolfo, chasing him from the room, and Bruno was caked with so much vanilla icing he looked like Santa.

Butlers poured into the room, ready to haul Mr. Hayes to the elevators, but they were forced to withdraw behind the kitchen counter under a barrage of frosting.

"Who IS this crazy bag of bones!" cried Grover, until an extra large strawberry cupcake connected so solidly with his face that he was knocked over backwards. "I'm allergic!"

"I am Lino Kang!" the ring master roared. "And you will stop—"

SMACK—a chocolate eruption coated his face.

Mr. Hayes hadn't emptied half his ammo yet. And so Lino King signaled for a retreat, the circus darting for the elevator under a hail of cookies.

"And don't come back!" cackled Mr. Hayes, his arm pumping out a final salvo.

The elevator dinged and they were gone.

Peter and Caroline slowly opened their eyes and peered around the Nook. It looked like a Mickey Mouse birthday party massacre.

Hawkins licked his fingers behind a chair. He said, "The old guy's got remarkable aim. Over ninety percent accuracy, I'd say."

Joey stared in disbelief at the mess. "I'm not so sure. He even got it on the *ceiling*."

Grover Ivory lay flat, looking like a casualty of war. A cupcake was lodged in his ear. He whined, "My eyes are going to swell shut."

Mr. Hayes grinned triumphantly at the advancing butlers. "Oh baby, I'm in trouble now. But at least Alexia is safe!"

THAT NIGHT, after spending two hours scrubbing frosting from the Nook, Peter lay in bed, listening to Hawkins snore. Caroline herself had asked Peter's parents if he could ride with her family to the circus. She'd fretted over the deceit, but ultimately decided the good outweighed the bad.

Peter's parents and Joey's parents had agreed, providing the perfect cover for the children to slip away unnoticed tomorrow night and hide inside the empty Crown, ready to call the police if and when the Red Masque appeared in force.

The plan seemed simple. Peter's friends would never be in harm's way and the Crown would be saved. And yet... plans seemed to have a way of going awry. Peter stared at the wall late into the night, his hand snaked below the bed and toying with the hilt of Dyrnwyn. The Phantom's sword, sitting dormant and useless.

Peter wished the real Phantom would appear. And soon. This had grown too big for him.

PART III

It's been said that courage is not the absence of fear, but rather the assessment that something else is more important than fear. I would add, sometimes courage is simply lionhearted determination. And love.

-Darci Drake
    New York Times

18

FRIDAY THE THIRTEENTH

Peter walked out of the bathroom, having fixed his hair with gel in the mirror. Hawkins was sitting on the bed, wearing formal clothes borrowed from the Laundry's lost-and-found. He said, "Peter, your mom's wearing that dress again."

Peter tucked in his black turtleneck. "Huh?"

"I think she's the prettiest woman I ever met."

"What! No she's not, she's my *mom*," Peter replied, nearly choking.

"I'm just saying—"

"Yeah, well don't. Cause it's super weird."

Hawkins looked down at the pageboy cap in his hands with a half grin. "Thought you'd be happy, my man. Got no idea what my mom looks like these days."

Funny, Peter thought, how he could so easily forget about Hawkin's past. Or rather, not funny. He placed his hand on Hawkins's shoulder. "Until you decide to find your birth mother, my mom is your mom. But that makes it even grosser."

"You're my best friend, Jumping Jack Peter. But that ain't my mom. Mine was nasty and kinda old."

"How old?"

"Who knows."

"It's time to go," said Peter. "We'll talk about finding your mom later. Okay?"

In the kitchen, Manos was adjusting his black tie in the microwave's reflection. He gave each boy a solid whack on the shoulder. "You rascals clean up well. I know you'll behave for the Crawfords."

Peter gulped guiltily.

Jovanna emerged from he bedroom, attaching sparkly earrings. "You gentlemen look so handsome," she said, and she stopped herself from ruffling Peter's hair. "You'll be safe, yes? You'll stay close to Caroline's parents?"

"Yes ma'am," said Hawkins. "Anything you say."

"We'll be safe," said Peter.

I hope.

"Okay boys, have a good time. See you tonight." Manos opened the door for them.

Joey waited for them in the hallway. To complete her disguise, she wore a red dress. "Took you two long enough," she snapped nervously.

"Joey's in a dress," marveled Hawkins. "And lookin' fly, too! Wonders never cease."

"I hate it. So unpractical." She shifted uncomfortably.

"A chiffon dress," noted Peter, recalling his lessons with Ms. Ernestine Parker. "With a princess neckline. Very classy."

Hawkins scowled at Peter like he'd spoken another language.

Joey muttered, "It's so bizarre you know that and I don't. And stop looking at me that way. Both of you."

Previously they'd decided that making an appearance in the Lobby would help cement their ruse. So, indulging themselves because of their formal attire, they rode the golden elevator to the Lobby. Guests and residents wearing tuxedos and silvery dresses waited in lines at the doors as taxis and Uber drivers shuttled them away from the Crown. The large reception area hummed with excitement.

"The piano's quiet," noted Peter. "The pianist must be going too."

"Look at zee children!" called Marlow Blodgett, approaching with a wide smile. He had dressed in his customary stylish jeans and fancy white shirt, looking flashy instead of formal. "Peter, you are excited for zee show, yes?"

"Yes sir, Mr. Blodgett," replied Peter, shaking Marlowe's hand. He couldn't be sure, but he thought Marlowe's hand might be trembling. "Very excited."

"Mr. Blodgett, you look nervous," said Joey. "Do you always get anxious before a show?"

"Not usually, Miss Joey. But zis is a big night, an important night! I do not perform but I want everyzing to be perfect."

"I'm sure it'll be great," Peter assured him.

"Let us hope so. Enjoy!" Marlowe turned and marched in the other direction.

"There's Leo." Hawkins waved but Leo didn't notice—he was wearing his virtual reality visor, his mother leading him by the hand.

Peter noted, "I suppose his parents got over their fear of circus diseases."

"D'you think enough people have seen us yet?"

"Yes. One too many, in fact," said Joey dryly. "Here comes Grover. Come on, let's hurry."

Before Grover could reach them and hurl insults at Peter, the three friends raced down the stairs, Joey doing her best in the uncomfortable shoes. "This way," whispered

Peter. He led them to a supply closet near the Laundry. He shoved Cypress's key into the lock and it clicked open. They piled inside and Peter pulled the door closed.

Hawkins turned on the small overhead light. The room smelled of lemon polish and moldy mops. "Oh man, this is really happening, isn't it. We're doing this. Did you know it's Friday the 13th? How appropriate is that?"

Joey was taking deep breaths, staring at the low ceiling. "It's not too late, you know," she said in a shaky voice. "We could still attend the performance. It's really not fair for the safety of the Crown to rest on three thirteen-year-olds."

Peter nodded. "Maybe you should go. I hate the idea of you getting in trouble."

"But you're staying here. Right?"

"I'm staying. It's not fair, but who says life is fair?"

Joey searched Peter's eyes a moment and seemed to find some strength from his determination. She snapped a nod. "Then I'm staying too. We stick together."

Hawkins checked his watch. "Circus starts in an hour. The Crown should be empty before long. We're like the army in that big trojan horse, waiting to spring our trap."

The hour passed agonizingly slowly. Hawkins called out the time every thirty seconds until they demanded he stop. Joey discovered an unsecured wooden shelf, so she inspected all the screws in the closet, tightening any that were loose. Peter wondered where Fara had flown off to.

After an eternity, it was eight o'clock.

As quietly as terrified mice, they crept from the closet and stole upstairs to the second-floor Nook. No televisions murmured from apartments, and no butlers talked in the kitchen. Their parents had gone and so had everyone else, all enjoying the final performance by the Circus of Doom. The Crown felt empty.

"So quiet," whispered Joey.

"Too quiet," said Hawkins. "I hate it. I'm glad this place isn't haunted anymore."

"It *is* haunted," said Peter with conviction. "But we're the ghosts. C'mon, I bet the Red Masque is already searching."

No matter how softly they moved, their footsteps echoed. Were they always this loud? Peter couldn't remember them sounding like such a herd of buffalo in the past. They reached the lowest level of the stairwell, emerging into the garage, and hid behind a gleaming blue Lexus SUV near the door.

The circus had turned off most of the lights, casting the garage into a dim gloom. Peering through the darkness, Peter detected the doors to the Caves were wide open, as he knew they would be. He pointed and whispered, "They're here."

"Can we call the police now?" asked Joey.

"And tell them what? We spotted an open door? We can't call until we see the Red Masque."

Hawkins tugged at his sleeve. "Look! It's Aggy."

Sure enough, the elephant stood contentedly near the door, munching on hay. Opposite him, and mostly hidden by heavy curtains, two enormous bears prowled restlessly inside their big steel cage. Judging by the bears' pacing, they were agitated.

Joey said, "Those poor animals. Should we give them food?"

"Or maybe ride Aggy?" asked Hawkins.

Peter clamped a hand around each of their mouths. He'd spotted movement—two figures hurried down the garage ramp from upper levels. Joey and Hawkins followed his gaze and froze. The darkness was too complete to make out details yet, but soon they heard footsteps attached to voices.

"...maybe not a good idea," said the first voice.

"What's the problem, chum? You said they were gone. This should be fun," said the second.

"What if we get in trouble?"

"Who cares? Your father can take care of everything."

The first voice said softly, "It's him I'm worried about."

"Isn't this what you wanted, Atticus? To be one of us? To be *somebody*? Then shut up. This'll be fierce."

The two figures snapped into focus—it was Atticus Snyder and his friend Capulet, the bully from the Ritz Carlton Hotel.

"What are those jerks doing here?" wondered Hawkins in a hush. "Told ya so, the Ritz kids are the worst."

The boys stopped at the bear cage and pushed back one of the heavy curtains. Aggy the elephant stood thirty feet away, but he still scooted backwards nervously, until the tether pulled tight.

"Get a load of these disgusting fleabags," cackled the taller handsome boy.

Atticus shuffled his feet, darting glances over his shoulder. "C'mon, Capulet, let's go. I don't like this."

"Pipe down, kid. Let me have my jollies." He picked up something from the pavement and chucked it at the bears. Peter heard a hard SMACK and the bear growled unhappily.

"Those jerks," said Joey from their hiding spot. "We should do something."

"Knock it off, Capulet," Atticus whined to his friend.

The Ritz kid didn't listen. He threw something else, further enraging the bears. This was the LAST thing Peter needed to deal with.

Hawkins whispered, "What do we do?"

Peter sighed. "I'll deal with this. You two stay here."

He started to walk around the shiny SUV, but Fara came zooming into view, bursting like fireworks. "Down down DOWN!" she cried. "Get down!"

Peter gaped and held his hands up, like—huh?

"Duck behind the car, you DOLT!"

Peter reluctantly obeyed, muttering to Joey and Hawkins, "Think I heard something. Let's stay here a sec."

Very soon they detected footfalls in the stairwell. To their surprise, a security guard walked out, his hands on his belt. It was one of the guards Peter didn't know personally.

"See?" said Fara. "I saw him coming."

"Hey!" the guard shouted at the two boys near the cage. "What're you two punks doing?"

Peter was filled with sweet relief; a security guard had been left to watch the Crown. Of *course* Mr. Conrad wouldn't leave it completely empty! What a fool Peter'd been to assume otherwise. This was perfect—Peter could tell the security guard about the Caves and let him call the police.

The guard pushed back his blue cap and closed the distance to the bear cage. "I asked you two boys a question. What're you doing here?"

"Take a hike, mall cop," scoffed Capulet. "You're not needed."

"You boys are in a heap of trouble."

"I'm a Snyder," said Atticus defiantly, with arms crossed. "You can't touch me. Besides, we were just leaving."

"Oh no you ain't," retorted the guard.

"Stay PUT!" Fara told Peter, pushing against his forehead. "Trust me. All is NOT as it seems."

From their hiding spot, they watched the guard raise a radio to his mouth and speak into it. "Ahhhh, found a couple kids up here. One is the Snyder boy. Please advise. Over."

Capulet smirked. "Okay, officer. We've had our fun. We'll be on our way, sorry to bother."

The guard blocked their path. "You two shoulda gone to the circus. I'm afraid you'll regret this."

"Snyders don't go to the *circus*," scoffed Atticus. "My parents flew to France for the opera, and I'm saying with friends. Now step aside."

"Sorry, kiddo. You're staying with me, until the boss says otherwise."

Peter, Joey, and Hawkins shared a befuddled glance. The boss? What was going on?

A giant emerged from the Caves. It was the bald man, with the mustache and black eyes. Peter's muscles tensed.

The security guard boasted, "Found these two trouble-makers poking around! Might cause trouble for the Red Masque. What should we do with them?"

"The *Red Masque*?" squeaked Joey.

Hawkins seized Peter's arm. "The guard! He's a turncoat, with the syndicate!"

Peter nodded grimly. No wonder Fara had been frantic.

The bald man glared murder at the guard. "You *should* have sent them on their way, you imbecile. These are the brats who stole Tandra's cub. They only returned to pull another juvenile prank. Now, because of you, we have to keep them."

Two more men emerged from the Caves, each wearing a crimson mask. The masks were of a scary face—thick eyebrows and trim goatee, smiling hideously. The men towered threateningly over the two teenagers.

Even at a distance in the dim garage, it was obvious Capulet had gone white in the face. He stammered, "The Red M-Masque? Hey now, w-wait a sec, chums..."

"Bring them," ordered the big bald man. "And hurry. We

don't have all night." Atticus and Capulet shouted indignantly as they were picked up and hauled inside the Caves. Their voices echoed off the steel rafters and the bears growled restlessly.

Suddenly alone once again, Hawkins muttered, "Crazy what goes on in rich-people hotels."

"It's not *always* like this," countered Joey.

"Nothing's changed, really," said Peter. "We still need the police. C'mon, we have to hustle, for Atticus's sake."

Joey kicked off her shoes and tore after the boys. They charged up the stairs, through the Nook, and into Peter's apartment. Peter yanked the phone off the wall and dialed 9-1-1, for emergency response.

He listened—nothing happened.

He hung up and dialed again. But there was only silence.

"What is it?" Joey asked.

"The phone's dead."

"The Red Masque cut the phone lines," said Hawkins with a sage nod of his head. "Saw it in a movie once. I shoulda guessed ahead of time."

"Our plan isn't working," said Joey anxiously. "I hate it when plans don't work. What do we do?"

Peter suddenly felt insignificant, huddled with two thirteen-year-olds inside the tiny kitchen. Who had he been kidding, thinking this would work?

"We need help. So we'll go for the Lobby phones," he answered. "If they don't work, we run outside and start shouting."

It wasn't an adventurous plan, but probably the wisest. "I guess so," said Hawkins.

Fara dropped into Peter's view. "You MUST put on the leather jacket."

"Eh? Why?" he asked.

"I dunno, I'm just agreeing with you," replied Hawkins.

"Trust me, Peter. Put. On. The JACKET," ordered Fara.

Peter rolled his eyes and growled. "Okay, hang on." He bounded to his closet, fetched the leather jacket off the carpet, and shrugged into it. For no reason he could explain, he felt a little more ready to face the danger.

"And the sword," directed Fara. "And the mask."

"No."

"YES!"

"Why?" he shouted.

"Because I am ORDERING you to and I've been doing this a LONG time! Pick up your WEAPON!" Fara shouted back, bursting with sparkles at each syllable.

"I don't even know how to use it!"

"I witnessed your training! You're a NATURAL!"

At his bedroom door, Hawkins and Joey stood with mouths hanging open. "Peter, this is truly an awful time for you to lose your mind," Joey observed with a kind of dumbstruck expression.

"Ugh, it's not...I'm just...arguing with myself," Peter said, raking fingers through his black hair.

"Arguing about what?"

"About whether to take the sword and the mask."

"Of COURSE you should," blurted Hawkins in disbelief. "I didn't even know you *had* a sword!"

"You're the Phantom, Peter," said Joey with a confident nod. "And he wears a sword and mask."

"I'm NOT the Phantom," Peter replied in a near-shout. "And I don't think this is a good time to pretend!"

"Pick up your sword, Peter," said Hawkins. "It's time."

Fara crossed her arms and her ball of light radiated smugness.

"This is ridiculous," he grumbled. Reaching under his

bed, Peter retrieved Dyrnwyn and attached the sheath to his belt. "See? It's too big for me."

"No it's not. But it's kinda old," said Joey with a disappointed wrinkle to her nose. "Do you have a newer one?"

"Pay her no attention, Peter. Wait till Dyrnwyn comes ALIVE," Fara told him. "Then she'll see. Where's your mask?"

"My mask is in my pocket," he replied, storming out of his apartment and into the hall. "Now let's call the police and let the professionals handle this."

They walked quickly to the Nook, and had almost reached the stairs when Dot leapt from stairwell door and surprised them. Hawkins jumped and fell backwards over a chair.

Dot demanded, "What are you CHILDREN doing here?"

"I could ask you the same question," said Peter, recovering from the shock. Dot had dressed in a black cape, her tight white leather jacket, and her sunglasses. Between the two of them, he hoped he looked less ludicrous.

"A CAPE?" hooted Fara. "Who wears a cape these days? And that jacket is so small she can barely move!"

"Is that my sword?" demanded Dot. "Give it here."

"This isn't yours. I got my own."

"Yeah, well, I forgot mine. I need it." She held out her hand expectantly.

Peter hadn't wanted to bring Dyrnwyn in the first place, but bestowing it to Dot didn't seem wise. Then again, Fara had acted taken aback when the sword failed to come alive in his hand, so it probably wasn't meant for him anyway. He was torn.

Fara said sternly, "Do NOT give her that sword."

Hawkins whispered to Joey, "Who's the weird girl in the shades?"

"No idea."

"Peter, the sword," repeated Dot, snapping her fingers.

"Peter, NO."

"This is my moment of glory. My destiny. You can't steal it from me. I've been training for years," said the girl in white, her volume rising with a surge of importance.

"Listen to her," snorted Fara. "She thinks this is about HER. Dot's not being brave, she's being selfish. The Phantom is a SERVANT, not a motion picture star."

Peter asked Dot, "Where's your family?"

"The circus. Ollie couldn't resist."

That was too bad. Peter could use some advice from Rory. He said, "We were about to use the Lobby phones to call the police."

"You can't. There are guys in red masks searching it," she told them. "They're everywhere upstairs."

Hawkins cursed, a bad word Peter'd never even heard.

"The Red Masque is already in the Caves," said Peter. "Lots of guys. They kidnapped Atticus and another kid."

"Then my time has come," she responded solemnly. "The sword, please. And I'll save the innocent."

Making up his mind, Peter unclipped the weapon and shoved it into Dot's hands. It wasn't going to do him much good anyway.

"Peter, no," groaned Fara, Hawkins, and Joey in unison.

He kept his eyes on Dyrnwyn, hoping something magical might happen. But nothing did. Instead Dot tried clipping it onto her belt before remembering she wasn't wearing one.

"Okay, kids. You stay here," she ordered.

"No chance. I'm going," Peter said. "Joey, Hawkins, find an exit. Run outside and call for help."

Hawkins fetched a frying pan from under the Nook's

kitchen stove and waved it like a crazy cook. "We're with you, my man! Gonna bust some Red Masque heads."

"I can't babysit all three of you," growled Dot, though Peter thought she looked relieved.

"Peter, take back your weapon," said Fara through clenched teeth. "Sometimes I think you're TOO selfless. That blade is not meant for her!"

Peter rolled his eyes and jogged back down the stairs, forcing the others to follow. There was no point in waiting any longer. The garage was still empty, except for the restive animals. They stole to the Caves' entrance and peered inside.

"I'm going in," he told them, indicating the murky gloom. "We'll find Atticus and Capulet, release them, and then all run for the police. Understood?"

Hawkins nodded, bouncing the frying pan on his hand. "Good plan."

"Our plans never work," muttered Joey and one of the nearby bears coughed. This close, they stank of rotten fruit.

"Stand aside," said Dot, striding boldly through the doorway. "The Phantom will see us safely to the destination."

Fara snorted in disgust. "Says the girl who forgot her own sword."

Joey found a flashlight and clicked it on. The small rescue team proceeded slowly into the Caves, guided only by the small cone of light. Every noise was magnified tenfold.

"Peter, how far into the Caves did you travel?" whispered Dot. She slid out Dyrnwyn and held it straight forward, as though she hoped nearby villains would be accidentally impaled.

"All the way to the end, the back of the third floor. How about you?"

"Only this far," she replied.

"That *it*? You told me you searched the Caves the whole night."

"I searched near the door," she said defensively. "It was dark!"

Encountering no resistance on their winding trek through the dusty mannequins and old furniture, they eventually reached the stairwell. Peter leaned far over and peered below. "I hear them," he whispered. "Second floor."

Dot nodded but her lip had begun to tremble. "Sure, Parker, no sweat... Great, I'm glad we found them. I'm ready, you know? This is it...this is really it..."

"We'll all go together—" Peter said but Dot bolted without warning. She descended the stairs in two jumps, touched down on the second landing, got caught in her cape, and tripped.

The Red Masque had posted a guard—two men wearing crimson masks and gloves, standing hidden near the stairwell. Initially startled by the girl in white's sudden appearance, they cackled and picked her up. Dot was too stunned to resist.

"What's this?" asked the first henchman, giving Dot a good shake. "Could this be the little Phantom causing us so much trouble?"

The second henchman snickered. "What's she wearing sunglasses for? Don't she know it's dark? Got caught in her own cape, the dummy."

Like a jaguar, Peter dropped from above and landed on the first henchman, who staggered and collapsed. The man's head thunked hard on the concrete floor, knocking him completely senseless. Hawkins swung the frying pan like a baseball bat, WHANG, and connected with the second henchman's head. The man toppled onto the body of the first, and neither moved.

"Always wanted to do that!" Hawkins said with a wild grin.

"I hope they're alright." Joey prodded them with her toe. "Concussions are no laughing matter."

Hawkins teased, "What, we should politely asked them to lay down? Think that would work?"

"My sword, where's my sword?" Dot frantically crawled on all-fours in the dark. "I lost it, fighting off the Red Masque."

"You lost it when you tripped, you mean," muttered Hawkins.

Fara hovered nearby. "It's directly below me, but my lips are sealed. Dot's a disaster! If she was a boat she'd be the TITANIC."

Joey cast her light around. "I can't believe all this is below the Crown. I had no idea. I feel so small."

"The Red Masque is thorough," observed Peter. He pointed at the the maze of wooden boxes, most of which had been pried open. "I bet they're almost done with the second floor."

"Oh this is DREADFUL," moaned Fara, shooting upwards to the ceiling. "This is bad, Peter, very bad."

He wanted to ask what Fara was worried about, what the Caves held that should remain a secret, but he knew she wouldn't tell him. Especially now that he'd forfeited Dyrnwyn.

"Let's find Atticus and get out of here," said Peter.

"Ah HAH," Dot half cried and half whispered. "Found the sword. Everyone follow me." And off she marched, sword outstretched.

Soon they started encountering Red Masque search teams, groups of two or three men with flashlights busting open crates and rousting through boxes. They slipped around the search teams and carried on, though they were once again required to rescue Dot when she walked smack into a sentry. While she fumbled with her sword, Peter tackled the guard and Hawkins used his frying pan again.

"The Caves are way bigger than the Crown's basement," said Hawkins in amazement. "I estimate a hundred thousand square feet, at least! We could be under the Ritz by now. No wonder it's taking them forever to search the place."

They stopped briefly to listen as a subway car passed nearby, shaking the walls and sounding like a dragon.

Joey clicked off her light. "There, look ahead."

They came round a large stack of wooden crates and discovered the Red Masque's temporary headquarters. Powerful spotlights had been erected, surrounding a clearing, and men in the scary crimson masks were bringing a steady supply of boxes and junk for inspection. There stood the bald man, shaking his head in frustration. "No, no, no," he barked. "We're looking for something larger, do you hear? Bigger! I'll know it when I see it."

Concealed in the darkness, the rescuers huddled up. "There's a lot of goons," whispered Hawkins.

Peter pointed to the side—Atticus and Capulet were sitting in the shadows, their hands and feet bound, and their mouths gagged. "Here's the plan. I'm going to confront the bald man, as a distraction," said Peter. "You three rescue Atticus and his friend. As soon as you're clear, we race for the exit. We can out run these fat grownups, right?"

Fara's light pulsated like a heartbeat. "I'm EXTREMELY anxious about that plan!"

"No, *I'll* be the distraction," said Dot in a wavering voice.

Peter had to give her credit—she was offering to do the dangerous work despite her obvious fear. "You rescue your friends."

"Dot, maybe it's time you quit arguing—"

"That's the Judge," said Dot. She took off her sunglasses to clean them and her eyes were huge. "The bald man. I'd recognize my old nemesis anywhere."

"How do you know?" asked Peter.

"Yeah, how do you know?" asked Fara curiously. Dot had told Peter previously she'd never heard of the Judge.

"What's the Judge?" asked Joey.

"Beats me. What's Dot?" asked Hawkins. "That her name? Kinda weird, right?"

"*That's* the Judge," said Dot, replacing her glasses with trembling fingers and pointing with the sword at the big man. "The leader of the Red Masque."

"But...you saw him at the Windsor Restaurant. You trailed him, remember? Did you know then?" asked Peter. "Or are you just pretending you know?"

She stared at Peter and gulped. "I'm going to meet my destiny. Goodbye, my friend."

"Dot, stop being weird!"

"Save your friends. And *run*." She took a deep breath and walked towards the bald man.

19

"I AM HIM."

Peter, Hawkins, and Joey stole through the shadows, careful to avoid tripping over old junk. The two captives, Atticus and Capulet, had been forgotten by their captors. Peter slid to a stop next to Atticus, who gasped and made a soft moaning sound. Not only had they been gagged, they were blinded with old rags tied around their eyes.

"Shush," Peter said. "We're here to help."

Fara landed on Peter's shoulder. "Dot's crazy as a loon but she's determined, I'll give her that. Look at her go!"

Dot strode into the light, raised the sword over her head and called in a shaky voice, "It is I...errr, I mean...It's me!"

The bald man raised up from his inspection of an old broken dresser. He gave a sinister half-grin. "It is you? Who is you, blondie?"

"I am...the Phantom of New York!"

The dozen men in scarlet masks chuckled. Dot glared furiously at them.

"You're not the Phantom I met upstairs in the hall," said the bald man darkly. "How many little Phantoms are there?"

"There's only me. And I know who you are...Judge," said Dot.

The bald man's eyebrows raised, creating a crease along his forehead. "Not many people remember that name. Where'd you learn it?"

"I come from a long line of Phantoms, Judge. And today you've met your match!"

Fara's ball of light hummed thoughtfully. "Could that be him? The Judge? He's certainly frightening enough."

Dot was directing the attention of every Red Masque henchman towards herself, so Hawkins and Joey worked unseen on the binding around Atticus's feet. Joey grumbled, "The knots are too tight!"

Peter removed the blinders from Atticus's face and pulled out the gag. "Atticus, as soon as we get you free, you gotta run. Okay?"

"You filthy garbage boy, hurry up!" he whispered, purple with panic. "What's wrong with you, baker girl? Move those fat little fingers!"

Peter rolled his eyes and shoved the gag back in. Atticus raged quietly. Hawkins told her, "Don't listen, girl, your fingers are fine."

Peter moved to Capulet and pulled on the bindings around his ankles, but Joey was right—the knots were stuck.

The bald man was walking towards Dot. He stared curiously at rusty weapon in her hand. "Where'd you get that sword, blonde little Phantom?"

"None of your business," she yelped, backing up. She couldn't go far, however, because the Red Masque had made a complete ring around her.

"Oh no," whimpered Fara. "This is the WORST case scenario. What have I done!"

"Your time here is through, Judge!" cried Dot, and she

launched herself at the giant man. He caught her hand easily, pried back her fingers, and removed Dyrnwyn. He tossed her to the side, like he would a pillow.

"Could this be..." He walked to one of the powerful lights and inspected the sword. First the cracked leather hilt, and then the notched blade. "This is *it!* See how the metal is dark? I feel the power. You brought me Dyrnwyn, little blonde Phantom. I've been searching for years and you...just walked in and handed it over."

Dot sat on the floor, watching with horrified eyes. She'd lost her sunglasses.

The bald man swished the sword twice. It looked like a large knife in his thick fist. "A pity. Left in the care of imbeciles, Dyrnwyn's life has been spent. But perhaps it's not to late," he growled to himself.

"Durr-what?" asked Dot weakly from the floor.

The bald man crouched next to her. With one hand, he held the sword; with the other, he snatched off his mustache. It was a fake. Then he placed his hand flat on the crown of his head and pulled. Peter felt sick, watching his scalp slide back. But it wasn't his scalp, yet another fake. His black fair fell into place. "Guess I don't need the disguise anymore, huh, little blonde Phantom."

Peter's eyes snapped open.

He was staring at The Evil Treasure Hunter. HOW could he never have noticed? The black eyes, the jaw that could chew rocks...

"Huh," said Fara, fluttering near Peter. "How unexpected. His grew hair REALLY fast."

Peter's head swam. "It was a plastic cap, hiding his hair."

"Wicked," said Hawkins.

The Evil Treasure Hunter was still crouched over Dot. He waved Dyrnwyn at her. "Where did you get this?"

"I'll never tell."

"Do you even know what this is, little girl?" He spoke soft and deep, like an earthquake. "Have you heard of Dyrnwyn?"

Dot refused to answer.

"This is an ancient blade, forged in a magical realm. There are only two or three like it left in existence. Once it was very powerful, wielded by great generals and kings of old. But, like the Phantom legend, it has turned to ruin." He twisted and examined the weapon from all angles. "Tell me. Where did you find it?"

"The Judge will never overcome the Phantom," she said defiantly.

Peter wondered, *Could The Evil Treasure Hunter actually be the Judge? It had to be, but that's a lot of nicknames, for one guy.*

"You truly believe you're the Captain of the Night?" The big man reached into his shirt and pulled a necklace over his head. Something dangled on the end, catching the light and gleaming. "Do you know what this is?"

Atticus startled Peter by releasing a muffled roar; they were so entranced with Dot and The Evil Treasure Hunter they'd quit wrestling with his bindings. "Heefhh eeee," he said, which probably meant "Help me."

Dot was examining the item held by the giant. "It looks like a ring on a necklace."

"Not just any ring, little blonde Phantom," he said. "This is Dragon Ring."

Fara gasped and her glow turned orange. "Oh no...oh no, OH NO! All is lost, we're ruined!"

"What's special about the ring?" Peter whispered.

Towering over poor Dot, the villain said, "The Dragon Ring has been around for centuries, mentioned in ancient tales. King Solomon once wore this ring, as did Genghis Kahn. In other languages it was called Andvaranaut, guarded by Fafnir the dragon and won by Sigurd. Do you know where I found this ring? Here, in the Caves. Exactly where legend said it would be. Now...tell me where you got the sword."

"I...I really don't know," said Dot in a small voice.

"Where's the magic gateway?"

"I don't know that either."

"Liar," he accused.

"I swear! I...I don't know what you're talking about. I've never even heard of a magic doorway."

He slipped the Dragon Ring's necklace back over his head. "My time is running short. I'll ask you one more time, little Phantom girl, and then it's going to get unpleasant. Is the magic doorway inside these Caves?"

"I...I...truly I don't know."

He stood and roared, "Take her! Grab the two boys, and take'em all to the bear cage! Let's see if we can't change her mind."

"To the bear cage?" Peter wondered. This was almost too horrible for his mind to accept. Red Masque henchmen hurried towards their hiding spot in the shadows. Too late Peter remembered he carried Bruno's throwing knife—he could have freed Atticus immediately. He shoved his hand into his jacket pocket, searching frantically, but Hawkins grabbed Peter's shoulders and hauled him deeper into the darkness.

"Quiet!" Hawkins whispered into his ear. "Or they'll hear you."

"I have a knife," he protested. "I can—"

"It's too late. Shhhh!"

While they watched from their hiding spot, Atticus and

Capulet were yanked up and carried away. Dot was being shoved toward the exit by The Evil Treasure Hunter. He called, "Everyone else, search the top floor of the Caves! We only have an hour left, and I WANT that portal!"

The Red Masque saluted—palms facing out— and quickly abandoned the headquarters, not bothering to cover their tracks. They followed their leader into the darkness. Soon Peter, Hawkins, and Joey were alone, staring guiltily at one another.

"Well that didn't work," said Hawkins.

"Our plans never do," muttered Joey. "I don't even know why we bother making them."

"Remember when that guy pulled his scalp off? So weird!"

"Peter, PLEASE," said Fara, flying in circles so quickly she was a blur. "You've GOT to get that ring and take back Dyrnwyn. And rescue your friends!"

"I don't know what to do," said Peter with a heavy heart. "Nothing has worked."

"But you CANNOT give up!" she cried.

"I'm not enough."

"But you're ALL we have!"

Hawkins asked quietly, "Do you think he'll feed Dot to the bears? Or maybe toss Atticus in?"

Peter said, "Well...c'mon. We can't stay here. We can...I dunno, we'll think of *something*."

"But what will we do?" asked Joey. "Feels like I'm asking that question every few minutes."

"I'll confront the bald man. Errr...the big scary guy. I'll tell him the sword came from me," said Peter. He picked up Joey's flashlight and clicked it on. He took a deep, shaky breath. And followed after the Red Masque.

It was the top floor's turn to be searched. Men in

crimson masks were tearing it apart, flinging junk in all directions. So focused were the henchmen that Peter snuck through easily, Joey and Hawkins directly behind. He raced as swiftly as possible and reached the double-door exit soon after The Evil Treasure Hunter. They remained just inside the Caves, hiding behind a stack of mattresses and peering out.

Atticus and Capulet sat back to back on the garage floor, and the big man held Dot's arm in his fist. But Peter wasn't looking at them. His eyes had snapped onto another man, standing near the bear cage with his hands on his hips.

It was Marlowe Blodgett, dressed like a pirate as usual, but now he wore a backpack.

The Evil Treasure Hunter said, "Step aside, Marlowe."

"Zis has gone far enough! You promised no one would get hurt," protested Marlowe, who looked small next to the Judge.

"Plans change," said the big man.

"You cannot hurt zee children! It's time we go. My bags are packed, let us leave zis place."

"You're the one who got us into the Crown," said Gordie Abaddon—The Evil Treasure Hunter—dangerously. "You can't back out. We leave in an hour. Now move."

From their hiding spot, Hawkins whispered, "It wasn't Lino Kang helping the Red Masque, it was Marlowe. I'm shocked!"

"I'm not," said Joey wisely. "I knew it all along."

"No you didn't," Hawkins snorted.

Marlowe shouted, "I'VE done all zee work! I contacted zee Snyders, I blackmailed Mr. Banks, I got you in! The Red Masque owes me, and I'm saying, let zee children GO!. I cannot watch you feed zem to zee bears."

"Then you better leave," snarled The Evil Treasure Hunter.

"You got zee ring! You got zee sword! What else do you—"

"SILENCE!"

Marlowe knew better than to press his luck. He shrunk under the murderous glare and hid with the henchmen.

"Now then," said The Evil Treasure Hunter, smiling evilly at Dot. "I'll ask you again. And if you don't answer, I'm throwing a little boy into the bear cage. You understand?"

Atticus, still wearing the gag, fainted. Capulet whimpered—blind because of the rag tied around his eyes, but his ears worked.

Peter's fists kept clenching and releasing. Of course he couldn't let Atticus be tossed into the cage, but how could he stop it? He felt like he was suffocating.

"Time's running out," growled a voice in his ear. Peter was so surprised he jumped two feet in the air. It was Rory, crouched next to Joey as though he'd materialized there. The old man coughed into a handkerchief and said, "Better do something. Quick."

"Rory!" Peter knelt next to him, marveling. "*When* did you get here?"

"Just now. Sorry it took me a while. I don't have the energy much longer."

"I need help, Rory. I don't know what to do," admitted Peter. "I can't beat him, I can't win."

"Yes you can. But your victory must come from within. You've got to believe. Nothing else matters."

Peter sighed in frustration. "That's what I keep hearing, but I don't know what it means! You used to be the Phantom! Give me all the advice you got."

"It's you, Pete," Rory said, and he coughed again. "That's

all there is to it. Nothing blasted magical about it, you have to believe."

Peter's heart sank. The words sounded like gibberish to him. He didn't know *what* or *how* to believe.

Hawkins tugged on Peter's sleeve. "Uhhh, Peter, my man? Who you talking to?"

Peter rolled his eyes. "Sorry, forgot the introductions. Hawkins and Joey, this is Rory Franklin. Rory, these are my friends. Rory used to be the Phantom, a long time ago. Now can we focus? Dot is about to be eaten."

"But...who is Rory?" asked Joey.

Peter frowned in confusion. "Huh?"

"Can you see him right now?"

"Yeah, it's like you're talking to thin air," said Hawkins. "Or to a ghost."

"But..." sputtered Peter in bewilderment. "But..." He pointed at Rory. "You can't *see* him?"

"See *who?*" asked Joey. "There's no one here."

Peter felt as though he'd been struck by lightning. Rory was INVISIBLE? Peter's mind rushed back to all his encounters with the Franklin family...

...When Peter had first spoken to him, Rory had been surprised and commented there weren't many kids with pure hearts anymore.

...When the fireworks erupted in the basement, everyone had ducked but Rory.

...Peter had witnessed Rory talking *to* Dot, but he'd never actually seen her reply.

...Ollie had never spoken to Rory.

...At dinner in the Windsor, Caroline had asked Peter why he was eating alone.

Because none of them could see the old man.

"Are you a *ghost?*" he asked.

Rory nodded. "You got it, kid. And I'm ready to move on, as soon as you save my great granddaughter."

Peter couldn't think straight. "I'm the *only one* who can see you."

"Only you, Pete. You got what it takes."

Fara said softly, "We are what we choose to be, Peter."

Joey and Hawkins watched Peter struggle with unseen forces, and they understood something important was happening.

Fara said, "It's you, Peter. If you'll trust us. And trust yourself."

Peter felt as though gravity pulled at him from weird angles, like he was dizzy. For a brief flash, he saw himself as if from someone else's point of view. He saw a boy, brave and strong, dressed like the paintings he'd seen, wearing the black key round his neck, talking to a ghost, being mentored by a faery...

It was him. How could he not have seen it before? All he had to do was believe.

"It's me," Peter whispered. "It's me, isn't it."

Had he been watching, Peter would've noticed that Dyrnwyn twitched on the villain's belt.

Hawkins said, "I don't know what's going on, Peter. But I believe. I believe you're him."

"It's me," Peter repeated, talking to himself. The sword twitched again. He said louder, "I am him. Cypress was right. I'm the Phantom."

"YES, Peter," sang Fara. "You're the Phantom! You have been since you arrived. You didn't need me to choose you. You chose yourself."

Peter stood. A tremendous surge of confidence mounted inside his chest. From his jacket's pocket, he removed the mask and pulled it over his eyes. "Stay here," he told Joey and Hawkins, and they nodded. The big man scared them, but at the moment so did Peter. He strode out from the Caves and called, "ENOUGH!"

The henchmen froze. So did The Evil Treasure Hunter and Dot.

Peter said, "That sword is mine."

Dyrnwyn began to glow.

The big man gave a half chuckle and muttered, "There are Phantoms everywhere tonight."

"Release her," ordered Peter. He felt as though he and The Evil Treasure Hunter were swelling in size, while everyone else shrank. "And you are banished from the Crown."

"You think you're the Phantom?"

"I know I am."

"We met, didn't we. You're the one from the fire," the giant said. "Last year."

Staring down his nemesis, Peter's stomach churned. "I know who you are. You're The Evil Treasure Hunter from New Jersey."

"You called me that name before," he growled. "But to the men surrounding you, I have a different name."

"The Judge."

"I am he." An evil smile. "Like my predecessors before."

"So you're the latest version," said Peter.

"The latest and the most ambitious. Soon all of New York will tremble at my name."

"I told you in the fire that I'd deal with you myself. You and the syndicate are finished here."

The Judge walked closer to Peter, dragging Dot after him. "Could it be true? The Masque's only true opponent, returned to die once more?"

Peter's hands itched. He needed a weapon. "I'm here. Because the city needs me."

"The Judge is far older than the Masque, did you know? Our ancestors clashed decades ago, legendary battles. I had hoped the prophecy was true, that you would return. But you're a teenager. Can you even drive yet?"

"You think age matters?"

"Before you're disposed of, you must tell me—how did you sneak through our halls and into our rooms? A fancy little trick."

Peter shrugged. "I'm the Phantom. I move unseen."

"We have you surrounded, Phantom. I have your infamous sword and the Dragon ring. Your friends will be fed to the bears. You lose."

Fara fluttered at Peter's shoulder. "Be brave, Peter. All is NOT lost." Peter's mind raced for solutions. He turned in a circle, but he was outnumbered at least twenty to one. It certainly *seemed* as though all was lost.

The Judge continued, "I know for a fact the bears have been mistreated by the circus. They haven't been properly fed in days." He jerked Dot's arm, giving her a jolt. "Let's see what they think of the girl."

"Don't fear the bears," said Fara. "I can handle them. ...Hopefully."

Peter stiffened. Suddenly he had an idea. It was crazy, but how could the situation get any worse? "I hope you're right, Fara."

The Judge paused. A pale knowing glint shone in his eye. "You're talking to someone."

"This is between you and me, Judge. Either surrender or throw *me* into the cage instead."

The audience of crimson masks cackled with glee.

"This new version of the Phantom won't last long," the

Judge said, with a sinister laugh. "Because I will defeat him. Tonight."

Marlowe Blodgett appeared again, holding his hands up. "Please! No, zis is madness! No children can be fed to zee animals!"

Peter's heart was hammering. "Release the girl. Take me instead."

"If you insist." The big man moved, quick as a cat. Flinging Dot aside, he gathered Peter's jacket into his fists. The sheer power of the giant was breathtaking. "Goodbye little Phantom."

Peter choked, "It's not too late for you to surrender." He was violently tossed upwards, crashing into the garage's steel rafters. The cage had been built with gaps at the top, too high for the animals to reach, and Peter easily slipped through.

"Peter, NO!" cried Joey from their hiding spot.

"Get out of there, my man!" Hawkins howled.

Peter landed on the floor of the stinking cage. His world turned to fur and darkness. The bears snarled and raged, and beyond them he heard the henchmen laughing. He tried to stand but a bear knocked him over. The stench of unwashed fur made him gag.

Fara swooped in, blazing with light. "I'm holding them off! But the Judge is right, they're hungry! And FURIOUS!"

Peter scrambled to his feet and backed away from the toothy maws and glaring eyes. The bears roared at Fara— they could see her. "Hope this works," Peter panted.

"What's your plan?" shouted Fara above the snarling. "They won't heed me long!"

"I need extra allies," said Peter, removing the magic key from around his neck. "The bears will have to do." He snaked an arm through the cage bars, jammed in the key, and heard a satisfying click.

"Oh wow," said Fara. "This is about to get WILD!"

The Red Masque suddenly fell silent outside the cage; they saw the key in the lock. Surely, they thought, he wouldn't... Peter threw open the heavy gate and shouted, "Release the bears!"

Fara's light blinked out.

With a mighty roar, the huge animals charged from their prison. Peter leapt aside. The men in masks screamed and scattered—they were carrying clubs and knives, pathetic against thousand-pound animals. Aggy the elephant trumpeted in terror, his wide eyes rolling.

"Stand your ground!" bellowed the Judge, but no one listened. The mistreated and savage animals rampaged through his ranks, snarling and clawing.

In the midst of the mayhem, Peter yanked free his throwing knife. He judged the distance and took two steps forward. He threw the deadly gift given to him by Bruno. The blade whistled through the air, sailed past the Judge, and neatly sliced Aggy's tether in half; Peter's mentor would've been proud. The elephant reared back on two legs, releasing an ear-splitting blast, and bolted. Marlowe Blodgett rushed forward to calm Aggy but the animal knocked him aside. Marlowe crashed into the wall and fell limply to the ground.

All was pandemonium.

Peter cried, "Dot! Get Atticus and Capulet to safety!" But Dot was overcome with the chaos; she ran senselessly in circles.

Peter bolted toward the two kidnapped boys. The Judge, however, got there first.

"You think you won?" he roared. "I came here looking

for powerful secrets and I'll leave with the sword and the ring! You've LOST! I don't need bears, I'll destroy you myself!" He gripped Dyrnwyn's hilt and slid the sword free.

As he raised it above his head, though, the blade ignited like the sun. A light so piercing Peter had to avert his eyes. The Evil Treasure Hunter's hand smoked and he screamed in pain. Releasing the sword, he tucked the burned hand under his arm.

Dyrnwyn soared through the air and landed in Peter's outstretched palm. The weapon vibrated hotly inside his fist, and Peter was astonished to see the rusty old blade was now one of brilliant fire. The edges were sharp and the metal sang. "I told you this was my sword!" he called.

The Judge snarled and swung his uninjured fist at Peter. He ducked it easily and whipped Dyrnwyn into the Judge's ribs. There was a burst of power and the giant shot upwards as though struck by a wrecking ball. Peter stared in awe at the pulsating blade; the giant landed thirty feet away and crashed through the fleeing Red Masque.

"Dyrnwyn's ALIVE!" screamed Fara.

"Peter, help!"

He whirled—a bear was nearing the entrance to the Caves. Joey and Hawkins would be nothing more than a light snack. Peter bounded to the double-doors, blocking the path, and raised the blade above his head. Piercing light blazed forth. The bear winced and turned aside in search of easier prey.

The sword's burst of light caused his enemies' hearts to quake within. Peter's voice rose to a terrifying pitch and filled the garage, "RUN AND HIDE, SYNDICATE! YOU HAVE NO PLACE HERE!"

The henchman scrambled over each other to obey. They poured up the garage, racing for the streets, fleeing the angry bears and the rioting elephant and the fiery warrior with the terrible voice. Peter scanned the retreating men, but of the Judge there was no sign.

Soon their section of the garage emptied. Peter hauled Dot to her feet and helped her to the stairwell. Joey and Hawkins darted to Atticus, tugging once more on his bindings.

"Looks like Atticus is still out cold, the wimp," Hawkins said, grinning.

Joey called, "Pet...I mean, Phantom! Someone will call 911 once the bears start charging up 58th. Maybe you should...you know, go change? Before you're seen by the police?"

"Yeah, my man! No one should know who you are."

Peter took a look around. Marlowe Blodgett groaned in the corner. The animals and men in masks had disappeared into the upper levels. The Judge had vanished in the mayhem. Dot would survive, and so would Atticus and Capulet.

His sheath was lost, so Peter shoved the sword under his belt. He glanced at Fara. "We're safe, you think?"

"Yes Peter. And I think Joey's correct, about hiding your identity."

"I can't believe you did that," marveled Hawkins, shaking his head. "You went all Batman on them!"

"He's not a BAT," Fara said, zooming excitedly over their heads. "He's a PHANTOM"

20

THE FLIGHT OF THE CIRCUS

Peter draped Atticus over his shoulder and carried him to the Nook and dropped him on a couch. Joey and Hawkins kept sneaking glances at Peter, as though seeing him for the first time, wondering what other magical surprises their friend had up his sleeve.

Peter dashed to 201 to shed his disguise. Out of curiosity, he picked up the phone and heard a dial tone. The phones had been restored. He punched in 911.

"*911 response, what is your emergency?*"

"I'm calling from the Crown Hotel," said Peter. "The Red Masque was here and circus animals are loose. We need police right away."

"*Thank you, sir, for alerting us. We're getting DOZENS of calls nearby. Cars have already been dispatched to your location. Are you in danger right now?*"

"I'm not. Thanks for your help." He hung up and proceeded into his room, shrugging out of the jacket.

Rory sat on his bed, giving Peter another jolt. Any more surprises tonight and his heart might stop. "Ya did good, kid."

"Rory, why didn't you tell me that you were a ghost?"

"Thought you knew," the old man said. "How'd you think I got into your apartment last time?"

"Good question." Peter held up Dyrnwyn and examined the weapon. The fire had cooled within, revealing a dark, gorgeous blade. It glinted in the light, as good as new. Unless Peter was mistaken, it had shrunk slightly in size to suit him better. The blade felt strong and powerful in his grip. "Did you see what happened to the Judge when I hit him with this?"

"I did. A mighty blow." He stopped to cough in to his handkerchief. "You're already a better Phantom than I was.

"Did you ever use Dyrnwyn?"

"Never. Cypress died before passing along the secrets. I did the best I could, but..."

Peter asked, "You're leaving, aren't you?"

"I have to. My energy's gone. Now that you're here, and my great granddaughter is safe, I'll be taken any minute."

Peter slid the sword under his bed, careful so his parents wouldn't be able to see it. "Before you go, can you tell me what happened? How you died?"

"Cypress was killed...I forget, somewhere in the 1920s or 30s. He was always too careless, that one. I was a blasted teenager, not ready for the role. But I carried on. In the 1950s, I finally came face to face with the Judge. A different villain than you met tonight. And...well, the monster won. I died in my late forties. My son, Ollie, was still a child. He was never cut out for the life."

Peter did some quick math. "You were the Phantom for thirty years."

Fara zipped into the room, sparkling and shining. "He was! He was excellent too, careful to never be seen. Of course I was holed up inside the Crown, stuck in that STUPID mouse. I wasn't much help to him."

"The Phantom legend died out because Ollie didn't know what to do," explained Rory. "And because he wasn't needed. The Judge and his Red Masque henchmen had receded into the shadows."

Peter hid his mask and throwing knife beneath the bed, next to the sword. He let the key remain on the chain around his neck. "Cypress still looked like a young man when I met him," said Peter. "Why have you aged, sir, and he didn't?"

"Maybe Fara can answer that, because I don't know. I expect it has something to do with the Crown. It's a magical place. But now...I think I'm ready to go."

"But I still have questions!"

"I'll answer them," said Fara, hovering near Rory's face. "He's earned his rest. Rory Franklin, I wish you a pleasant trip to the next life. The land of milk and honey awaits."

"Take care of Dot, please," said Rory, looking younger and fading like a mist. "I'm proud of you, Peter. The legacy of the Phantom is in good hands."

Then he was gone.

～

ATTICUS WAS PACING the Nook when Peter returned. "What were you three twerps doing down there?" he demanded in a shaky voice. "You should've been at the circus."

Hawkins muttered, "I think you meant to say, 'Thanks for untying me,' and 'sorry for being a humongous twit' and you're welcome."

Joey crossed her arms. "We could ask you the same

question, Atticus. We saw you and the Ritz kid throwing stuff at the bears."

Capulet sat in a nearby chair, pale-faced and quiet.

"Okay, okay." Atticus held up placating hands. "I propose a deal. You keep my secret, I'll keep yours. None of us was ever here."

"You kidding? What about the security guard? Or Marlowe Blodgett? They both saw us," said Hawkins.

"Those two will be long gone, probably." Peter glared thoughtfully at Atticus; the Snyders were the reason the circus stayed at the Crown. Almost certainly they were in league with the Red Masque. But did that mean Atticus was too? Or just his parents?

Joey offered, "There are no security cameras in that level of the garage. Unless we get unlucky, I think we can get away with it."

"Very well, it's settled," said Atticus, looking relieved.

"He was there," murmured Capulet softly from his chair. "I mean...I thought he was only a legend."

Atticus turned to his friend. "What's that, chum?"

"You fainted, Atticus, but I heard. The Phantom of New York. He's returned. He...he was there."

"Be serious, Cap."

"I *am*!" insisted Capulet.

Atticus scoffed and turned to the three friends. "He's loony, right? You didn't see the Phantom, did you?"

"Nope," said Peter.

"No way," agreed Joey.

"I *definitely* saw him!" cried Hawkins. "He chased away a bear with his glowing sword! It was so wicked awesome!"

Peter and Joey rolled their eyes and groaned.

Capulet remained quiet, staring at his hands.

THE CROWN'S residents and guests returned from a splendid evening at the Circus of Doom's final performance. Peter, Hawkins, and Joey filtered in with the crowd and found their parents, doing their best to describe their favorite parts of the show. Caroline Crawford spotted Peter, and he shot her a thumbs-up sign. She lit up with a smile—Caroline had been worried sick; she was so relieved to see him she blew him a kiss.

Capturing the two bears and Aggy the elephant turned out to be an arduous task for Animal Control—the chase lasted all night and ended at the foot of Trump Tower. Not only were the animals apprehended, but so were a couple Red Masque henchmen, who turned themselves in rather than get eaten by a bear. Soon afterwards, police arrived at the Crown and demanded an explanation, only to find the Circus of Doom in disarray. None of the circus staff knew how their animals had escaped, and a significant number of performers were suddenly missing. Shaman, Keith, and Adolfo hadn't even returned to collect their luggage—they were gone. Lino Kang appeared to be genuinely mystified.

A thorough inspection turned up clues in the basement of the garage. The police discovered a handful of crimson masks and Marlowe Blodgett, who'd been knocked so sense-less he hadn't run away. From the confusion, police were able to assemble the puzzle pieces—the Red Masque had been at work in the Crown Hotel, in league with the Circus of Doom.

It's about time someone figured it out, thought Peter, who'd known it for months.

The apprehended henchmen refused to divulge any information about their criminal syndicate but both agreed

—the Phantom of New York had disrupted their plans. Marlowe, not totally in his right mind and having forgot much of the night, admitted to working with the Red Masque in their crusade for ancient and powerful weapons. "And zen," he raved to the police, "out of no where, zee Phantom appeared, waving his sword of fire and directing zee animals! He can talk to zem, I saw it with my own eyes! He's ten feet tall and strong as zee bull!"

Over the weekend, newspapers had a field day with the story. How long had the Red Masque been cooperating with the Circus of Doom? No one knew. Lino Kang was being held for questioning, but so far he appeared innocent—he'd been manipulated by Marlowe into staying at the Crown and chasing ghost stories.

The circus dissolved in disgrace, canceling further shows in subsequent cities.

Stories and rumors and gossip about the Phantom's return were splashed over the newspapers and television reports. Darci Drake went delirious with the tale, chasing down every lead she could. Where had the Phantom come from? And where had he gone? But no clues could be found. The Captain of the Night remained a mystery.

THE FOLLOWING MONDAY, Peter helped carry the Franklins's luggage to the street. Dot had given Ollie a few details about that scary night, including the ring stolen by the Judge. Ollie looked despondent at having missed his chance. Of the Phantom's sword, Dot made no mention, because she was completely unable to admit to her grandfather that she'd failed as the Phantom and that Peter had saved the day.

On the sidewalk, Ollie smiled good-naturedly at Peter.

"So long, Preston! Very glad to have helped drive off the Red Masque. No need to thank us."

Peter shook his hand. "Well, thank you anyway, sir, for... err, you know. Something."

Ollie ducked into the waiting yellow taxi while Dot stared at her shoes, wearing a glum frown. "I guess we'll return to our hole in the ground. Though it belongs to the Phantom, I suppose, not to us."

"You mean, the lair under the Chelsea? You keep it," Peter said, shivering. "Did you see how many goons the Judge has? I'll need your help."

"I'm not much good, though," she mumbled.

Peter loaded bags into the trunk and slammed it closed. "Come visit every few days, okay? You're a part of this."

"Really?" she asked, finally meeting his eyes. "You want me back, even after I failed?"

"Of course."

She wrapped him in a fierce hug. "Thanks, Pete. You're already great at this." Then she climbed into the cab and motored out of sight.

Caroline Crawford surprised Peter in the Nook later that very day. He and Joey were working on math when she swooped in, fresh out of school and still dressed in her uniform.

"Did you *see* him?" she asked breathlessly.

"See who?" asked Peter.

Joey quickly hid her notebook under the table, inexplicably embarrassed it was covered with rainbow unicorns.

"Everyone is talking at school," explained Caroline. "They believe me, now. About the Phantom. Earlier today I realized—I can't believe I didn't think of it sooner—you two were there! At the Crown, with the Phantom! Did you see him?"

"No, definitely not," Joey replied, a little too quickly. "Did Hawkins tell you we did? Cause...he's lying. We didn't...we never...we, um, had our eyes closed."

Caroline arched an eyebrow, trying to decode Joey's gibberish. After a moment she said, "Your eyes were closed? I don't understand."

"What are people saying?" asked Peter.

"That he's *real*," gushed Caroline. "Just as I said he was. It's so nice, being vindicated. You never saw him, Peter?"

"I'll be honest, Caroline. During most of the action, we were hiding. Behind boxes. Because it was scary."

"That's a shame." Caroline lowered into a chair and set her chin on her palm. "Where do you suppose he went?"

"Not far, I bet."

"You think?" she asked, a hopeful gleam in her eye. "I do hope he's nearby. He's very dashing."

"Yeah." Peter grinned. "He's dashing as heck."

Joey groaned.

Marcellus, the swarthy son of Lino Kang, emerged from the stairwell. He stopped at their table and gave them a somber bow. "The Sheriff is releasing my father today. And so I must go, my friends."

Peter stood and stuck out his hand to shake. "I hope everything works out for you, Marcellus. You're always welcome here."

"Yes! Visit again soon," said Joey, going a little red in the cheeks.

Marcellus ignored the offered hand and kissed Peter on the forehead, the traditional sign of friendship. He kissed Joey too. "I was lonely and you gave me friendship. Thank you. You are special to me," he said, and he returned to the stairwell.

Caroline smiled. "Josephine, what's with the goofy grin?"

"Just...you know," she said, fussing with her pencil. "I'll miss him."

"Oh yes? Are you a little sweet on the cute circus boy?"

There began a ten-minute conversation between the girls, discussing Marcellus and other cute boys they knew. Caroline kept shooting glances at Peter, who found the discussion so awkward and off-putting that he was on the verge of fetching a pair of headphones when his father stuck his head into the Nook.

He said, "Peter, I'm heading to the Caves, and I could use a hand."

"Sure, Dad!" cried Peter, glad to leave the girls, who'd begun to debate the difference between a boy being sweet versus shy. Pure madness, in his opinion.

The two Constantine men ventured once again into the depths of the Crown basement. Seeing the disaster within, Manos ruffled Peter's hair. "I should've believed you about the Red Masque. You were right and I was wrong."

"S'okay, Dad. I wouldn't have believed me either."

"Any idea what they were searching for?"

"No idea." Peter was lying easier than he used to, primarily due to the large volume of secrets he kept. "But I'm glad the Phantom stopped them."

"Yes," agreed Manos, inspecting Peter suspiciously. "I should have trusted you, son, but I hope you know you can trust me. With the truth. You think he's really back?"

"Dunno," Peter said. "Men in masks are usually just little kid stuff, right?"

"Then why're you wearing an Iron Man shirt?'

Peter shrugged. "Cause he's super cool."

They travelled all the way to the bottom and closed the door to the underground tunnel one more time. Even though Peter hadn't felt the tension beforehand, the muscles in his neck relaxed; the Crown was secure again.

That afternoon, Peter went for a walk in Central Park. It was warm for January and he needed the air. Fara, still exhausted from Friday night's adventure, rested comfortably in a sock inside his leather jacket pocket. She'd been gone a lot recently.

Peter sat on a bench with a view of the sparkling Crown and he said, "Okay, Fara. I need some answers."

Her voice came muffled from his jacket. "Ask me anything, Phantom."

"You've dealt with the Red Masque before. What do they want?"

She answered immediately. "To control New York City! And then maybe everything else. They are power hungry. And possibly insane."

Peter had one hand in his jeans pocket, and the other pulled thoughtfully on his lip. "Do you think that man is really the Judge?"

"I believe so, yes."

"He found the Dragon Ring, which has you scared. He called it Andvaranaut. I looked it up in the library, but it's considered a myth."

"There are VERY few magical items in this world, Peter. But one of them is Andvaranaut, a ring that's been passed around and found its way into many legends. Look up any famous ring in history, and it's usually about the Dragon Ring," said Fara. "It's older than ME."

"What's it do?"

"First, Peter, it's important you understand something. There's MORE to your universe than what you can see.

When earth was created, it was built with light and love, and with many dimensions. There is an unseen world."

Peter nodded. "After what I've been through, I believe it. Are you talking about heaven?"

"No, although heaven is BRILLIANT—you'll love it. The unseen world I'm referring to exists *next* to yours. It's beside —but also merged with—your own world. It has been called many names. The ancients called it Elfhame, which you would translate into Elfland, or Elf Land."

"Is that where you go? When you disappear for hours?"

"Yes, Elfhame is my true home. Not many believe in it, these days. But the Judge does, and that's what he's after— one of the portals into the unseen world."

"But we scared him off before he could find it, right?" Peter asked, watching a family walk past, pushing a stroller. They looked curiously at the boy talking to himself.

"Yes, the Judge failed to find the gateway. But...he found the Dragon Ring," she said with something of a shiver.

"What's it do?"

"Lots of AMAZING things. But mainly, it acts as a key. Wearing the ring, he'll be able to pass into Elfhame, the unseen world. And there's no telling what evil he'll cause."

"So we'll protect the portal. It's in the Caves, right?"

Fara replied, "Unfortunately there's more than one portal. In New York City alone I know of three, including the one in the Crown."

"Do you know where the other two are?"

"Sort of, yes. But it's guarded."

His skin crawling at the thought, Peter asked, "By what?"

"I'd rather not say. Not until I know for sure."

"Three in the city," Peter thought to himself, shuffling his feet. "There must be hundreds of portals in America, then."

"New York City is a special place, Peter. Our worlds come close to touching here, which is why there are three. I know of no other portals on this side of the ocean. But the point is, Peter, your work has just begun."

"Is that what Cypress did? Guard the portals?"

Her glow inside Peter's pocket strengthened. "YES, although he didn't fully understand. Remember, Peter, you're the first Phantom that I've been able to speak to. The other Phantoms...well, we did our best, without them knowing the secrets."

"So the Phantom legend, it's always been about you and the guys you picked to protect the city?"

"Guys and girls, yes. Few wee people care about your world. I'm one of the only, mainly because I was chosen the same as you. I've been working for CENTURIES to protect the people and the land, to keep the worlds separate! Along the way, the protectors I chose became noticed and the newspapers and historians cooked up the name Phantom. Kinda silly, really, you humans."

"And you equipped the protectors with Dyrnwyn, and eventually with Cypress's key," guessed Peter.

"Yes!"

"One more question. Before Cypress left, he touched me and *something* happened. Ever since then, I have a weird connection with the Crown. What'd he do to me?"

"He did something he should NOT have, Peter. In FACT, I didn't know it could be done, and I'm not *entirely* sure how to explain it," Fara sang.

"Try."

"Very well! Cypress turned you into a ghost."

"*What?*" Peter cried.

"Hmmm, you're right, I should rephrase. Cypress was the Crown's ghost. LOTS of old buildings are haunted, and your hotel belonged to him. Or at least, no other ghosts were *allowed* as long as he was here, because he and the Crown had a bond. Kind of. It's COMPLICATED, and I don't fully understand. Ghosts are from your world, not mine. But before he left, he transferred his haunting powers to YOU."

"What are haunting powers?"

"You haunt the hotel, I suppose. You see ghosts that others can't, but it's MORE. Cypress had a mystical relationship with the Crown, and that belongs to you now. It's QUITE an honor, even though I'm *certain* he wasn't supposed to do it. You're the new ghost. You *haunt* the hotel," explained Fara.

"But I'm alive."

"CORRECT. Now you get it!"

"I do *not*. Does this have anything to do with the Dragon Ring?"

"NO. The Dragon Ring is something else. It's remained a secret, too powerful to be used safely. No Phantom has ever crossed over to my world. I don't know HOW the Judge learned of it," said Fara angrily. "You NEED to get it back."

"We can do it, Fara. Together."

"Yes, Peter, we can."

～

THE NEXT MORNING, Peter woke early and remained in bed. Life had grown so bonkers recently that he felt most at peace under the covers. He pulled Cypress's magic key over his head, and let it dangle on the necklace. He watched it swing side to side, over and over, as he pondered magical artifacts and the fantastic creatures who made them.

"I bet the Judge wants to get his hands on you too," he told the key softly.

Hawkins snorted in his sleep.

Eventually Peter got up, stepped over Hawkins, and shuffled into the bathroom. A moment later he returned, yawning sleepily, and the misty ghost of Captain Kidd materialized, perched on his dresser.

"You ARE him, aren't ye," growled the pirate captain. "That's why y'can see me!"

Peter kept his distance, but he nodded warily. "Yes Captain, I'm him."

"Let's be off then, ya swab."

"Be off where?"

"To the treasure! I kept it hidden these many decades, but those lubbers are closing in fast!" growled Captain Kidd.

"Maybe I can help, Captain, and maybe I can't. I need to figure all this out. But not today," said Peter.

"And why bloody not?"

"Because I have a test today at the assessment center, and I don't want to miss it. It's all the way across town," said Peter simply. "And also, I haven't eaten breakfast yet."

"Argh! My fate rests in the hands of a mere SCAMP," roared the pirate and he vanished with a poof.

Hawkins sat up and rubbed his eyes. "Peter, be honest with me. Did you...were you just...I wasn't dreaming that, was I?"

Peter winced. "Thought you were asleep. You heard me talking?"

"You don't have to tell me if you don't want, I guess. But... can you see things that I don't?"

Peter pressed his lips into a hard line. Released a breath through his nose. He debated lying, but eventually he nodded. "Yes."

"Like just now? And the ghost back in the Caves?" asked Hawkins.

Peter nodded again. "Yep, both times."

"Was that a ghost on your dresser you were talking to? What'd it say?"

"He wants me to help him with buried treasure," said Peter, worried about what his friend would think.

Hawkins jumped to his feet and stretched. "Oh. Probably it was Captain Kidd, then."

"You know him?" marveled Peter.

"Sure, everyone in New York's heard of him! He's an urban legend round here. C'mon, I smell waffles."

Manos and Jovanna sat at the little kitchen table. There was just enough room for four chairs and four plates, and so they squeezed in and shared the syrup.

Jovanna smiled at the boys, clutching her robe sleepily. "Good morning, you two."

The boys nodded, their mouths already too full to talk.

Manos set his cup of coffee down. "Hawkins, I think you should attend school today. You've been missing too much. We'll ride with you on the bus later this morning, because Peter and Joey have to take a test near Trinity."

Hawkins shrugged and said, "Mkay."

"That'll give us a chance to talk," said Jovanna, smiling. "About something very important to us."

Peter washed down the waffle with some orange juice. He asked, "What about?"

Peter's father grinned at Hawkins, and set a strong hand on the boy's shoulder. "You belong here, Hawkins, with us. I think it's time we talk about adoption."

THE END

～

DEAR READER,

I HOPE you enjoyed the second volume of The Phantom of New York! I particularly enjoyed the surprises at the end. (I have a favor to beg—try not to spoil the surprises for those who haven't read the book yet.)

BOOK THREE IS available here - releasing in January or February of 2020.

YOU'RE WELCOME to text me with your thoughts— I respond to as many as I can. (260) 673-5450

YOU MAY HAVE NOTICED that I've written other books, under the name Alan Janney. These books are YA, and I think you'll like them. However, I recommend readers be at least thirteen before beginning.

MANY MANY THANKS TO DEBBIE,TERESA, and Liz for finding so many errors. Thank you to Elise, Anne, Larry, and Megan for the beta reads. To Danny, Luke, and Nick for reading volume one at bedtime. And especially to Jackson and Chase, for listening and offering feedback.

IF YOU HAVE TIME, leaving a review for the book makes a huge difference for writers like myself, who'd rather not sell their work to big fat publishers. I appreciate your support!!

. . .

FUN FACTS:

-I RECORDED the Phantom of New York audio book in my closet with the door closed. I spent hours in total darkness (the overhead light produces an annoying faint buzz) shouting into a microphone.

-THE BOOKS themselves are written in the most remote corner of the local library, or at a coffee shop, over iced vanilla coffee and an omelet.

-THE BOOKS I am reading as I write this: *Cross Vision*, by Greg Boyd (about theology); *The Tale of Despereaux*, by Kate DiCamillo (about a heroic mouse); *Inevitable*, by Kevin Kelly (an optimistic book about our future. I'm listening to this one on audio in the car); and *The Mauritius Command*, by Patrick O'Brian (about naval warfare during the napoleonic wars). That might be one too many.

-THE CROWN HOTEL is loosely based on the Plaza Hotel in NYC. I've never been inside.

ORDER VOLUME III of The Phantom of New York here!

Made in the USA
Coppell, TX
08 July 2020